A Light in the Dark

Mysteries of Sparrow Island™

A LIGHT IN THE DARK

Charlotte Carter

Guideposts Books
CARMEL, NEW YORK

www.guideposts.org
(800) 431-2344
Guideposts Books & Inspirational Media Division

Cover and interior design by Cindy LaBreacht
Cover art by Gail W. Guth
Map by Jim Haynes, represented by Creative Freelancers, Inc.
Typeset by Nancy Tardi
Printed in the United States of America

Special thanks to Barbara Jensen, president of the San Juan Audubon Society. Rest assured, any mistakes made regarding bald eagles are wholly my own.

Likewise, my thanks to Chuck KN6H, my very own "old man," for his help with ham radio questions and other technical assistance.

And an extra hug for grandson Andrew KI6AOT, who really did get his amateur radio license at age ten.

ORCAS

To
U.S.A.

LUMMI

N
W E
S

CYPRESS

GUEMES

To
ANACORTES

FIDALGO
ISLAND

*SPARROW ISLAND IS FICTITIOUS

CHAPTER ❦ ONE

IT WAS A DARK AND STORMY . . .

That silly thought had Abby Stanton chuckling to herself as she dashed out the front door to grab *The Birdcall* newspaper, which had just been delivered. It wasn't actually stormy, more like a steady mist that had been falling off and on for almost a week. Nor was it dark, although the morning overcast made it seem that way.

Regretfully, this was typical weather for early February on Sparrow Island in the San Juan Islands of Washington.

Abby was more than ready for a bit of spring sunshine.

Back on the porch, she shook out her umbrella and propped it near the door. Then she pulled the weekly newspaper from its plastic wrapper and read the headlines as she went back into the house.

"*Hmmm*, that's interesting," she mumbled to herself as she went into the kitchen.

Her sister Mary was already preparing oatmeal for their breakfast, and the table was set with her favorite bright red place mats, a glass of orange juice at each place. It continued to amaze Abby how easily her sister accomplished almost any task, despite being confined to a wheelchair. Her handicap had happened when she'd tried to avoid hitting a deer and had gone off the road.

Mary's cat, Blossom, a beautiful white Persian, neatly avoided her mistress's wheelchair as she made her way to her dish to discover whatever tasty morsels might be there. Across the room, Finnegan, Mary's handsome service dog—a golden Labrador retriever mix—waited patiently to be asked to help.

After Mary's accident, Abby had returned to Sparrow Island, where she and Mary had been raised, to help her sister. Her initial task had been to remodel the first floor to make the house accessible. That included lowering the kitchen counters, so Mary could be as independent as possible in the home where she and her late husband Jacob had raised their family.

Later, with God's help and the offer of an exciting new job at the Sparrow Island Nature Conservatory, Abby had decided to accept Mary's invitation to return to the island permanently and make her home with Mary.

"Anything interesting?" Mary asked, wheeling around to scoop up two bowls of oatmeal from the pot simmering on the stove.

"The lead story in *The Birdcall*," Abby said as she sat down at the table. "It says that there have been three near misses of ships in the strait between Sparrow Island and San Juan Island in the past two weeks. In each case a ship has almost gone aground or hit another ship."

Mary delivered Abby's steaming bowl of oatmeal and placed it on the table along with one for herself. "Gracious, people could have been hurt. Why aren't the ships more careful?"

"According to all three ships' captains, the Wayfarer Point Lighthouse wasn't working."

"No! How could our lighthouse go out? That doesn't seem reasonable."

Adjusting her glasses, Abby quickly skimmed the newspaper article. "The commander of the Coast Guard Station at Bellingham, who's in charge of the lighthouse, says their monitoring equipment has shown no interruption in service and that the Coast Guard is investigating the incidents."

"That sounds like a lot of bureaucratic double-talk to me. Surely a ship's captain would know whether or not the lighthouse was working." Mary rolled her chair into place at the table and bowed her head briefly in prayer. Her neatly styled silver hair shone beneath the overhead light as she looked up. "I can't ever remember our lighthouse going dark, if that's what they're saying."

"It's what they're saying, all right."

Setting the newspaper aside, Abby said her own grace before taking her first bite of oatmeal, which was seasoned with cinnamon. Mary had also added bits of dried apples and apricots to spruce up the flavor. Although Abby could hold her own in a kitchen, Mary was by far the better cook.

"You don't suppose William Jansen at *The Birdcall* has got his story wrong, do you?" Mary asked.

"William is usually very good about checking his facts." William hoped to someday win a Pulitzer for his reporting and make up for the years he had spent in his family's diaper business, instead of pursuing his dream of being a reporter for a major paper. As a result, their small-town newspaper was generally a creditable source of information.

Mary spooned a few bites of oatmeal into her mouth, her brow furrowed.

"It just seems so . . . I don't know . . . unreasonable to think the lighthouse would go dark after all these years without the Coast Guard acknowledging there's a problem," she said.

Abby tended to agree. But she had other matters on her mind today. She was due at Friday Harbor later that morning for a meeting with members of the San Juan Islands Birding Society. She planned to ask the group for help with a census to locate bald eagle nesting sites and catalog transient non-nesting eagles here on Sparrow Island. She intended to create a display at The Nature Museum, where she worked as Associate Curator, that would show where people could most likely spot the ever-popular eagles.

"You must be going into the shop this morning," Abby said, noting her sister was dressed in a bright, flowered skirt and a complimentary sunshine-yellow sweater with a boat neckline. She looked as fresh as the flowers she sold at Island Blooms, the shop she owned.

"My, yes! The phone's been ringing off the hook with people wanting to send flowers for Valentine's Day. Mostly, it's men calling, of course."

"Has Sergeant Cobb placed his order for flowers for *you* yet?" Abby teased.

A blush crept up Mary's neck to color her cheeks. "Now, why would Henry send flowers to a florist? It'd be like coals to Newcastle." Embarrassed, she waved off the idea of the deputy sheriff sending her flowers, although her twinkling blue eyes suggested she was hoping to receive a bouquet no matter how much she might deny the possibility.

"Maybe because he likes you," Abby suggested mildly as she got up to carry her bowl and glass to the counter, where she rinsed them out.

"Before I forget," Mary said, "Sandy McDonald's great uncle Robert arrived yesterday, and we're invited over for coffee and dessert tonight to welcome him to the island."

"Perfect." Knowing that Sandy, their next-door neighbor, was extremely fond of her great uncle, Abby was happy to share in the gentleman's welcome.

She also knew Sandy made really tasty desserts, which meant Abby would have to eat both a light lunch and dinner if she didn't want dessert to show up on the scale tomorrow morning.

"You recall that Sandy's uncle was recently blinded," Mary said. "A terrible accident, I understand."

"Yes, she mentioned she wasn't sure how well he was adjusting to his new circumstances. I imagine that's one of the reasons she invited him to visit her for a while."

With a knowing nod of her head, Mary silently confirmed that adjusting to a disability of any sort wasn't an easy—or a short—process.

LESS THAN AN HOUR LATER, with Abby onboard, the ferry sounded its horn and eased away from the Green Harbor dock into the open water of the strait. Cloud cover spread like gray flannel across the top of Arrowhead Hill in the center of Sparrow Island. The sea took on the same gunmetal gray as the sky, so that at the horizon there was little to define the earth from the heavens.

Generally when she traveled by ferry, Abby enjoyed standing

out on the deck to watch the passing scene, hoping to catch a glimpse of the pod of killer whales that remained in these waters year round or to see porpoises playing in the ferry's wake. But it was less than fifty degrees outside and still drizzling. Staying in the main cabin with a cup of coffee seemed a better choice today.

She was looking forward to meeting with the San Juan Islands Birding Society. One of the joys of her previous job at Cornell University Lab of Ornithology had been the opportunity to share her love of birding with so many knowledgeable people in the field. From what she'd heard, the members of the local birding society were very much experts on the species that called these islands home, either permanently or as a migration site—the same birds she'd always had a proprietary interest in because she'd grown up observing their behavior.

Since Friday Harbor was the county seat, there were several businesspeople onboard the ferry. This time of year there were few tourists and only a handful families traveling together to the neighboring island. It made for a quiet journey, so she took advantage of the opportunity to pull out her book of daily devotionals and commune with God.

She was so absorbed in her meditations about the myriad ways the Lord brings light into the darkness, that the loudspeaker announcing their arrival at Friday Harbor startled her. Putting her book away, Abby went downstairs to the lower level where she'd left her car, a compact hybrid that served her needs well and did little damage to the environment.

A few minutes later, the front of the ferry yawned open and she drove up the ramp onto solid ground again.

Board members of the Birding Society were to gather at the home of Leanne Van Hoesin, the president of the group.

Abby knew from conversations she'd had with Leanne, that the Van Hoesins owned a boat rental and tour guide service in Friday Harbor. They'd raised two sons on the island, one of whom was active in the family business, the other son still in college. Until fairly recently, Leanne had taught high school biology and spent her summers helping her husband.

Driving a short way out of the town, Abby found the Van Hoesin house, a two-story clapboard structure with brick facing and flower beds on either side of the walkway to the front door.

She parked on the street behind a pickup truck, grabbed her briefcase and walked up to the house through the continuing mist. She imagined the flower beds would be bright with color during the summer, but now there was only a little greenery, and winter moss grew in the cracks in the walkway.

The woman who answered the door was strikingly tall, perhaps five-foot-ten, and about Abby's age, in her mid-fifties. She looked very trim and fit.

"You must be Abby. It's so good to meet you at last." With a welcoming smile, Leanne extended her hand.

Abby reciprocated, noting the woman's firm grip. "It's good of you to have me here. I've been looking forward to meeting you and the board members."

Leanne ushered her into what appeared to be a family room with warm wood paneling that held original oil seascapes and bookshelves with handmade models of ships of all sizes. The focal point of the room was the sliding glass door that opened onto a redwood deck, much like the one at Mary's house. Below the deck and visible from the window, the sea throbbed against the rocks.

"What an incredible view," Abby commented.

"Fortunately we bought the house long before Friday Harbor became so popular, or we never could have afforded the view, much less the house." Leanne cupped Abby's elbow and introduced her to the board members who were attending the meeting.

Abby concentrated hard in an effort to remember their names, using the memory tricks she'd picked up from a fellow professor at Cornell.

Wulf Walkenhorst had shaggy gray hair that made him look very much like his namesake, an aging gray wolf, and his accent spoke of his European roots. Fortyish, Maureen O'Leary had the telltale red hair of an Irish girl, enhanced, Abby suspected, by her beautician. Nothing came to mind to help her remember Susan Beck's name, so Abby simply tried to memorize her heart-shaped face.

Pamela Folz extended her hand, although her dark glasses and the golden retriever guide dog at her feet gave away the fact that she was blind—a surprising disability for someone so involved with bird watching.

"I'm glad to meet you," Abby said as she took Pamela's hand. "My sister's confined to a wheelchair and has a mixed Labrador retriever as a service dog. His name's Finnegan."

"This is Harriet," Pamela responded, her free hand finding its way to her dog's head and gently stroking her. "Perhaps sometime we can arrange for Harriet and Finnegan to have a play date."

Abby laughed, as did the others in the room. "I'll be sure to mention that to Mary. I'm confident Finnegan would be delighted."

The last board member was by far the youngest, Justin Foote. Barely out of his teens, Justin had an intensity that belied his youth as he came to his feet to shake Abby's hand. His blue eyes flashed with laser sharpness.

"It's sure good to have a professional on the team, ma'am."

Suddenly feeling old, Abby winced inwardly at the *ma'am* part. "I've found that amateur birders are often as skilled at identifying birds as some of the professionals in the field. I certainly couldn't do the project I have in mind without the help of your group."

Justin appeared taken aback by her enthusiastic support of volunteers. "Yeah, well . . ." Shrugging, he finger-combed his straight blond hair away from his forehead.

Leanne offered coffee, tea or juice to those interested, and put out a plate of cookies, crackers and cheese for snacks. Then they got down to business.

Spreading out a detailed map of Sparrow Island, Abby said, "There hasn't been a complete inventory of bald eagles on the island for nearly a decade. I'm hoping to update the information and locate nesting sites, as well as catalog the most likely spots to view itinerant eagles."

"So you can keep the tourists away, right?" Justin asked.

"No. Actually, I'd like people to be able to see the birds in their natural habitat, without disturbing them, of course. I think they gain a greater appreciation of a species if they can see and understand them."

Justin didn't look entirely convinced.

"That's sure true of bald eagles," Wulf said, backing up Abby's position. "Once you've seen an eagle swoop in to snatch a herring right off the top of a wave, you can't help but want to cheer him on. Beautiful creatures."

Nodding, Pamela vigorously agreed.

Susan spoke up. "You still may want to put up signs to warn

people to stay a hundred yards away from nesting sites. Sometimes, out of ignorance or curiosity, people get too close and upset the birds."

"That's a good idea, particularly along the most popular hiking trails."

Justin seemed somewhat mollified by that decision.

"I've noted on the map the half dozen nesting sights previously identified," Abby continued, returning their attention to the map. "I believe there are more now, however, and we'll need to confirm those already marked."

"The general population of bald eagles in the islands is increasing," Leanne confirmed. "Last year we noted the prior year's young were staying around to help raise the new chicks, which is quite unusual in this area. And breeding territories are getting smaller too."

"That's because boats and people are encroaching on their food sources." Justin reached for a chocolate chip cookie, popped it in his mouth in two bites, then took another.

He was so slender, all lanky arms and legs. Abby decided the extra calories would do him some good.

"Habitat encroachment's a problem," Pamela agreed. "But at least we've stopped landowners from cutting down large, old-growth trees that could serve as nesting sites."

"It's interesting," Leanne said, "how every human action has a reaction in nature. Since we reduced the use of DDT, eagles have been better able to reproduce, and their population, at least in the Northwest, has grown. But now, the increase in human population has affected the eagles' habitat and they can't strike out on their own. Yet, the population continues to grow because last year's hatchlings are increasing the chances of this year's chicks surviving."

"The environment and its effects are a complicated subject." Unable to resist, Abby took a cookie from the tray. "In every case, nature attempts to adjust to changes, man-made or otherwise. It's just that we can't always tell what the long-term impact will be on changing bird populations. Sometimes it's neither good nor bad. Just different."

For a while, they discussed environmental pressures on the bird population, then Abby returned to the topic of the upcoming eagle census.

"I've identified twelve routes on Sparrow Island that should be covered," she said. "But I'm not sure if you have enough members willing to hike through the woods on a Saturday morning, particularly if it's raining."

"Oh, we'll easily have more than a dozen volunteers. A little rain won't stop them." As if to confirm her prediction, Leanne glanced at her fellow board members, who seemed to agree. "I imagine we'll be able to go out in pairs and maybe even some threesomes so we can include newer club members."

"That would be perfect! I'd like to include some of our conservatory volunteers, too, if that's all right with you."

"The more the merrier," Wulf said.

"I'll map out the routes I have in mind," Abby told them, "then divide them up depending how many people show up."

"When you get the sites located," Justin said, "I can put it all in the computer and generate a full-scale map, if you'd like."

"That would be terrific," Abby said, loving the enthusiastic response of the group. "I admit that computer work, particularly graphics, is not my strong suit."

Blushing slightly, he smiled in a way that said "no big deal."

Together they selected a week from the coming Saturday as the census date. Volunteers from the Birding Society and those from Sparrow Island would join up at the ferry landing at eight thirty that morning, then spread out across the island to do their counting. They'd regroup at The Nature Museum for lunch, and Abby would arrange to have sandwiches and soft drinks brought in by Springhouse Café.

After a little more talk about indigenous birds in the region, Wulf excused himself to return to work. That seemed to break up the meeting. Maureen, who had been quiet throughout the meeting, stood.

"I'm probably the least skilled birder of the group," she said apologetically. "But I'm ever so excited to be a part of this. Until Pamela dragged me into the Society, I had no idea birds could be so much fun. Now I love to spend time in the woods just watching them flit around."

"She's been a quick learner too. Another few years, she'll know more than any of the rest of us do." Pamela stood, and her dog Harriet responded immediately, taking up a position on her left side. "She's also become my eyes when we go birding, as well as my personal driver on all sorts of expeditions."

"That's wonderful," Abby said.

"I don't really do much. When we're birding, Pamela hears a birdcall, points where I should look and tells me what bird to look for."

"And usually she tells us which branch or stump the bird is sitting on and who its mother was," Leanne added with a chuckle.

Pamela denied she was that good at spotting birds.

With a shake of his head that said he wasn't quite buying that, Justin excused himself as well and left with the women.

Turning to Leanne, Abby said, "I'm very impressed with your group. What an interesting mix of people."

"Pamela lost her sight to macular degeneration a couple of years ago, but she absolutely refused to give up birding, so she learned to rely on her other senses."

"She seems like an amazing individual." Both Abby's sister and Pamela Folz were living examples of overcoming handicaps and thriving in the process. "I'm also impressed with Justin. Sometimes it's hard to get young people involved in activities like birding." Abby was quite proud of the small cadre of teenage volunteers she'd recruited for the conservatory.

"Yes, he's a brilliant young man and quite enthusiastic. He has brought in a couple of his young friends, too, who've joined the group. The good Lord knows the Society can use some new blood now and then to keep us on our toes. The rest of us aren't getting any younger."

"Too true."

Abby thanked Leanne again for her hospitality and the willingness of the Birding Society to be a part of her census effort.

Just as she stepped out the front door, a column of sunlight streamed through a break in the cloud cover and a rainbow appeared in the north against a backdrop of darker clouds. Abby's spirits immediately rose.

Thank You, Lord, for promises made and kept, and for the coming of spring.

CHAPTER ✿ TWO

Every florist in the country was vying with wholesalers for deliveries of red roses, including Mary at Island Blooms.

Hanging up after her latest call to her Seattle supplier, Mary exhaled a long, troubled sigh.

"Will they be able to get us the flowers we need?" Candace Grover, the shop manager, popped out of the back workroom to check on Mary's progress. With only three more days to go until Valentine's Day, the large walk-in refrigerator was nearly bare of roses and had limited supplies of carnations, flock, daisies and marigolds. Even the stock of baby's breath, gerberas and assorted greens looked short.

"Antonio says he'll get us all the flowers we need. I'm just not sure he'll get them here for Valentine's Day." Worried, Mary wheeled herself away from the front reception desk and rolled toward the dangerously empty refrigerator. "He sounds so harassed, it may be Easter before he fills all of his orders."

"That doesn't sound good." Frowning, Candace glanced at the stack of Island Blooms orders to be filled, a pile of more than forty slips of paper on the desk. "Maybe I should take the ferry to the mainland tonight and get to the flower market first thing in the morning."

"You'd have to be there by three or three-thirty to have any chance of picking up what we need. You wouldn't get any sleep at all, and couldn't get back to the island until the early ferry departs."

Mary remembered her frequent visits to the wholesale market when she first opened the shop. It was an exciting place filled with the scent of an unimaginable variety of blooms, somehow enhanced by the darkness and chill air of early morning. Nowadays flowers were brought in literally from all over the world, often by plane. Depending upon the season, they arrived from California or South America, even Israel. The pace of the workers—both buyers and sellers—was frantic as florists, wholesalers and individuals vied for the best and freshest flowers they could find.

"I'll be all right," Candace insisted. "Brad will let me nap on his couch and I can sleep on the ferry ride back home."

Although Mary was confident Candace's boyfriend wouldn't object to her visit, she hated to impose on the young woman's willingness to make the trip to the market. She'd been such a godsend since Mary's accident, taking on much of the responsibility of running Island Blooms. And it was possible that Antonio would be able to fill her order by tomorrow or the next day. In which case, they might end up with double the amount of flowers they needed and twice the expense.

That would be better than not having enough and being unable to satisfy her customers, Mary realized.

Candace plucked a fading leaf from a white African violet plant and tossed it in a trash can under the counter. As she often did while working at the shop, Candace was wearing a colorful smock over her blouse and broomstick skirt. A beaded necklace completed the hippie-era outfit. Her long strawberry-blonde hair hung nearly to her waist.

"I think I should go," she said. "Brad's been so busy with a big case he's working on that I haven't seen him in a couple of weeks. This would be a good time to remind him that Valentine's is coming and girlfriends should not be forgotten."

Mary chuckled at the mischievous twinkle in the young woman's eyes. Despite being very much opposites, Candace and her attorney boyfriend had a loving relationship, but so far there'd been little talk of marriage. At least Mary hadn't heard of any.

"If you're sure you don't mind," Mary said.

"Not at all, I promise. The trip will be a nice break for me."

"I don't want to lose Antonio as my supplier or end up with a double order of everything. Maybe you can coordinate with him when you get to the market so there won't be duplicates."

"Sure, that should work." She glanced toward the front of the shop just as the bell on the door jingled to announce the arrival of a customer. "Speaking of boyfriends," she said with a conspiratorial grin.

Mary experienced a little flutter of pleasure as she turned to find Henry Cobb striding into the shop, looking spiffy as always in his deputy sheriff's uniform of dark-green pants, tan shirt with a tie and matching green jacket.

"Good morning, ladies. How are you this fine day?"

"I'm great, sergeant." Still grinning, Candace shot a knowing look in Mary's direction. "But if you'll excuse me, I've got some work to do in the back room."

Embarrassed, Mary watched as her shop manager fled into the workroom, leaving her alone with Henry.

Smiling warmly, he crossed the room and leaned against the counter, thumbing his Smokey-the-Bear hat farther up on his forehead. "I hope she didn't leave because of anything I said."

"Subtlety may not be Candace's strong suit."

"Perhaps not, but I appreciate her timing. How are you today, Mary?"

"I'm quite well, thank you, sir. Though I could use some sunshine. If you could arrange that, I'd be most appreciative."

"I'll do my very best. Meanwhile, I dropped by to invite you out to dinner on Saturday night. The Dorset is having a special menu for Valentine's Day and live dinner music. I thought you might enjoy that."

"How sweet of you to ask." Mary flushed, flattered by his invitation to dinner at the nicest hotel in Green Harbor. Henry was a handsome man of sixty-two, four years older than she, and a good friend. They'd been seeing each other socially for quite some time, and her feelings for Henry were more than platonic. But where they would lead, she wasn't quite sure. "Let me make a counteroffer, though. The Dorset is always so crowded on holidays and even with a reservation we'd probably have to wait. Why don't I cook dinner for you instead?"

He looked surprised by her suggestion. "Won't you be too tired to cook that night? I know Valentine's has got to be one of your busiest days of the year."

"It is, that and Mother's Day. But I can start something in the slow cooker before I come into work, and it'll be ready for us by the end of the day. All I'll have to do is pop some rolls in the oven, put together a salad, and we'll be able to eat."

"Well," he said hesitantly. "If you're sure. We can go to the Dorset another night when they're not so busy."

Pleased, she let her smile tell him so. "I'll consider that a rain check and take you up on the offer later in the year. Let's say seven o'clock Saturday then, shall we? At my house?"

"Perfect." Straightening his hat, Henry started to leave.

Remembering her morning conversation with Abby, Mary stopped him.

"Henry, what do you know about our lighthouse going dark?"

"Not much," he conceded. "Mostly just what I read in *The Birdcall.* It doesn't fall under my jurisdiction. That's the Coast Guard's bailiwick."

Her forehead tugged into a frown. "I know, but it just seems so strange to me that the Coast Guard denies there's anything wrong when all the ships' captains agree the lighthouse wasn't working."

"Mary, you're not trying to drum up a mystery to solve like your sister's always doing, are you?"

She sputtered a denial. "Well, it *is* curious, don't you think?"

He laughed at her comment. "This is a real quiet time of year here on the islands, without tourists getting themselves into a mess or making mischief. Trust me, I'm not one to go looking for trouble on my own. I'll wait till it comes to me. I suggest, with Valentine's Day coming so soon, that you have enough to worry about without taking on the Coast Guard too."

Mary supposed he was right. But it did strike her as peculiar. . . .

Hush, she told herself as Henry went out the door. Abby was the amateur sleuth in the family and she hadn't seemed all that concerned about the lighthouse problem at breakfast. She should just leave it at that.

RETURNING HOME FROM FRIDAY HARBOR, Abby bought a salad on the ferry for lunch, then headed for The Nature Museum after she disembarked at Sparrow Island. The clouds had lifted considerably since morning and there were bright patches of blue sky peeking through the clouds, promising a beautiful afternoon.

Hugo Baron, a world-renowned naturalist, had established the Sparrow Island Nature Conservatory in 1981 to protect and conserve nearly ninety acres of virtually untouched land on the island, including areas of old-growth forest and an extensive shoreline. A few years later he added The Nature Museum, where Abby now worked.

From her perspective, working for Hugo as Associate Curator was an ideal job.

Abby parked her car in an almost empty parking lot and started toward the two-story, stone-and-stucco building that housed various natural history displays as well as her office. A shadow passing across the ground and the sibilant whisper of wings overhead caused her to look up.

Two immature bald eagles—no doubt itinerants recently arrived from the Fraser River salmon spawning area on the mainland—flew by en route to their new feeding grounds near the shoreline.

She smiled to herself as she walked by the bigleaf maple in the center of the circular drive, still stripped of leaves this time of year but with a hint of the buds to come. The timing of the eagle census ten days from now would be perfect for catching the birds at their maximum population on the island. Although those two young eagles hadn't yet acquired the distinctive black-and-white markings of an adult, their wingspan was still nearly eight feet wide.

In the Center's reception area, Wilma Washburn, the museum's secretary, bookkeeper and general go-to gal, greeted her.

"Hi, Abby. Sure nice to see a little sunshine, isn't it?"

Apparently even Wilma, who, like Abby, had been born here on Sparrow Island, was tired of the recent spate of gray skies and rain. "It is indeed. And I just spotted a pair of newly arrived eagles, so they must appreciate the sunshine too."

Wilma's characteristically dark eyes and Native American features became animated. "Ah, eagles are always a good omen. It means the tourists can't be far behind."

Raising her brows, Abby said, "Is that what your ancestors told you?"

"I'm sure they must have."

Abby laughed as Wilma had no doubt intended. "Then I'll remind you of that *good omen* this summer when you start complaining about too many tourists cluttering the streets of Green Harbor and taking all the parking places."

With good humor, Wilma waved off her threat, and Abby, still chuckling, headed for her office through the doorway marked Private.

She was about to hang up her jacket when her phone rang. Noting the caller ID was Island Blooms, she quickly picked up.

"Oh good," Mary said when Abby answered. "You're back from Friday Harbor. How'd your meeting go?"

"Fine. Is anything wrong?" Her sister didn't often call Abby at work, and she always felt a stab of worry for fear something might have happened to their parents, who were both in their early eighties, or to Mary herself.

"Not a thing. Except getting red roses this year is a real struggle," she added as an afterthought. "But I called to let you know Henry's coming to dinner Saturday night."

"That will be nice for Valentine's Day."

"And I thought, as long as I was going to do up a big pot of Swiss steak in the slow cooker, you might want to invite Hugo to dinner too. We'll make it a foursome."

"Hugo? Oh well, I don't know . . ." Although Hugo was a true gentleman and Abby was very fond of him, he was her boss. Valentine's Day, a day generally reserved for sweethearts, seemed an awkward time to invite him to dinner.

"Of course, Hugo. Unless there's some other man you'd rather invite."

Abby frowned. "You're not trying to play matchmaker again, are you?"

"No, Abby, I know better than that."

Mary sounded offended by the remark, despite the fact she'd tried her hand at matchmaking before, and not only with Abby.

"Hugo's been a good friend to both of us," Mary continued, "and to our parents. Henry enjoys his company too. We always have a pleasant time when we're together."

All of which was true, Abby conceded. "All right, I'll invite him, but he may have other plans. I'll let you know what he says."

"Good. You can tell me this evening."

After hanging up, Abby checked her messages, returning one to a professor at the University of Washington, whose

Wildlife Biology students did some bird-watching field studies on Sparrow Island under Abby's supervision.

That project's schedule confirmed, Abby headed for Hugo's office to see if he was in.

Although he was on the phone, he waved her inside through the open doorway. As always, his office was as neat as a pin. Only a polished granite pen and pencil holder and one yellow pad, on which he was writing notes, rested on his desk as he listened to his caller.

On top of the bookcase near his desk were a few mementos he'd brought back from some of his many travels: a whale bone from a Baja California beach; a photograph of himself with a group of Masai tribesmen; and a drawing of a moose done on birch bark by a native Alaskan.

Dressed with his usual care, Hugo wore a business suit and a silk maroon tie precisely knotted at the neck of his white shirt. With his white hair and mustache and regal manners, nothing detracted from his overall appearance of elegance.

In contrast, Abby's navy business suit and pale blue blouse seemed to lack the class and sophistication that was second nature to Hugo.

Concluding his phone conversation, he smiled at Abby and gestured toward the chair in front of his desk. "Sorry to keep you waiting."

"No problem."

Leaning forward in an interested way, he tented his long fingers under his chin. "How'd your meeting go at Friday Harbor?"

"Very well, I'd say." She related her morning's activities, concluding with her plan to let the conservatory's volunteers know about the eagle census program and encouraging them to participate.

"Excellent. It sounds like a morning well spent."

"It was indeed. I'm very impressed with the group." Feeling slightly ill at ease, she adjusted her position in the leather chair. "When I got back to the office, I had a call from Mary. She's invited Henry Cobb to dinner on Saturday night and would like you to join us, if you're free."

A sparkle lit his blue eyes. "On Valentine's Day. A perfect way to spend such an evening, dining with good friends."

Abby felt the tension ease from her shoulders and realized it was odd she'd been nervous about extending the invitation. He was, as Mary had said, not just her boss but a good friend of the family as well.

"Good," she said as she rose. "I'm glad you can make it. Mary will be pleased too."

Hugo stood as well, his posture erect. "I'm looking forward to it."

Returning to her office, Abby finished up some paperwork and then generated a flyer to post to notify volunteers about the census activity. Her computer skills might not be as finely tuned as Justin Foote's apparently were, but the flyer would get the message across.

The sun was already slipping below the horizon as she drove home and there was a lovely silver lining on the bottom of the retreating clouds to the west. She hoped that boded well for a sunny day tomorrow. The weather report she'd heard on the news, however, suggested another storm was coming in from the north.

Shuddering a little, she thought of the problems that could

occur if the Wayfarer Point Lighthouse went dark in the middle of a severe winter storm. It could be disastrous.

As she pulled into the driveway of the house she shared with Mary, she pressed the automatic door opener on the car's visor and drove into the garage. She parked next to Mary's specially equipped van that allowed her sister to drive, despite the fact that she no longer had the use of her legs.

It was just one of the many adjustments Mary'd had to make since her accident.

Abby hoped, given a little time, that Sandy's great uncle, who they'd meet tonight, would be able to adjust to his new limitations as well.

It occurred to Abby that macular degeneration, which had stolen Pamela Folz's eyesight, had no doubt come on her by degrees, which allowed her time to adjust to her changing situation. In contrast, apparently Sandy's great uncle had gone from normal vision to blindness in an instant.

Little wonder he was having trouble adjusting to his new circumstances.

AFTER A LIGHT DINNER of homemade chicken soup, Abby and Mary headed for the McDonald's house next door. The clouds had cleared, leaving the sky carpeted with shimmering stars, but the air was still damp with the threat of renewed rain.

The uneven roadway made it difficult to maneuver the wheelchair, so Abby pushed and Finnegan helped by pulling Mary along. Once there, Sandy's husband Neil helped get Mary and her wheelchair into the house, then took their jackets to hang them up.

Sandy bent down to give Mary a hug, then gave Abby a hug too. "I'm so glad you could join us."

Grinning in his usual proud way, Neil said, "Sandy's desserts are worth going a lot farther for than just next door."

"Mom made chocolate cake," Bobby, their ten-year-old son announced. "*Three* layers!"

"Wow. Her famous Chocolate Wonder cake, I bet. I sure hope you didn't sneak a piece before we got here," Mary teased. "I may want to eat it all myself."

"We have to share," Bobby assured them. "But I told Mom she could make another one tomorrow for just us."

Everyone laughed, and Neil gave his son an affectionate tap on the top of his dark-brown head.

Going to the couch, Sandy took the arm of the gentleman sitting there, urging him to stand. He looked to be in his seventies, with an athletic physique, salt-and-pepper hair cut short and a stubble of whiskers as though he was growing a beard. His eyes were invisible behind dark glasses.

Sandy made the introductions. "I'd like you both to meet my great uncle, Robert Weatherford. Mary Reynolds and Abby Stanton."

"He's how come I'm named Bobby," Bobby announced quite proudly. "Well, Robert Neil McDonald, really, 'cuz he's my mom's favorite uncle, but I got named after my dad too."

"It's a pleasure to meet you." Abby took Robert's hand, which he hadn't really offered, though she suspected that was because he hadn't yet learned how to deal with his blindness. "I'm Abby." She placed his hand in Mary's outstretched one. "And this is Mary, my sister."

"I imagine Sandy mentioned that I'm in a wheelchair and not really as short as I seem," Mary said in a light tone. "Of course, all the ruckus of Neil getting me into the house was probably a clue too."

"Right. Good to meet you." Without a smile, he dropped his hand to his side.

"I also have my service dog with me. Finnegan, meet Mr. Weatherford."

Finnegan *chuffed* his greeting and wagged his tail, but Robert appeared unimpressed.

"Uncle Robert has traveled all around the world, building dams and bridges and all sorts of fascinating things." Looking distressed, Sandy spoke quickly, as though trying to cover for her uncle's lack of enthusiasm. "He has a world of stories to tell."

"Which nobody cares one whit about anymore. It's old news."

"Uncle Robert—"

He shuffled two steps backwards to the couch and sat down heavily.

Sandy looked like she might burst into tears. The stress of holding her emotions in check tightened her lips. Apparently they had been having a difficult time since her uncle's arrival yesterday.

Her heart aching for Sandy, all Abby could do was to smile encouragingly. She doubted Sandy's uncle had always been this grumpy. But drastic changes in one's life could change a person's outlook, at least temporarily.

"Uncle Robert," Bobby said softly as he sat down on the three-cushion couch next to his uncle. "I care about your stories. I've never, ever been to all the places you've been. Sometime, maybe, I'll go, but I'm not big enough yet. So you gotta tell me about 'em. Okay?"

Moved, Robert reached out blindly and hooked his arm around the boy's shoulders, tugging him closer. "I'll try, junior."

Although Abby knew Bobby wasn't 'officially' a junior, the nickname seemed especially appropriate coming from the man who had inspired his name.

"You're gonna teach me ham radio, too, right?" Bobby asked.

"Now don't push your Uncle Robert too hard about that," the boy's father warned.

The ghost of a smile hovered at the corners of Robert's lips. "We'll see about that."

"You're an amateur radio operator?" Abby asked. She'd seated herself in the matching chair next to the couch, both pieces of furniture upholstered in a subdued wine-color fabric that picked up the highlights of the pattern in the Oriental-style rug.

He nodded. "Since I was fourteen years old. My stateside call is W7PQ."

"Wherever he traveled, even in the jungles of South America, he used to take a radio with him," Sandy explained. "When he could, he'd call us and we'd all get to talk to him. I especially remember him calling when I was little, and Mother would get so excited." She lightly touched her uncle's shoulder, no doubt recalling with some sadness that her mother had died when Sandy was only eight years old. "You called here a couple of years ago. Remember?"

"I remember. It's called a phone patch," Robert said. "It only works when I can raise a ham operator fairly close to the person I'm trying to call and he makes the call for me." After the explanation, Uncle Robert fell silent again.

"You folks visit a bit." Sandy forced a smile. "I'll serve the cake."

"May I help you?" Abby asked.

"No, no. It'll just take me a minute."

"Uncle Robert knows Morse code and everything," Bobby bragged as his mother left the room.

Finnegan stirred, apparently thinking Mary might be on the move, too, then settled down again next to her wheelchair.

"Really?" Abby chuckled slightly. "When Mary and I were little, we learned a little Morse code and sent secret messages back and forth to each other with our flashlights. One of us would be in the tree house out back and the other one inside. Not that what we had to say was all that secret, of course. Usually it was something about bring me a cookie or a soft drink."

"Goodness. I'd almost forgotten about that. And I know I'd be hard pressed to remember much Morse code now," Mary said.

"I'm gonna learn to send code too," Bobby said. "I got a book from the library and Uncle Robert is gonna help me."

"You don't need Morse code to get a technician's ham radio license nowadays," Robert said. "Just another way they've made the requirements easier. In my day, you had to be able to send and receive code at thirteen words a minute, and know something about electronics, too, not just be a fool appliance operator."

"I want to learn code anyway," Bobby said. "It'd be cool to send secret messages from my tree house."

"Who are you going to send messages to, son?" Neil asked.

"I dunno. Maybe Mary and Abby will learn code again."

"How about your imaginary pirates?" Abby asked. "They'd have something interesting to say, like where they've buried their treasure."

Bobby scowled. "It'd be better with a real person."

Sandy returned carrying a tray with slices of rich chocolate devil's food cake on dessert plates.

Coming to his feet, Neil offered his help. A big man with broad shoulders, he worked on the ferries that plied the waters of the Northwest. His oversize hands were strong enough to handle the thick lines that held the ferry to the dock, yet gentle enough to deliver delicate china plates to his guests.

"Thank you, honey," Sandy said. "While you do that, I'll bring the coffee. This time of night, I made decaf."

"Perfect," Abby said.

Neil served Mary a slice of cake first.

"Thank you, Neil. This looks wonderful." She accepted the plate, troubled by Robert's barely disguised anger and his glum expression. Although he might feel his anger was justified, she knew for a fact it was a self-defeating emotion in the face of adversity.

"Here you go, Robert." Neil put the plate directly in Robert's left hand. "The fork's on the right side of the plate."

"I shouldn't be eating in the living room. I'll get crumbs all over."

"It doesn't matter, Uncle Robert," Sandy assured him. "That's what vacuums are for."

"Cleaning up after blind old men who can't even feed themselves. *Humph!* Lucky you."

Mary exchanged a sympathetic look with the others in the room, her heart going out to all the McDonalds.

Wheeling her chair forward, she moved closer to Robert. "I remember after my accident, when the doctors told me I'd never walk again, I was angry at the entire world, including myself, the deer that I *didn't* hit, the doctors and every able-bodied person I saw. I was even angry with God."

Stabbing a bite of cake, Robert tried to get it into his mouth, but it fell off, dribbling into his lap. "You had every right to be angry, if that's how you felt."

"I may have had the right, but it certainly wasn't a very productive attitude. All it did was make me feel miserable. I was hurting myself as well as those who were trying to help me."

"At least you ended up in a wheelchair because of an accident. The people who did this to me, did it on purpose!"

She closed her eyes, sending up a quick prayer asking God to give her the right words to say.

"When God takes something away from you," she said to Robert, remembering the words her father had spoken during one of her darkest days in the hospital, "it's because He intends to give you another gift that will bring you great joy."

"*Humph!* What's He going to give me that will replace my eyes, huh?"

"I'm sure I don't know. But He does. He's just waiting until you're ready to accept the gift He has in mind."

CHAPTER ❦ THREE

AN UNCOMFORTABLE silence filled the room. The family photos on top of the fireplace mantel were more animated than the people sitting there holding their breath. Even Robert had no comeback for Mary's comment because it had so obviously come from the heart.

Abby wanted to cheer for her sister. She had traveled a long, hard path before coming to grips with her limitations. At the same time, Abby prayed Robert's journey would bring him the inner peace he so obviously lacked at the moment.

"I lost a friend once," Bobby said solemnly, breaking the silence. "When Matt Bender moved to Los Angeles, I was real upset and almost cried and stuff. Then the very next day, José Bondevik showed up in my class. Now he's my very best friend ever. Guess he was God's gift, huh? Dad's even gonna take us fishing, aren't you, Dad?"

Neil's smile was filled with both love and pride. "I am, along with Uncle Robert, *if* the weather is good."

Obviously relieved to have gotten past an awkward moment, Sandy said, "Tomorrow's a short day at school for a teacher inservice and Neil's taking the day off. The boys will have a good time."

Everyone seemed excited about the arrangement except Robert. Abby suspected he felt as though Neil had been assigned to babysit him and that didn't sit well with his pride.

After enjoying a couple of bites of rich chocolate cake, Abby decided to return to a safe topic. "Robert, did you bring a ham radio with you?"

"Just my two-meter rig," he answered. "I didn't think Sandy'd want me putting up a sixty-foot tower in her backyard for my twenty-meter antenna. Not for such a short visit."

"My, goodness," Mary said. "That sounds so technical. I have no idea what you're talking about."

"It's not that hard. Easy enough for junior here to learn if he works at it. Two meters is for line-of-sight communication, not long distance. There's a repeater on top of your Mount Ortiz, here on the island. So I can talk all around the San Juans and probably to the mainland. If I had anything to say, that is."

"I don't know how active the local repeater is," Sandy said. "But I thought he might find some buddies to talk to so I encouraged him to bring his radio."

"And have you? Found anyone to talk to?" Abby asked.

"Mostly listened so far. I'm not all that good at sitting around all day rag chewing."

Abby didn't need a translation for that bit of jargon. Robert had been active all of his life and probably rarely just sat talking with friends on the radio to pass the time. That could well be another adjustment he'd have to make.

"Can I show 'em your radio, Uncle Robert?" Bobby asked.

"Don't know that they'd be interested in an ordinary hand-held radio," he said.

"I'm interested." Glancing toward Mary, Abby hoped her sister would chime in too.

"If Bobby could bring the radio out, that would be very nice," she said.

"Hugo Baron—my boss at The Nature Museum—and I use a small family radio to communicate around the conservatory when we're out in the field working."

"Those things only work at about five miles and you don't need a license." Rubbing his whiskered chin, Robert finally relented. "Okay, junior, go get my radio. But be careful."

Like he'd been goosed by a wayward spring in the couch, Bobby hopped up and raced from the room, which caused Finnegan to come to his feet as well. Bobby returned with somewhat more dignity, carrying a radio not much bigger than the one Abby had used. This one, however, had a longer antenna rather than the four-inch one on her radio.

Mary whispered, "Sit, Finnegan," and the dog resumed his position, although he remained alert for any change of orders.

"Can you show us how it works?" Abby asked Robert.

He shrugged with indifference. "Turn it on, Bobby. You know how to do that."

Bobby complied.

"What's the frequency?" his uncle asked, and Bobby read off the number on the face of the radio.

To Abby's surprise, a disembodied female voice spoke. "Negative fish in the sea."

"Copy that," came a male response. "No bait tonight."

Then the radio went quiet.

"What was that about?" Abby asked.

Robert shook his head. "I don't know. Fool operators didn't even identify themselves by their call signs like they're supposed to."

"Maybe it was a commercial fishing boat," Sandy suggested.

"Shouldn't be. They've got their own marine frequencies."

"Was it someone here on Sparrow Island?" Mary asked.

"Can't tell. Could be anyone who has a radio that can bring up the local repeater."

No one knew what to make of the odd radio transmission, if anything, and Robert didn't seem very forthcoming. Only Bobby appeared fascinated by the radio, examining it in detail and fussing with the knobs.

Finishing her cake and coffee, Abby gathered her plate and Mary's, putting them back on the tray. They visited a few more minutes, mostly talking about the weather, then said their thanks and good-byes.

As they were returning home, Abby noticed fog had drifted in, muting the street lights and blanketing the normal sounds of the neighborhood.

"At least the rain stopped long enough for us to get to the McDonalds and back again," Mary commented as Abby pushed her toward their front door.

"But I don't think we've seen the last of the rainy weather," Abby said. "Another storm's coming in from the north."

"No doubt the good Lord intends us to really appreciate spring this year, after all the rain we've had."

Once inside, Abby hung their coats in the front closet, then followed Mary into the living room.

"Mary, I can't tell you how proud I was of what you told Robert."

"Told him about what?" After taking Finnegan's service

cape off, she wheeled herself across the hardwood floor to the chair where Blossom napped, picking her up and cuddling the cat in her lap. Meanwhile, Finnegan gave himself a big shake and yawned.

"About when God takes something from a person, it's because He's going to give them another gift."

Idly, Mary petted the long-haired cat. "I'm afraid the thought wasn't original to me. It's what Dad told me in the hospital when I was so discouraged I wasn't sure I could go on."

Abby felt a pang of sympathy that Mary had been so disheartened after her accident. How terrible it must have been for her to wake up in a hospital bed and learn she would never walk again. She'd been a woman who had lived life to the fullest, even after the death of her husband, Jacob, whose collection of hand carved scrimshaw was still proudly displayed in an oak and glass showcase in the corner of the living room.

"Well, in any case, it sounded very wise on your part," Abby said. "Although I'm not at all sure Robert's ready to listen to any advice about his disability just yet." Sitting down on the damask couch, Abby stretched out her legs and rotated her head to work out the kinks in her neck. "What did he mean by someone blinding him on purpose?"

"From what Sandy told me, Robert's taking the situation a bit too personally, though I can certainly understand why. He was consulting on the construction of a dam in Mali, a country in Africa where the people have experienced terrible drought and starvation. Apparently, a small group of environmental extremists decided the dam was an affront to the natural course of things and they tried to blow it up,"

"Good heavens!" The thought of someone blowing up a

structure as large as a dam, and as potentially important to an impoverished country, brought a stab of regret to Abby's chest.

"Robert had the misfortune to be touring the site that day. He was injured, along with several other people. In addition to that, the project was set back by a year or more, which means more people will die of hunger."

"Sounds like a tragedy for everyone involved. But the people responsible for blowing up the dam weren't targeting Robert specifically."

"No, it was a question of misguided extremists, unintended consequences and Robert being there at the wrong time."

Taking off her glasses, Abby cleaned them with a tissue, then slid them on again. "You know I'm a great believer in protecting the environment, but not at the cost of injury or loss of life to others. Sometimes it's a fine line we walk. There has to be a balance between all of God's creatures."

"Including humans."

Abby agreed with a nod. "Well, I certainly hope Robert will find a way to cope with the loss of his eyesight. You've adjusted so wonderfully well to your situation—"

"Not every day is all that easy," Mary confessed. "I still have my moments of frustration."

"I'm sure that's true."

"You're one of the gifts that God has sent to me. You and our rediscovered sisterhood."

Abby tried to wave off the thought, though her return to Sparrow Island and the closeness she'd found with her sister had been a blessing for her too.

"I've received other gifts too," Mary said. "From where I sit, I've gained a new perspective. Maybe it's that of a child, looking up. I see new things, like a hive the wasps have created in the eaves of the house that I might otherwise miss or a spider web that's caught just right in the sunlight. And I'm closer to the ground, so in the spring I smell the flowers even more intensely than I did when I could stand upright." Mary seemed pensive, wrapped up in her memories, in the changes she had experienced. "Those are all His gifts to me. They're things I might have missed if it hadn't been for my accident. And *most* days my heart is filled with gratitude for what I've received."

Tears burned in Abby's eyes. She felt humbled—grateful for the gift of her sister's insight and wisdom. And filled with love.

Her throat tightened. "I don't know what to say."

With a flick of her hand, Mary wheeled around and smiled. "I think we ought to pray that Robert finds his peace and learns to *see* in a new way."

"I met a woman today who has certainly found a different way to see since she's lost her eyesight to macular degeneration." Standing, Abby walked over to her sister and placed a loving hand on Mary's shoulder. "In fact, Pamela Folz is eager to arrange a play date between her Harriet and Finnegan."

Mary's head snapped up in surprise. "A what?"

Laughing, Abby related her meeting with Pamela and her guide dog, and the woman's amazing gift for identifying bird songs.

Together they decided, if and when the time was right, they would try to introduce Robert to Pamela Folz. She just might be the catalyst that would open him to the possibilities, the gifts from God, that he hadn't yet recognized.

Later, when Abby went upstairs to bed, she found she wasn't quite ready for sleep yet. Instead, troubled about Robert Weatherford, she sat in the chair next to the window and picked up her Bible, turning to the first chapter of Job, which related the ways in which Job's faith was tested. Even after losing all he had—his wealth, home, servants and family, he could still pray to the Lord.

"Naked I came from my mother's womb, and naked I will depart. The Lord gave and the Lord has taken away; may the name of the Lord be praised" (Job 1:21–22).

Lowering her head in prayer, Abby asked God's blessing on Mary, Robert and Pamela for tests of faith they had suffered, and prayed that they would find the strength to endure.

THE NEXT DAY, Abby organized the routes the volunteers would use during the eagle census and mapped them out using existing roads and trails throughout the island. She also noted the difficulty of each route, not wanting to assign those who were less physically fit to a trail that would demand too much of them.

Making sure the census was a pleasant experience for everyone would help to make it a success, one that volunteers would be happy to repeat in subsequent years.

When Saturday arrived, one of Mary's busiest days of the year at Island Blooms, Abby offered to pick up some last minute items at The Green Grocer for their Valentine's Day dinner.

She parked in front of the store on Kingfisher Avenue. For the first time in several days, the sidewalk was dry, although the awning in front of The Green Grocer was still open to protect pedestrians from the rain. It was likely to be needed again before the rainy season was over.

As she went inside, she waved at Archie Goodfellow, the owner of the store, who was behind the cash register. Wearing his usual green apron with a caricature of himself stenciled on the front, he nodded in acknowledgment.

Selecting a cart, she headed for the bakery. Kari Dryson,

who made the hearty, whole-grain rolls that both Mary and Abby loved, was behind the counter. As usual, a black mesh hairnet held her graying hair in check. Abby couldn't remember ever seeing the woman without it on, which made her wonder if she slept in it too.

"Hi, Kari. How are your rolls today?"

"Better than anything you'll get from those factory bakeries on the mainland, I'll tell you that. They wouldn't know a healthy product if it reared up and hit 'em with a whole sheaf of freshly harvested wheat."

To avoid laughing out loud, Abby cleared her throat and suppressed a smile. Kari definitely had her own opinion about what made for proper nutrition. Most of the time, Abby agreed with her.

"Sounds good to me," Abby said. "Why don't you give me a dozen of the whole-wheat rolls then."

Kari leaned across the glass enclosed display counter. "You and Mary planning a party?"

"Just a small dinner party for Valentine's Day."

"*Humph.* Bet Mary invited Sergeant Cobb. He's got one big crush on her."

"I think you're right about that."

Glancing up and down her display case, Kari zeroed in on her pies. "Henry's right fond of my cherry pie. Would save Mary the trouble of making dessert if you bought one and took it home. They're real popular around this time of year with George Washington's birthday and all."

That was probably true, and Abby wasn't sure what Mary had planned for dessert. She only knew that the Swiss steak was already in the slow cooker and she'd been asked to get rolls and the makings for a nice salad.

"In that case," Abby said, "I'm sure a cherry pie won't go to waste. I'll take one."

Apparently satisfied with Abby's decision, Kari bagged the rolls and slipped the pie into a box, taping it closed.

"Now don't tip that pie over," Kari warned. "It'll leak juice and make some awful mess."

Abby agreed to use care, then headed for the produce section. She was selecting a cucumber to slice for the salad when Margaret Blackstock joined her. In a small town like Green Harbor, the grocery store was one of the places where the paths of local residents often crossed, providing an opportunity to keep up with their neighbors.

"Say, now, those cucumbers are *beyoodyful*," Margaret said with a Brooklyn accent she hadn't lost in the dozen years she'd lived on Sparrow Island. "It's something else, isn't it, that Archie can get good-looking vegetables this time of year?"

"Sure is," Abby agreed. "He probably intimidates his suppliers so they know to bring only the best of their produce."

"Of course, he charges plenty for 'em too." Picking up a cucumber from the neatly stacked pile, Margaret used the granny glasses that hung on a chain around her neck to examine her selection. "Did you hear what happened to Neil McDonald and his boy?"

"No. What?" Although Margaret was probably one of the biggest gossips in town, she was good hearted. And as the school secretary, she often heard news around town that escaped Abby's notice.

"A certain party told me Neil and Bobby and that boy, José Bondevik, and Sandy's uncle were out fishing yesterday when the fog came rolling in."

"Did they have a problem?"

"They sure did. They were coming back in, out by Wayfarer Point, and the lighthouse just plain went dark. Like somebody blew out a candle. Third or fourth time that's happened in the past couple of weeks."

"Did they get home all right?"

"Made it home fine, I hear, but it must've put a scare into them."

"Thank God they're safe. But what on earth is happening? From what I read in *The Birdcall* the Coast Guard denies there's a problem with the lighthouse."

Margaret dropped the cucumber into a bag and selected a second one with the same care. "Well, I say the problem doesn't have anything to do with the Coast Guard. The *problem* isn't earthly at all." She lowered her voice to a whisper. "It's the ghost of Terrence Pettigrew who's making mischief out at Wayfarer Point."

Thinking she'd surely heard Margaret wrong, Abby shook her head. "You mean Bryant Pettigrew who owns that derelict boat at the marina is messing with the lighthouse?" The man was in his seventies and lived on the old fishing boat alone and rarely ventured farther from the marina than the Springhouse Café to have a meal.

"Not *Bryant*," Margaret emphasized. "His daddy, Terrence. He was the last man who was lighthouse keeper out there at Wayfarer Point, and I hear he was none too pleased back in '61 when they automated the light and fired him. They even moved him out of his house, leaving him no place to live after all those years. It's a spite thing, don't you know."

Margaret's suggestion stunned Abby. Although she didn't

doubt Terrence Pettigrew had been upset about being let go, she certainly couldn't imagine his *ghost*, for heaven's sake, was sneaking about getting revenge after all these years.

"Margaret, ghosts don't exist. And they certainly don't wait around for more than forty years to start haunting whatever it might be they'd want to haunt."

Margaret planted her fist on her hip. She was wearing a neon-orange jogging suit that would have warned off any approaching driver if she'd been running along a street, which wasn't something Margaret ever did, based on her rather full figure.

"Now I know you're far more educated than I am, but I'm telling you there's no other explanation for what's happening. Everybody knows ghosts like to flicker lights and scare people. And that's exactly what's going on at Wayfarer Point Lighthouse."

"There's another explanation, Margaret. We just don't know what it is yet."

Margaret snorted a rather unladylike sound. "That's good to know, 'cause the whole town will be happy to find out what our local Miss Marple thinks is causing all the trouble."

Abby winced inwardly at the Miss Marple comment. She had always enjoyed mysteries, fictional and otherwise, which had led her to investigate a good number of strange goings on since her return to Sparrow Island. But that didn't mean she was going to stick her nose into this situation.

After all, she had the eagle census to worry about as well as her other responsibilities at the conservatory. She also checked in on her parents regularly, and she'd been remiss in that department lately, despite the fact they lived quite near the conservatory. Dropping by for a visit wasn't that hard to do.

She was sure the Coast Guard was perfectly capable of determining the cause of the periodic blackouts at the lighthouse.

Except so far they had denied there was even a problem, much less that they were culpable.

And whatever was happening had now put her dear friends and neighbors at risk.

Sighing, she said good-bye to Margaret, moved onto the display of bright red tomatoes and idly picked one up to test its firmness.

Maybe she could just ask a few questions of Neil McDonald. Surely that wouldn't do any harm.

That was a lot wiser approach to solving a mystery than deciding the lighthouse was haunted by the ghost of Terrence Pettigrew.

CHAPTER ❦ FOUR

ABBY HURRIED HOME with the groceries, put them away, then took the shortcut path to the McDonalds' house. Undeterred by the damp grass, she crossed her yard and ducked through a row of fir trees that separated the two properties. She knocked on the backdoor.

A moment later Sandy appeared. She wore a frilly pink apron over a nubby sweater and pants. "Hey, Abby, what brings you out today?" Smiling, she stood back to let Abby inside.

Abby wiped her feet on the mat, noticing the shortcut had left its damp mark on the hem of her jeans.

"I was hoping Neil might be home," she said, stepping inside. The warm air in the kitchen engulfed her along with the scent of cookies baking in the oven. This was the heart of the McDonald house—a walnut table with just enough clutter to make it feel homey, snapshots of Bobby and handwritten reminder notes stuck on the refrigerator with cute little magnets, a window box featuring African violets in bloom despite the time of the year.

"I'm sorry. Neil's at work today. He traded days off with a friend so he could take Robert and Bobby fishing the other day. Now Bobby's with Uncle Robert learning Morse code." The timer on the stove dinged. Sandy found a hot-pad, opened the oven door and pulled out a pan of freshly baked chocolate-chip cookies.

"Good for Bobby," Abby said. "How's your uncle doing?"

Her expression full of dismay, Sandy shrugged and put the cookie sheet on top of the stove. "It's been hard for him."

"I'm sure that his being here with you, being part of a loving family, will help him."

"I hope so."

Giving her a smile of encouragement, Abby said, "Those cookies smell heavenly."

"Neil's favorite. I made him some for Valentine's Day. I have one batch cooling already so I've got plenty to bag some up for you to take home, if you'd like."

"No, you don't have to do that. In fact, I just bought a cherry pie. I really wanted to talk to Neil about what happened out by the lighthouse."

"Oh, that." Her brows, the same dark blonde as her hair, pulled together in a frown. "He told me they'd stayed out longer than he'd planned because they hadn't caught anything. He'd wanted to show Uncle Robert a good time. And then the fog rolled in and they headed back home." Using a spatula, she lifted the cookies one at a time on to a sheet of waxed paper to cool as she talked.

"The lighthouse wasn't on?" Abby asked.

"It was at first, according to Neil. And then *poof,* it went out and so did the foghorn. You know how quiet it can get when there's a low fog. Bobby said it was spooky."

Which meant the boy had been frightened. Abby didn't like that and it made her want to know all the more what had caused the problem, including the foghorn going silent. She hadn't heard that that had happened before, only the light going dark.

"Neil kept telling me they weren't in any danger. The boat has a GPS—a Global Positioning System—so there wasn't any chance they'd go aground on the point or anything. The sea was perfectly calm, hardly any swells. But still . . ."

"Lighthouses aren't supposed to go dark."

"More than that. There was a big oil tanker in the straits coming toward him at the time. Our boat isn't all that big. Twenty feet. If their radar didn't pick up our boat or the ship's pilot missed seeing it, they could have rammed our boat, barely noticing they'd hit anything in the fog."

"I'm sorry, Sandy. Just hearing about it frightens me. I can imagine how you felt, knowing Neil and Bobby were in danger."

"Plus little José, who's a real sweetheart of a kid, *and* my Uncle Robert too." She set down the spatula and looked at Abby. "What on earth do you think is going on?" Picking up one of the cooling cookies, she took a bite and chewed thoughtfully.

Abby shook her head. "Neil would have a better idea than I do. Margaret Blackstock thinks it's the ghost of Terrence Pettigrew out for revenge."

Sandy choked and began coughing.

Quickly, Abby grabbed a glass from the counter and ran some water into it. She handed the glass to her neighbor.

Slowly, Sandy regained her breath and took a sip of water. She wiped the tears from her eyes with the back of her hand.

"Good grief, don't do that to me when I'm eating."

"I'm so sorry." Abby couldn't help but chuckle—at Sandy's expense or Margaret's, she wasn't sure which.

"Margaret really thinks—"

"That's what she told me when I met her at The Green Grocer earlier this morning."

"That there's a *ghost*?"

"Mom! I learned *e* and *t* in Morse—" Bobby popped into the kitchen and looked around. "Where's the ghost, Mom?"

"There's no ghost, sweetheart."

"But I heard you say."

"I was just telling your mother what Margaret Blackstock had said," Abby explained.

Bobby's eyes rounded with excitement. "You mean she saw a ghost? A real one? At school?"

"Oh dear." Abby laughed aloud this time. "Things seem to be getting out of hand. I'll leave you to sort it out, Sandy. Keep up your good work on Morse code, Bobby."

Sandy rolled her eyes. "Thanks so much."

Still chuckling, Abby left the way she had come, via the backdoor. She had the troubling feeling everyone in Green Harbor, adults and youngsters alike, would soon hear the tale of a ghost haunting the Wayfarer Point Lighthouse. A few might even believe it.

Abby didn't.

Unfortunately, at this point, she didn't have an alternative answer for what was happening.

But her natural instinct to solve a mystery—any mystery—had certainly kicked into high gear.

BY THE TIME Mary returned home, Abby had the house dusted and vacuumed, and the dining room arranged for dinner. She'd selected one of Mary's nice white linen tablecloths and used red napkins to match a pair of red, cinnamon-scented candles she'd placed in crystal holders. That accomplished, she'd changed into a long beige hostess skirt with a matching knit top that she wore with a gold necklace and earrings.

"The table looks very festive and you look very nice," Mary said as she wheeled her chair in from the garage. Her hair looked mussed, her blouse wrinkled, as she took Finnegan's harness off.

"How was your day?"

"Brutal." She exhaled a weary sigh. "I think next year I'll hire an extra assistant. In fact, maybe I'll do that starting with Mother's Day. I'm getting too old for all that pressure."

"I think that's a good idea. No need to wear yourself out." Affectionately, Abby rested her hand on her sister's shoulder. "Why don't you take a few minutes to freshen up and rest a bit. We still have time before the men come. All that's left to do is put the salad together, mash the potatoes and warm the rolls."

"You're a saint, dear sister. I don't know what I'd do without you."

Abby chuckled. "I don't think I'm quite ready for sainthood yet. And you'd probably do just fine. But I do like being here with you. I'd say we're pretty compatible housemates."

"After all the times we fussed at each other when we were teenagers, it's amazing all right." She wheeled toward her room. "I think I will freshen up a bit, then I'll come out and help you with whatever's left to be done."

"Take your time."

Abby watched her leave, Finnegan right behind her, then returned to the kitchen. She turned off the slow cooker, knowing the Swiss steak would stay warm, and retrieved the salad makings from the refrigerator.

She and Mary'd had their differences when they were adolescents. On the surface they'd been almost opposites, Mary the gregarious sister, Abby more introverted and studious while loving the outdoors. But their parents had instilled in them the same basic values of God and family.

It was those values that became the glue that brought them back together again. *Not sainthood*, Abby thought, smiling to herself.

She'd finished the salad and mashed the potatoes by the time the doorbell rang. Grabbing a tea towel, she wiped her hands and hurried to answer it.

"Hugo!" She smiled at him and then felt her face flush at the bouquet of red roses *and* a floral table arrangement he held. "Gracious, it looks like you've been keeping Island Blooms busy all by yourself."

"I fear I can only take credit for the roses, which Candace recommended. The arrangement was here by the door when I arrived. I thought it prudent that we bring it inside."

"Yes, of course." She stepped aside so he could enter. "The roses are lovely, but you needn't have—"

"My late wife would insist every woman deserves roses on Valentine's Day. Certainly you and Mary are among the most deserving."

"Why, thank you." She took the long stemmed roses from Hugo, which left him holding the floral centerpiece. "Those must be from Henry."

"That thought did occur to me."

"Well, do come in. I'll find a vase for these lovely roses."

She inhaled the sweet scent of them. "And we can put the centerpiece on the table to enjoy during dinner."

Mary wheeled into the room from her bedroom, looking more rested than she had a few moments earlier. She was wearing a colorful floral skirt that flowed gracefully over her knees and a bright red top with a boat neckline. "Good evening, Hugo. We're both so glad you could join us for dinner."

"My pleasure, Mary."

Finnegan trotted over to Hugo and sat down right in front of him, no doubt expecting a head scratch, which was immediately forthcoming.

"What beautiful flowers." Mary cocked her head, studying the arrangement. "Candace mentioned you were bringing roses, Hugo, but she didn't say anything about a table arrangement."

"They're not from Hugo," Abby explained. "We think they must be from Henry."

"Really?" Surprise and pleasure colored her cheeks. "Candace didn't say anything at all about that."

"Perhaps he wanted it to be a surprise and told her mum's the word," Hugo commented as he handed Mary the flowers. "There's a card."

"Yes." With the arrangement on her lap, Mary plucked the small envelope from its holder and pulled out the card, reading it. Her flush deepened. "How sweet."

Abby tried to peer over her shoulder. "What does it say?"

"If you must know, it says 'Love Always' and it's signed with only a squiggle." Mary frowned. "I guess that's an *h*. Henry's handwriting isn't very clear."

"Maybe Candace wrote out the card for him," Abby suggested.

"No, it doesn't look like her writing. Though we were both so tired by the end of the day, we were seeing double."

A firm knock on the front door announced Henry's arrival. Abby opened the door and gaped at him.

"You brought flowers," she said, staring at the huge bouquet of red and white long-stemmed roses, a dozen of each, plus ample baby's breath and Boston ferns. A spare-no-expense bouquet.

Dressed in a spiffy leather jacket, sport shirt and slacks, he smiled smugly. "I figured a florist probably didn't receive flowers herself very often. I had them sent over from Bellingham so it would be a surprise."

"Yes, well . . . please come in."

With Abby still carrying the red roses and Mary with the centerpiece in her lap, it didn't take Henry long to notice the abundance of flowers. He presented Mary with the red-and-white bouquet, bending down to kiss her briefly.

"I guess the thought wasn't original," he said.

"Oh, these are exquisite," Mary told him. "But really, you didn't have to send an arrangement too."

"It appears Henry has outdone my small token of affection," Hugo said.

Henry looked from the arrangement in Mary's lap to the roses in Abby's arm, then back to Mary. "Those roses are the only flowers I brought. I don't know anything about these other two."

"I have already confessed responsibility for the smaller bouquet of roses," Hugo said.

Everyone exchanged confused glances.

"Then who's this arrangement from?" Mary asked.

"And who's it for is another question of interest," Hugo added. "With two such charming ladies in the household, it could be for either of you. Or both."

"I can't think of anyone who would send me flowers." Puzzled, Abby took the small envelope from her sister. "This doesn't say who they're for. It's blank."

"And the signature is illegible." Holding up the card, Mary turned it around to study the back. "This enclosure card didn't come from Island Blooms. We use a different source and have for years. I didn't notice that at first. And there's no way to tell what florist the arrangement came from."

Hugo slipped his hand into his suit jacket pocket in a gesture that mimicked one a college professor might make when he was about to challenge his students to a test of logic. "It appears, my friends, that we have a mystery on our hands."

"A beautifully scented mystery," Mary said. "Thanks to you two gentlemen and our unknown benefactor."

Unknown benefactor indeed, Abby thought as she went in search of vases for the roses. She had to get out the step stool to look in the highest cupboard.

"You should have let me get that," Henry said, coming into the kitchen. He'd taken off his jacket and his shirt sleeves were rolled up to reveal his muscular forearms.

"I've got it. Thanks." Climbing down with a cut glass vase in hand, inspiration struck Abby.

"I bet I know who those flowers were meant for," she said. "Sandy, next door. Neil probably had them sent."

"And he didn't send them from Island Blooms? You'd think he'd be loyal to Mary when he's ordering flowers."

"*Hmmm,* yes, you would." Still, it was logical to think the flowers had simply been misdelivered.

Placing the vase on the kitchen counter, she went to the phone and dialed Sandy's number.

"Hi, Sandy," she said when her neighbor answered. "I was wondering, did Neil happen to give you any flowers for Valentine's Day?"

"He certainly did. A pink African violet. It's a hybrid and quite lovely really. He picked them up in Bellingham on his last run. Why did you want to know?"

"Oh, no particular reason. We just seem to have a surplus of flowers tonight and thought maybe an arrangement had been misdelivered."

Sandy was of no further help, and offhand, Abby couldn't think of anyone else in the neighborhood who might have gotten flowers from out of town. She'd have to go door-to-door in sort of a reverse trick-or-treat with the centerpiece to locate the rightful recipient, *if* the flowers had reached the wrong destination. But it was long past dark outside and she had two guests who expected to eat dinner in the not-too-distant future.

So she went back to arranging the two sets of roses, then finished preparing the dinner. Mary helped by dishing up the Swiss steak and mashed potatoes. When they were ready to serve, Abby called the men into the dining room. Hugo had removed his suit jacket but still wore his precisely knotted tie. Even so, for Hugo he looked quite casual and at ease.

In the flickering candlelight, Hugo said grace. "Lord, we thank You for good friends, bountiful food to eat and a new mystery for Abby to solve. We ask You to care for those who are sick and hungry around the world and ask Your aid in protecting the world and all Your creatures in it. Amen."

They echoed his *Amen*, and Mary urged Henry to start with the Swiss steak and Hugo to serve himself some potatoes.

"I'm not sure which mystery you're hoping I'll solve," Abby said to Hugo as he passed her the potatoes. "Discovering who sent us the floral centerpiece or finding out what's going wrong with the lighthouse."

"Uh-oh," Henry said. "The Sparrow Island amateur sleuth is off and running again."

"Hush, Henry," Mary scolded with mock fierceness, and Abby laughed.

"I know I'm always sticking my nose in where it might not belong, but you did hear what happened to Neil McDonald, didn't you?"

"I did," the sergeant admitted.

When Hugo indicated he'd been thinking of the unexpected flowers while saying grace and that he hadn't been apprised of the lighthouse situation, Abby filled him in on the details.

Taking a bite of Swiss steak, Hugo chewed thoughtfully. "It could be disastrous if one of the oil tankers went aground in the straits. The damage to the environment could well be more extensive than it was in the Valdez oil spill. I can barely imagine the loss of habitat and water fowl."

"I hadn't thought about that," Abby admitted. She served herself some salad and passed the bowl on to Henry. "I was thinking more about the people who might be hurt or even die because of an accident."

"What does the Coast Guard say?" Hugo asked.

Henry handed the salad bowl to Mary. "Coast Guard says there's nothing wrong with the lighthouse, but I suspect this most recent incident has got them listening a little more closely to the complaints."

"I bet," Abby said under her breath.

Finally, Hugo said what surely was on everyone's mind. "If the Coast Guard doesn't claim responsibility or even that there's a fault in their system, then what else could be happening?"

Abby studied her plate. "You mean besides Margaret Blackstock's theory that it's the ghost of Terrence Pettigrew getting his revenge?"

Hugo smiled indulgently. "Perhaps there's another reason."

They all ate in silence, then Henry spoke up.

"There's a marine recovery operation in Port Angeles. Could it be the owner, who I've heard isn't all that scrupulous, is trying to sink ships that he can later salvage?"

"Henry! That's a terrible idea, but a real possibility if the man's truly greedy," Mary said.

Abby shuddered at the thought that anyone would intentionally try to sink a ship for financial gain. Taking innocent lives, destroying the environment. It made no sense that a rational human being would do that. Yet she knew not all people were rational.

"Maybe, instead of Terrence Pettigrew, it's his son who's disrupting the lighthouse service," Hugo suggested.

Abby shook her head. "You're thinking about Bryant? He's a harmless old man who can barely hobble up from the marina to get his breakfast at the Springhouse Café."

"Revenge is a strong motivator," Hugo commented as he carefully forked a bite of Swiss steak into his mouth. "Of course, I'm not accusing Bryant. I was just brainstorming ideas."

Abby understood that. Yet she couldn't quite get her head around the thought of Bryant—or his long-deceased father—having the power to turn the Wayfarer Point Lighthouse on and off at their will. *And* the foghorn. Although Bryant, having lived there as a youngster, would certainly be familiar with the layout of the place. But that wouldn't explain why he'd take such an action more than forty years after the lighthouse was automated.

Henry dipped his forkful of mashed potatoes in the Swiss steak sauce on his plate. "In the past there've been some smugglers active in the Northwest. Some smuggling drugs, some other illegal contraband like untaxed cigarettes. Maybe there's a smuggler who thinks he won't get caught if the light is dark." He shrugged almost apologetically.

"That's a good thought, Henry," Hugo said. "At this point, we don't want to eliminate any possibility."

"Frankly," Mary said, "while I'm troubled about the lighthouse, I'm just as curious about who sent that centerpiece. Unless Abby has a secret admirer we haven't heard about."

Abby started and leaned back from the table.

"Not me." She'd ended her most recent relationship some time ago. Hugo, she admitted, might hold her interest but their relationship wasn't romantic. Other than that . . .

"Maybe you can decode this card." Mary handed her the enclosure card. "You've always been good at codes and whatnot."

Abby wasn't so sure. The signature, if it could be called that, wasn't much more than a swirling line. An *h* maybe, but it could also be a *d* or an *n*. There was simply no way to tell who'd signed the card.

Or who the flowers had been intended for, Abby realized.

Love Always was a pretty strong statement from a stranger. So either she or Mary must know the sender.

Beyond that, she didn't have a clue.

CHAPTER 🌹 FIVE

THE FOLLOWING MORNING, Mary drove them to church. The van was far more convenient than attempting to get Mary in and out of Abby's car and then worrying about where to carry her wheelchair. Abby knew the van also enhanced Mary's sense of independence and gave her the ability to be in charge of her own life.

Finnegan seemed to enjoy the van ride as much as Mary, sitting up alertly, watching the scenery through the windshield.

It was only a short drive to Little Flock Church, a wooden structure painted white with a weathered metal cross at the peak of the shingled steeple. The Stanton family had been members of the church for as long as Abby could remember, and it had felt very much like coming home when she was able to rejoin the congregation and become an active member again.

After parking in the handicapped slot, Mary and Finnegan exited the van by the lift while Abby climbed out of the passenger side. She helped push Mary's wheelchair up the walk to the main entrance with its welcoming double doors. Even before Mary returned home from her stay in a rehab center following her accident, Rev. James Hale had arranged for one of the pews to be altered to allow space for her wheelchair where she wouldn't block the aisle.

Inside, they discovered their parents had already arrived and were sitting in Mary's special pew.

"Hello, dears," Ellen Stanton said softly, giving them a finger wave as they joined their parents. She wore a light-gray suit, which nearly matched the color of her hair, with a gold pin in the shape of an *s* on the lapel. "Hope you had a nice Valentine's dinner."

Abby slid into the pew next to her mother and took her hand, giving it a squeeze. "We did. Mary's Swiss steak was wonderful. Tasted just like your recipe. Delicious."

"I'm so glad," Ellen said with a trace of pride in her voice.

George Stanton leaned forward to greet his daughters. "Happy day after Valentine's."

Abby smiled her thanks just as the pianist began the prelude to the service.

Settling back on the pew, Abby looked up at the circular window with bands of stained glass above the pulpit and focused her mind on the worship service about to commence and her undying faith in the Lord.

Rev. Hale, who looked more like a surfer than a forty-five-year-old preacher, talked about the various kinds of love in his sermon: love not only between a man and a woman, but also for the Lord, for family and for friends as well, and all that was in His domain. Abby thought that was a particularly appropriate topic for the day after Valentine's Day, since her love for both family and the environment were so strong.

That thought brought her up with a start. As the recessional began, she leaned over to her sister.

"I bet Mom and Dad sent that floral centerpiece," she whispered. "You know, *Love Always*, works for them. And that signature could have been an *S*."

Mary gave her a puzzled look. "As far as I know, they didn't buy it from Island Blooms."

That was true and suggested Abby might have guessed wrong. But it did seem like a reasonable possibility. Except Abby couldn't imagine their parents would buy flowers from anyone except Mary. "Maybe they did and Candace didn't mention it."

Mary shrugged. "We could ask them."

Abby did just that after church when many of the members of the congregation were standing outside visiting.

George Stanton shook his head. "It would have been a nice idea to send you girls flowers, but I didn't think of it. Ellen?" He turned to his wife and took her hand in the affectionate way long-married, loving couples did, as though simply touching one another reaffirmed their marriage vows. "Do you know anything about the flowers the girls received?"

"I imagine Henry gave Mary some." She looked to her older daughter for confirmation.

"Yes, he did, and they were lovely," Mary answered. "Red and white roses."

"But a centerpiece for the table arrived, too, and we can't figure out who sent it," Abby told them. "I thought maybe you two had."

"My, my." Ellen's blue eyes sparkled with excitement. At eighty, she was still energetic, helping out at the Visitors Center in town regularly, and her complexion was as smooth as that of a much younger woman. "One of you must have a secret admirer."

"So secret we don't have any idea who he is." Abby glanced

around at those members of the congregation who had gathered to visit after the service. It was a cool morning, and most were wearing jackets or warm sweaters. There were lots of smiles and laughter as friends chatted and reflected on the week's activities. But she saw no one who might have sent them a floral tribute for Valentine's Day.

Margaret Blackstock caught Abby's eye and hurried toward her. The hem of her winter coat flapped around her calves as she all but ran across the lawn.

"Did you hear?" she said, somewhat breathlessly. "There's going to be a séance out at the lighthouse."

Abby's jaw dropped. "A séance? Whatever for?"

"There's some in town who think if we can contact Terrence Pettigrew's ghost and apologize for firing him as keeper of the lighthouse, then he'll stop his shenanigans and the light won't go popping on and off all the time."

"Are you still talking about the lighthouse being haunted?"

"You'd better believe it, hon. Everyone says so." Margaret's arm-waving gesture encompassed the entire congregation and probably all of Sparrow Island too. "They're going to hire a psychic from Seattle to make contact with the other side."

Abby could barely believe what she was hearing.

His expression more amused than shocked, George spoke up. "I suspect the problems at the lighthouse have a more rational explanation than ghosts."

"Well, if it isn't a ghost, then I'm betting it's that no-goodnik, Terrence's son, Bryant."

"I'm sure the Coast Guard will figure out what's wrong soon," George said.

Abby wasn't quite that confident. Last she'd heard, the Coast Guard was in denial about the incidents at Wayfarer Point Lighthouse.

Maybe what the Coast Guard needed was a bit of public pressure so they'd sit up and take notice of the problem.

Margaret flitted off to visit with other parishioners, and George gave an indulgent chuckle. "Woman's got some imagination."

Sandy McDonald and her Uncle Robert, who was wearing dark glasses and holding her arm, were among the last to exit the church. Robert was so unsure of his steps, it made him seem like a much older man than his seventy-two years. Abby was sure that before the disastrous explosion, he'd been far more agile and fit than he appeared now. And had more self-confidence too. She suspected he could use some extra help with mobility training from a group that dealt with people who were recently blinded. But she wasn't sure where those services might be available locally or if he'd be willing to take advantage of such services.

"Hi, Sandy. Robert." Abby called to them and waved them over. "Come meet my parents, Robert."

Smiling, Sandy angled in Abby's direction. With his hesitant steps, Robert communicated his reluctance to meet anyone.

"Good morning, all," Sandy said, giving Ellen Stanton a quick hug before introducing her uncle.

Ellen welcomed Robert to the island, as did Abby's father, shaking his hand.

"We'd better go now, Sandy," Robert said before any real conversation could get started, in an obvious effort to not engage with others.

A typical reaction for someone newly disabled, Abby imagined. From what Mary had told her, the bombing incident had only occurred two months ago.

"Perhaps you can all come to our house one night for dinner this week," Ellen offered.

"I'm fine at Sandy's house. Thanks anyway."

Her shoulders sagging, Sandy shook her head. "Thank you, but—"

Arriving at a run, Bobby was bursting with news. "Uncle Robert got me a practice code generator, Abby. Now I can send my *dits* and *dahs*, just like I was really on the radio."

"Your *dits* and what's?" Abby asked, astonished.

"You know." He proceeded to demonstrate by saying *dit*, *dit*, followed by *dah*, *dah*, holding the *dahs* slightly longer than the *dits*. "That's *i* and *m* in code. Right, Uncle Robert?"

"You got it, junior."

"Ah, the dots and dashes. I remember," Abby said, smiling.

"He's been driving us crazy," Sandy said with some dismay. "If this keeps up, I'm going to be dreaming in *dits* and *dahs*."

Neil arrived and slipped his arm around his wife's shoulders. "Seems to me there's a pot roast cooking in the oven, honey. And I know Uncle Robert must be hungry."

Sandy leaned into her husband. "I'm sure he is, but it was your stomach I heard growling during the sermon."

Neil looked sheepish, but everyone else laughed.

Ellen admitted she had to get home, too, in order to finish her preparations for the family's usual Sunday supper. Together, they all walked toward the parking lot. Abby couldn't help hoping and praying that Robert would soon find a way to regain the joy in life that he surely must have once had.

A verse from the Bible came to her, Proverbs 14:10: "Each heart knows its own bitterness, and no one else can share its joy."

Robert seemed to be experiencing a full measure of bitterness recently. Abby could only hope, in God's time, the joy would return.

MONDAY MORNING, Mary went in to the flower shop a little late. She had paperwork to complete after their busy Saturday, and she knew Candace would be handling the cleanup that they hadn't been able to tackle at the end of the Valentine's rush. Otherwise, she anticipated a slow day.

After parking in the lot behind the shop, she wheeled into the workroom, Finnegan trotting along beside her. As expected, Candace had nearly filled a big trash can with leftover bits and pieces of flower stems, ferns and buds that hadn't been needed for the last-minute arrangements, but were too tattered now to be used.

"Gracious, what a lot of debris," Mary said.

"What a lot of sales we had." Using a broom, Candace swept some greenery into a dustpan and dumped it into the trash. "I'll take all this out to the composting site at the conservatory later."

"Perfect. At least we can give something back to the environment."

"I like to think of our work as being part of nature's cycle of life, with the added benefit that people can enjoy nature right in their own homes for a while."

Mary knew Candace had a solid grip on her faith, and it seemed to encompass all of creation.

"You certainly saved our bacon by going to the Seattle flower market," Mary said. "With what few flowers Antonio was able to deliver, we wouldn't have had nearly enough product to meet all of our customers' needs."

"Hey, it was great to hang out with Brad for an evening. He tends to work way too hard . . . and not take time to smell the roses."

"Did he come over to celebrate Valentine's with you?"

She smiled rather smugly. "He did. He brought an orchid

corsage, which I wore, and a picnic dinner, which we ate at the top of Mount Ortiz, after we hiked up there. We watched the moon rise."

"Very nice." Mary laughed. "It's not exactly my idea of a fancy dinner, but if it works for you and Brad . . ."

Leaning back against the workbench, Candace sighed. "It's funny, I know. Brad's such a straight-laced guy, but he tries so hard to do the things he knows I'd enjoy. He's really sweet about that sort of thing."

"Do you think you might get married?" Mary asked gently.

"*Hmmm*," Candace said thoughtfully. "I'm not getting any younger, am I?"

"I didn't mean to imply—"

Candace waved off Mary's apology. "The fact is, I've been thinking about the big *M*. I just can't decide if that's what I want out of life."

Mary knew her marriage to Jacob had been the best thing she'd ever experienced. Even though she'd lost him far sooner than she'd expected or hoped, she wouldn't have given up a moment of the love they'd shared together.

"Say, we received a lovely centerpiece Saturday night. I don't think it came from here, but I wondered if you have any idea who might have sent it to us."

Thoughtfully, Candace shook her head. "Hugo Baron came by and picked up a bouquet of roses. I didn't see Sergeant Cobb. I hope he did something—"

"Oh yes. A lovely bouquet of roses he picked up in Bellingham so I'd be surprised and wouldn't have to arrange my own flowers."

Frowning, Candace seemed to be thinking back through the orders she'd filled on Saturday. Lifting her gaze, she shrugged.

"I can't remember any centerpiece that had been ordered for you or Abby. And I would have remembered, I'm sure."

Mary was sure of that, too, particularly since the enclosure card hadn't come from Island Blooms.

"Then I guess our mysterious gift giver will forever remain anonymous," she said. That, in itself, seemed quite odd. Who would want to keep the fact that they'd given someone flowers —with a notation of *Love Always*—a secret?

ABOUT MIDMORNING, after handling some tardy paperwork at The Nature Museum, Abby placed a call to the Coast Guard Station at Bellingham and asked to speak to the commanding officer. A female voice answered.

"Senior Chief Bosnik's office. Seaman Holland speaking."

"I'd like to speak to the senior chief, please."

"I'm sorry, ma'am. Chief Bosnik's not in today. May I ask what this is about?"

Abby introduced herself to the seaman, making it a point to use her title as Doctor Stanton, Associate Curator of the conservatory. Over time, she'd found her official title gained her more attention than simply being Ms. Stanton.

"I'd like to talk with him about the problems that have been happening to the lighthouse on Sparrow Island."

"Yes, ma'am. We have been investigating the reports of alleged malfunction. I can connect you with our PIO, our public information officer, if that would be acceptable."

"No, it wouldn't. I'd really like to talk with the chief directly. When do you expect him back?"

"He'll be off the station all day today, ma'am. I'm sure our public relations—"

"This matter is of increasing importance to those of us who

live on the island." Abby knew when she was getting a run-around and didn't like it a bit—polite *ma'ams* or not. They only made her feel somewhere near ancient. "I think it might be best if I met with the commander in person. Would he have time to see me tomorrow?"

"I'm not sure, ma'am. Are you by chance with the press?"

Abby smiled at the opening the young seaman had given her. "I'm a concerned resident. But if it takes a member of the press for me to get in to see Senior Chief Bosnik, I'd be happy to invite the editor of the local paper to join me." William Jensen, editor of *The Birdcall*, would be tickled pink to go with her to Bellingham if he had a chance to get a story.

"Just a moment, ma'am." Seaman Holland put Abby on hold.

Keeping the phone to her ear, Abby tapped the eraser end of her pencil on top of her desk. As she repeated the gesture, she realized she was tapping out the alphabet in Morse code—*dit-dah, dah-dit-dit-dit, dah-dit-dah-dit. A, B, C.*

"Oh for heaven's sake," she said with a laugh. Bobby's enthusiasm for Morse code must be contagious.

"Ma'am?"

"I'm here." She straightened.

"Chief Bosnik can spare you a few minutes tomorrow morning at zero-nine-hundred-hours. That's 9:00 AM civilian time, ma'am. He says it won't be necessary for you to bring the press with you. Will that be satisfactory?"

"Perfect." She knew William would be upset if he found out he'd missed a chance to interview the Coast Guard, but she wasn't about to tell him.

The seaman gave her instructions about how to reach the station. From there, the person on watch would direct her to the chief's office.

Feeling satisfied with herself, Abby leaned back in her chair. So far, the San Juan Islands and everyone who lived there, including the fish and fowl, had been fortunate that no major accident had occurred because of the failure of the Wayfarer Point Lighthouse. Abby hoped she could emphasize the importance of keeping it that way to Senior Chief Bosnik and encourage him to get to the bottom of the problem.

As she sat alone in the office, she became aware of the silence in The Nature Museum. During the winter months the museum often remained closed on Mondays. There were none of the usual sounds of visiting school children, no tourists dropping by to learn a bit about the varied ecosystems on the island. Even Hugo wasn't in his office this morning.

Outside, the day was overcast and little light crept in through the high windows of her office.

Suddenly, the electric power flickered off. The overhead lights went dark, submerging the room in shadows. The uninterruptible power supply, which was designed to keep her computer going until the electricity returned, beeped loudly, as did a similar device in Hugo's adjacent office.

She shook her head. It wasn't all that unusual to lose power, but it was annoying. And it usually happened during a storm when a tree fell down across a power line or lightning struck a transformer.

As unexpectedly as the electricity had failed, it came back on again. The uninterruptible power supplies quieted.

From somewhere in the exhibit area came a wail that sounded so filled with pain that Abby was on her feet in an instant. She ran, searching for whomever was in trouble, adult or child, she couldn't tell which. And no one should be in the museum at this hour.

The displays were turned off, the lights dimmed, as she

raced past the diorama of extinct and endangered birds, and the Native American exhibit.

"Hello!" she called. "Where are you? Do you need help?"

The only response was the sound of her own rapid breathing.

She reached the holographic display of the 1980 Mount Saint Helen's eruption, a cutaway with computer generated special effects. Slowly the model turned under its dome. Lava balls exploded into the air; fiery red lava flowed down from the crater left by the explosion.

Halting abruptly, she looked around. The Mount Saint Helen's display was the only one operating.

Had it been on when she arrived this morning? She couldn't remember. But she didn't think so.

"Hello," she said again, but this time her voice quavered. A shiver ran up her spine; the hair on her nape prickled.

Slowly, she walked over to the display and switched off the power. The lava fell back into the crater and the eerie light of the hologram faded. Spooky. Even ghost-like.

She'd found no sign of anyone in the building. So who had turned on the display?

"It certainly wasn't a ghost," she said aloud. Her voice bounced back at her in the empty room.

Goodness! Now she felt like she was having another debate with Margaret Blackstock about ghosts on Sparrow Island.

Somehow the power surge must have affected the display, not one of Margaret's phantoms, she told herself.

Nonetheless, since she wasn't busy, and the museum felt suddenly creepy, this seemed like a good opportunity to go visit Bryant Pettigrew at the marina. Maybe he did know something that would shed a little light on the lighthouse problem.

CHAPTER ❧ SIX

ON THIS COLD, DREARY Monday, the Green Harbor marina seemed empty of life. Not a soul sat drinking coffee at the rustic tables outside the sundry store. Pleasure boats tied to the dock rose and fell with the gentle swell, their masts barely moving. Heavy blue canvas covered the cabins, protecting the boats from the elements. Many of the boats wouldn't set to sea again until spring was well under way, their owners snug in their warm homes either here on Sparrow Island or on the mainland.

The weathered planks moved up and down with each step as Abby strode toward the far dock where Bryant Pettigrew kept his boat. Wavelets lapped softly against the pilings and the sandy shore. From the top of a mast, a seagull announced with a shrieking call that he was the alpha male, his favorite roosting spot would be shared with no other.

She pulled her jacket more snugly around her against the chill, damp air.

There wasn't much chance Bryant's fishing trawler, the *Princess Lola*, would be heading out to sea ever again. From the look of it, the boat was waterlogged and permanently resting on the bottom in this shallow end of the marina. As far as Abby knew, Bryant was content with that. This was his home.

At the moment, he was sitting on a low stool on the dock, his back against a light post, a pipe clenched between his teeth and a paperback book that looked as old as he was in his hand. He wore a knitted cap pulled down over his ears and a Navy pea jacket buttoned up to his chin.

"Hello, Bryant."

He took a moment to finish reading the page, then he looked up at her with watery blue eyes. A smile creased his leathery face, revealing teeth gone yellow with age.

"Hello yourself, young lady."

She squatted down beside him. "What are you reading?"

He showed her the cover. *Hamlet*, by William Shakespeare.

Abby's mouth all but dropped open in surprise. "That's an interesting selection."

Using an old matchbook cover to save his place, he closed the book. "My dern TV fizzled out on me the other day. This here book's got about as much blood and gore as most of them TV shows anyways. It'll keep me occupied for a time."

"I imagine so." Abby chided herself for assuming an old fisherman like Bryant wouldn't enjoy reading. He'd probably spent months at sea with only his books to entertain him.

"What brings you down to the marina?" he asked. "Not much goin' on here abouts."

"I wanted to ask you some questions about the Wayfarer Point Lighthouse."

He looked at her for a moment, then reached into his

pocket to bring out his bag of tobacco. With fingers knotted with arthritis, he filled his pipe, tamped down the tobacco, then struck a safety match with his thumbnail. He sucked the flame into the pipe bowl.

"So? Whataya want to know?" A stream of smoke drifted up toward the faded No Smoking sign on the light pole behind him.

"Have you heard about the trouble they've been having with the lighthouse?"

He glanced away. "Some, maybe."

"It's been erratic lately, going dark for no apparent reason."

"I wouldn't know nothing about that."

"But you would know the layout of the lighthouse. Is there any way someone could get inside to turn out the light?"

"The Coast Guard has the place pretty well boarded up, leastwise it was last time I saw it."

"How long ago was that?"

His brows lowered and his watery gaze narrowed on her. "A long time ago, missy."

Apparently she'd hit a sore spot. "The problem is, a few people in town have gotten the foolish notion in their heads that your father is haunting the lighthouse."

To Abby's astonishment, Bryant virtually leaped to his feet, at least as nimbly as possible for a man whose body had been treated harshly by time. He angrily tossed the paperback book onto the boat deck.

"Ain't nobody haunting nothing out there."

"I know that, Bryant. I'm just trying to figure out what could be going wrong with the lighthouse. If a ship should run aground—"

"Everybody ought to stay away from the lighthouse. It's

none of their dern business what's goin' on." He threw one leg over the boat's railing and hoisted himself onboard. "Let the Coast Guard worry about it. They own the property. It's their worry, nobody else's. Tell the rest of 'em to stay away."

With that, he stalked across the deck in his heavy boots and opened the hatch to the cabin, then stepped inside, leaving Abby gaping after him. A faint ray of sunshine glinted off the porthole on the closed door.

Slowly, she stood. Her knees protested the movement with a crack.

Something she'd said had certainly upset Bryant. Probably he didn't like the thought of his father being a ghost or the town talking about him. She could understand the feeling, of course.

But her instincts told her it was more than just an aversion to ghost stories—or even being talked about in town.

Bryant was hiding something.

Abby didn't know what it was yet. And she still couldn't imagine Bryant would have the knowledge to control the light at Wayfarer Point from here, assuming that was even possible. She also doubted he was physically able to walk to the lighthouse, climb the narrow stairs to the top, do some sort of mischief and get back to his boat before someone spotted him. And he didn't have a car.

Although he'd moved agilely enough to get onto his boat, she'd seen him hobbling around town. His years at sea had no doubt left him with arthritis in his knees as well as his knotted fingers.

It made no sense that he'd be the culprit.

Still, she couldn't cross him off the list of suspects.

She'd simply need to get more information.

Thoughtfully, she walked back up the dock to where she'd parked her car. The seagull reminded her again that the top of the highest mast belonged to him despite his equally assertive buddy who had decided to challenge his rights. The second gull made a pass at taking over the perch, but the alpha male held his ground with a piercing shriek.

What kind of person would shut off the light at Wayfarer Point and risk injury to both people and the environment?

Greed was often a motivator for ill-gotten gains. Revenge could inspire desperate measures as well. Or a prankster might not understand the ramifications of his or her actions.

But turning off the light was no joke.

Perhaps tomorrow when she met with Senior Chief Bosnik she'd gain some insight into the operation of the lighthouse and who or what might be interfering with the light.

Instead of getting in her car, she decided to walk the short distance to Island Blooms. Since it was after twelve, perhaps she could get Mary to go to lunch with her.

As she turned onto Shoreline Drive, she noticed a man coming out of Holloway's Hardware a half block down the street. She squinted, thinking there was something familiar about him. He was wearing a suit, and the almost arrogant way he walked reminded her of—

Roger Harris?

Goodness, she'd dated Roger in high school and hadn't seen him in years. She didn't particularly want to now either, since he'd dumped Abby to go with her more popular sister to a school dance. It had nearly broken Abby's adolescent heart and caused a strain between her and Mary until they had talked it out years later.

Canting her head to get a better look, Abby watched as the

man in question stepped off the hardware store's porch and turned in her direction.

Not Roger, she realized with a sense of both relief and disappointment.

Now why would she have that reaction? she wondered.

Because ever since that floral arrangement arrived for Valentine's Day, I've been looking at every *man, wondering if he was the one who sent the flowers.*

"Foolish woman!" she said aloud, redirecting her feet toward Island Blooms. What utter nonsense that she felt obliged to discover the source of those flowers. It really didn't matter. They might not have even been intended for her. She certainly wasn't the type who engendered a following of secret admirers.

Oh well, as Margaret Blackstock would say, "Forget about it!"

The bell over the door tinkled as she went inside her sister's shop. As always, the scent of every variety of bloom filled the air, making Abby think of this as a natural perfume factory.

Finnegan rose from his spot behind the counter, *chuffed* a greeting and came over to welcome her, his tail signaling his pleasure at seeing her. Bending down, she gave the dog a scratch behind his ears.

Although she was on the phone, Mary waved her welcome as well. A moment later she finished her call and hung up.

"Hi there. I didn't expect you to drop by." Mary completed an order form before setting it aside.

"I was in the neighborhood. Thought I'd try to talk you into going to lunch with me."

"*Hmmm.* Sounds like a plan. I've got a couple of things I need to finish up here, then I'll be ready to go."

"No rush." Tempted by the velvety leaf of an African violet,

Abby brushed the back of her fingers against the soft texture. "You'll never guess who I thought I saw just now."

A teasing look came into Mary's blue eyes. "Since I'll never guess, why don't you just tell me."

"Roger Harris."

Mary's eyes widened. "*Our* Roger?"

"Not exactly *ours*, I'm afraid. Anyway, I saw this nicely dressed gentleman coming out of the hardware store and something about him reminded me of Roger. But it was a stranger."

"How odd you'd think of Roger."

"Odd, indeed. I think I'm so curious about who sent us that floral arrangement, that I'm beginning to imagine things."

Placing the azalea on the counter, Mary made a note on the order form and tucked it into the center of the plant. She looked up at Abby.

"And you thought Roger could have sent them?"

"See? Isn't that the most ridiculous thing you've ever heard of? If anything, he'd more likely have sent the flowers to you. Between us, you were the last one who dated him."

"But I didn't like him very much."

"For good reason, as I recall."

"Well, yes."

"And that scrawled initial on the card could have been an *h*. Or an *r*."

Candace appeared from the backroom. She wore a knitted top featuring a bouquet of spring flowers on the front, a long skirt and sandals. "You two still trying to figure out who sent the mystery flowers?"

"Abby thought she saw her old boyfriend in town," Mary said.

"Your boyfriend, not mine." Abby countered.

"Uh-oh. Sounds like a sisterly rivalry to me."

"Long past and over with," Abby insisted.

"So if he's in town, has he called?" Candace looked from Abby to Mary and back again.

"It wasn't him," Abby informed her. "A total stranger."

Candace looked disappointed. "That's too bad. I was kind of hoping for a little romance around here."

"Not very likely with me," Abby said. "You'll have to count on Mary for that."

"Oh hush," Mary said, color flooding her cheeks.

Candace grinned at Mary's embarrassment.

Abby was just as glad Roger hadn't sent the flowers. But her curiosity about the sender remained unsatisfied.

She also wished she knew who or what was messing with the lighthouse.

This appeared to be a day of continuing questions, not answers.

"Are you ready to go to lunch?" she asked her sister.

"If you're all right on your own," Mary said to Candace, "I'll get my coat. I think a bowl of clam chowder at Springhouse Café is exactly what this gray day needs to brighten it up."

AFTER A LEISURELY LUNCH, Mary returned to Island Blooms and Abby went home. She had some personal correspondence she wanted to take care of, notes to her friends at Cornell.

Blossom greeted her arrival, winding her way between Abby's legs.

"Surprised to see me this time of day?"

The Persian responded with a contented purr. Then, her tail lifted into a perfect hook, she ambled off toward the kitchen to have an afternoon snack.

With her laptop, Abby settled into the chair beside the couch in the living room. The view out the sliding glass door revealed a slate-gray ocean under a matching sky. For once she could appreciate the vibrant colors Mary preferred in her house. They seemed to bring the sunshine inside when there was none to enjoy outside.

She'd lost track of time when she heard a knock on the back door. She glanced at her watch. Based on the time of day, she suspected her visitor was Bobby from next door.

Saving her letter, she set her laptop aside and went to see what her young friend was up to.

He greeted her with a big grin. "Hi, Abby. Mom says I have to ask you if you're busy before I bother you."

"You're not bothering me." She chuckled. Since she'd never had children of her own—or been around them much—she'd been surprised by how much she enjoyed Bobby's company. "Come tell me what's up."

"I wanted to practice my code but Uncle Robert's taking a nap and Mom has school papers to correct."

"And you thought you could sucker me into helping you?"

"Yeah." Shrugging, he looked up at her sheepishly. "You know, if you're not busy. I've got my code generator 'n stuff."

She hooked her arm around the boy's shoulders. "Then it seems like a perfect afternoon to drag out my rusty Morse code skills. Let's sit at the kitchen table and we'll learn together."

Happily, he pulled out a chair and put a small metal box on the table along with a slender paperback study guide for amateur radio licensing. Taking off his warm jacket, he draped it over the back of the chair.

"You're really getting into this ham radio business, aren't you?" she asked.

"Yeah, it's great. Uncle Robert's teaching me all about volts and watts and electrical resistance and Ohm's law and stuff like that. Before I can take the test for my license, I've gotta know the answers to like five-hundred questions."

"Goodness, that's a lot." She sat down opposite him at the table.

"It's okay. I can do it. I'm pretty smart."

She used her hand to cover her amused smile. "Yes, you are smart." Lack of self-confidence was not one of Bobby's problems. Rightfully so. He had a sharp, inquisitive mind and so much intelligence that his school studies often bored him. A new challenge like ham radio was perfect for him.

"Uncle Robert had Mom order a code practice tape for me. And I can take practice exams online for the written test so I'll be able to pass really easy."

"I'm sure you will." She pulled his study guide toward her and flipped through the pages. A good deal of the information and drawings were unfamiliar to her. "What do you want me to do? Ask you the questions and see if you can answer them?"

"Could we start with code first? I mean, could you send me some code and I'll write down the letters?"

He gave her a sheet of paper that listed the Morse code alphabet and numbers and showed her how to use the code generator.

At first it all sounded like indistinguishable beeps, but she finally got the hang of it. Awkward at first, she sometimes held the *dit* too long, turning it into a *dah*, and sending the wrong letter. Eventually she tried sending a few short words like cat and mat. It was like learning a whole new language.

Before she knew it, more than an hour had passed and Mary had arrived home. She wheeled herself into the kitchen.

"Gracious, I heard all that beeping going on and thought a giant cricket had gotten loose in the house."

Abby laughed. "A very smart cricket. One who's learning Morse code."

"Abby's been helping me," Bobby explained.

"Yes, I can see that." She rolled over to the refrigerator. "But what she hasn't done, I bet, is offer you milk and cookies. I'm an expert at that. Would you like some?"

"Yeah, sure." Bobby's eager nod of approval indicated he thought that was a great idea.

"Well, you know where the cookie jar is," Mary told him.

While Mary retrieved a carton of milk from the refrigerator, the boy hopped up from his chair and headed for the Rhode Island Red ceramic rooster on the counter where Mary kept an endless supply of homemade and bakery cookies, mostly as a lure to keep Bobby coming around, Abby suspected. Mothering her own children and others seemed to be a natural instinct of Mary's.

Abby leaned back in her chair, removed her glasses and rubbed her eyes. "You called it a day earlier than usual."

"Not much happening right after Valentine's Day. In fact, I told Candace to close early and go home herself."

Smiling, Abby watched Bobby consume two peanut butter cookies with gusto, then down half a glass of milk in one gulp. By the time he became a teenager, she imagined both Sandy and Neil would have to work two jobs to keep the boy properly fed.

He finished the rest of his milk, leaving a white mustache above his lip. "Can I take Finnegan outside to play?"

"Of course. I'm sure he'd enjoy that."

He grabbed his jacket and shrugged into it, then scooped up his code practice equipment. "Thanks for helping me, Abby."

"You're more than welcome. We'll do it again another day."

"Bye." In a burst of energy, the boy was out the door, Finnegan at his heels. The door slammed behind them.

Abby winced. "Do you think you and I ever had that much vim and vigor?"

"Oh, you did. A regular tomboy you were, racing around the neighborhood. I, on the other hand, was nothing but demure and always a lady."

Sputtering a laugh, Abby got up to put on water to heat for tea. "It's possible your memory has been dimmed by the passage of time. I remember one time when you threatened to 'clean the clock' of a girl who was trying to bully me and get me to fight her. That seemed pretty tomboyish to me."

"A brief moment of weakness, I confess."

They laughed together, and the richness of their shared love filled the room with a special kind of warmth. The sensation was so powerful, Abby couldn't help but send up a quick prayer of thanksgiving for the blessings the Lord had brought her by her return to Sparrow Island and her family.

When the water had boiled, she poured it into Mary's favorite teapot.

"I'm going to have to get up early to make the first ferry in the morning," Abby said.

"Oh? Where are you going?"

"To Bellingham, to the Coast Guard Station. I have an appointment with the senior chief in charge of the station. I'm hoping to get to the bottom of whatever's going on out at the lighthouse. Or, at the very least, get him to admit there's something wrong and nudge him into investigating what's causing the light to go off."

Mary lifted her thumb in approval. "Go get 'em, sis. I don't like it any more than you do that our friends and neighbors are being put at risk by the problem at the lighthouse."

Abby planned to carry her sister's words with her the next morning. She would not accept the Coast Guard's claim that there wasn't a problem.

CHAPTER ❦ SEVEN

Abby checked the directions to Coast Guard Station Bellingham and drove off the ferry, following a line of cars up the ramp before turning right. Most of the occupants were daily commuters who lived on the islands and worked in the city. She considered herself fortunate not to have to commute to her job. Instead, the cross-island drive to the conservatory took no more than fifteen minutes.

The hour-long ferry ride from Sparrow Island had been uneventful, the sea calm and the sky overcast. She read her morning devotionals, strolled around the deck as she meditated, and now she was ready to meet Senior Chief Bosnik.

Within ten minutes of driving off the ferry at Bellingham, she arrived at the Coast Guard Station. On either side of the entrance, chain-link fencing with rows of barbed wire on top protected the facility from intruders. A young seaman wearing a navy-blue uniform and jacket stepped briskly out of the guard shack. Leaning down to talk to her through the car window, he touched the brim of his ball cap with a hint of a salute.

"Abby Stanton for Chief Bosnik."

"Yes, ma'am. He's expecting you." Pointing, he directed her to one of the two buildings on the property. Beyond the structures, three boats were tied up to the dock, their crew members apparently engaged in training drills and maintenance activities.

Following the guard's instructions, she pulled into a parking spot, got out and walked into the building. Inside, two seamen were working at their desks, including Seaman Holland, the young woman with whom Abby had spoken on the phone.

"I'll show you to Chief Bosnik's office, ma'am."

The young seaman led her upstairs to the second floor and down a hallway to the last office, then gestured for Abby to go inside.

The chief stood to greet her and Abby was struck by two things. First, she'd expected an older man to be in charge of a Coast Guard station. Eric Bosnik—blond with a deeply tanned face—looked to be in his mid-thirties and very fit. Secondly, his office window provided an extraordinary view of Bellingham Port with the ships tied to the wharfs and huge cranes off-loading cargo.

He came around his desk and extended his hand.

"Thank you for taking the time to see me," she said.

"I'm glad you decided not to involve the press. We don't need that kind of distraction." He gestured toward the chairs in front of his desk.

"I understand. But as an unofficial representative of the residents of Sparrow Island, we want you to know we're very concerned about the lighthouse at Wayfarer Point."

His narrowed gaze was that of an experienced leader who liked to be in charge, no questions asked. He held that look of intensity for several heartbeats before returning to his chair behind his desk. He wore the same uniform as the seaman at the gate, but his sleeves were rolled to above the elbow and contained more stripes. His name was embroidered just above his right shirt pocket, just above the U.S. COAST GUARD insignia.

"Wayfarer Point Lighthouse is our responsibility," he conceded. "However, we've investigated the reports of malfunction and have found no evidence that any error occurred."

"But you have several eye-witness accounts. They can't all be making it up."

"We don't have an explanation for that, ma'am. It may be that the fog was particularly heavy on the nights in question and the ships weren't close enough to see the light. Or the ships' navigation systems were off."

"That would be dangerous, wouldn't it?"

"It would, yes, ma'am."

"I'd have some difficulty believing four ships, at least three of them commercial vessels with seasoned captains, would all experience the same navigational problem within two or three weeks of each other."

His expression turned into a scowl. "It does seem unusual."

"Have you visited the lighthouse yourself?"

"Two of my men, including my electronics specialist, have investigated the reports. They checked the connections at the power station as well as at the lighthouse. Everything is perfect. No problems."

"Yet we know something is going wrong."

Growing visibly impatient, the chief stood. "Ms. Stanton,

I want you to see our monitoring equipment. Perhaps that will satisfy you."

He marched out of the office, and she had to hurry to keep up with him as he led her downstairs and then to the basement. They entered a dimly lit room with all sorts of dials and meters on the wall, black cables crisscrossing the ceiling.

"Petty Officer Houston." At the bark of his name, the petty officer in question jumped to his feet. "I want you to show Ms. Stanton the monitoring records for Wayfarer Point Lighthouse. When you're done, escort her to her car." Bosnik turned to her, gave a curt nod, then left the room. His footsteps pounding up the stairs.

"I think your boss is not pleased with me," Abby said.

"He's been getting a lot of static about that lighthouse. Whatever the reports are saying, I sure as heck can't find anything wrong. Of course, intermittent outages are the toughest to pin down."

Abby was as puzzled as the Coast Guard was. She knew that Neil McDonald's report was accurate; the light had gone off. There was no question in her mind about that.

"Could you start by explaining how the lighthouse works?" she asked.

He proceeded to talk about old Fresnel lenses, the frequency of the white flashes the lighthouse emitted and how fog horns worked. It was far more information than she could absorb in one sitting.

"Does the lighthouse require electrical power to operate?" she finally asked.

"Yes, ma'am. We have a dedicated line from the power substation on Sparrow Island. And we monitor that through a cell phone telemetry link. There've been no glitches in the power at the times the ships reported their problems. It just didn't happen, ma'am."

But it did. "Can you show me the monitoring equipment?"

"Sure." He took her across the room to another set of meters. He tapped one with his knuckle. "This is Wayfarer Point Lighthouse. The dial's straight up, meaning everything's A-OK. There's also a record printed out every twenty-four hours." Pulling open a drawer, he showed her sheets of paper with squiggly lines that looked very much like the results of a heart-monitoring test when the patient had died. The line was virtually straight.

"No glitches, ma'am," he concluded.

"There was a power surge at my office yesterday. Would that show up on your monitor?"

"Not unless your power source was drawing power from our dedicated line."

"Could someone be doing that? Stealing electricity from the Coast Guard?"

Slowly, he shook his head. "We'd see a decrease in the power output. So, no, that hasn't happened."

Abby could understand why the senior chief was upset by her inquiry. Apparently they'd checked everything they could and hadn't found an answer.

"Could someone here at the station be interfering with the operation of the lighthouse in some way?" she asked.

"Sabotage from an insider? I don't see how, ma'am. It would show up on the monitor as if we'd lost power to the lighthouse. There'd be a record. And this position in the monitoring room is staffed 24/7."

Discouraged, Abby thanked Petty Officer Houston for his

help and returned to her car. As she headed back to the ferry landing, she thought again that just because no one had found the answer to the problem didn't mean the problem didn't exist. It simply meant they hadn't found the right answer yet.

As she sat in the ferry parking lot waiting for her turn to board, she thought of Psalm 120:1: "I call on the Lord in my distress, and he answers me."

She lowered her head. "Lord, I know there's an answer somewhere. Please help me or the Coast Guard to find it before any permanent damage is done. Amen."

Lifting her head, she realized there was another lead she hadn't yet followed—the possibly unscrupulous maritime salvage company in Port Angeles.

Digging her cell phone out of her purse, she punched in the number of the sheriff's substation on Sparrow Island. Fortunately, Henry Cobb was there. He provided her with the name of the owner of Marine Recovery, Inc., Mr. Sigfried Hoppe.

As the ferry crewman signaled that it was time for her line of cars to board, she thanked Henry and started her engine. The problem now would be to get to Port Angeles. It was thirty nautical miles from Sparrow Island across open ocean and there was no direct ferry service there. Driving would mean a long trip clear around Puget Sound, so the better choice was to find someone with a fairly fast boat who would be willing to take her.

Giving that some thought as she walked upstairs to the main deck of the ferry, she smiled. Rick DeBow, the handyman and general jack-of-all-trades at the marina, had access to a lot of different boats. During the off season he wasn't usually pressed for time. And not only was he knowledgeable about a good many subjects, he was an all-around nice man.

She pulled out her cell phone again and made the call.

IN LESS THAN TWO HOURS, she was onboard a sleek cabin cruiser, *My Settlement*, with Rick DeBow at the wheel as they slowly eased past the marker buoys, leaving Green Harbor.

Rick was a muscular man in his late fifties, his hair a mix of brown and gray, his face well tanned from the amount of time he spent outdoors. Seeing him dressed in faded jeans and a plaid wool shirt, it was hard to imagine him wearing suits every day in his former life as a stockbroker. But his new life in Sparrow Island seemed to agree with him. Abby had never known him to be anything but quietly content.

"You're sure the owner of the boat won't mind us borrowing it?" she asked, for probably the third time.

"No problem. Since he doesn't come to the island during the winter, he specifically asked me to take her out once a week or so to keep the engine oiled up and running smoothly. A quick trip to Port Angeles makes a perfect outing for the ol' girl."

"How long will it take us to get there?"

"Couple of hours, give or take a bit. She can do ten knots, more if we push her."

"Perfect."

They reached the outer marker and he shoved the throttle forward. The throbbing of the two large engines increased, the deck vibrating beneath Abby's feet. She'd taken the time to go home to change into slacks, a warm sweater and deck shoes, and had called both Mary and Hugo to let them know what she was up to. Now, as they rounded the point to head south, she was having second thoughts.

"This may be a wild goose chase," she warned Rick. She'd perched herself on a stool near him where she could get a good view out the front window of the boat.

His calloused hands resting comfortably on the wheel, Rick shrugged. "I was bored anyway. Not much activity around the marina this time of year. Good day to go for a boat ride."

"What do you think is happening at the lighthouse?"

"Hard to tell. I sure don't think Neil McDonald imagined the light going out. Or that some screwy ghost is pulling the plug when the mood strikes him."

She chuckled. "That rumor's certainly getting around."

"That's what happens in a small town. Rumors are like the flu. One person gets it, the next thing you know everybody in town is sniffling and coughing."

"The truth is the only cure for that kind of a rumor. The electronics specialist at the Coast Guard told me an intermittent problem is the hardest to find."

"That's true. When I'm troubleshooting electrical equipment, it can turn out the problem is as simple as a loose connection or a wire that some mouse has chewed through."

"A mouse?"

"Sure. It could be that there are mice in the lighthouse and they've been chewing on the wiring. Or maybe some other rodent has gotten into the underground cable and done some damage. The least little movement could affect the connection. That'd be hard to track down until the break is complete."

"Now that's a happy thought. We can wait 'til the light goes off permanently."

"Easier to find and fix the problem that way."

That wasn't exactly what Abby wanted to hear, despite how reasonable it sounded.

"What are you going to say to this Sigfried guy you hope to see?" Rick asked.

"I'm not sure. I can't very well go blazing into his office, metaphorical guns drawn, and accuse him of intentionally trying to run ships aground in the strait so he can get a recovery fee."

"No, I don't imagine a man would react well to that."

"I think I'll have to play innocent. I'll ask him his advice, what he thinks the problem might be and hope I'll instinctively know if he's lying."

"Ah, the dumb blonde routine."

She slanted Rick a frown. "I'm more like a rapidly graying, middle-aged woman."

His lips hitched up into a half smile. "Abby, you're a very attractive woman. The bit of gray in your hair makes you look distinguished and intelligent. In fact, it'll be hard for you to pull off a dumb act, I'm afraid."

"Why, thank you, Rick," she murmured, embarrassment warming her cheeks. She hadn't expected that sort of a compliment from Rick. They'd worked together on several projects, and he'd never been anything more than a valued friend.

Suddenly she thought of the mystery floral arrangement and the enclosure card. That scrawled initial could have been an *r*, but for Rick, not Roger.

With a shake of her head, she rejected the thought. Rick had never expressed any romantic interest in her. Certainly not enough that he would sign a card *Love Always*. The flowers couldn't have come from him.

DERELICT SHIPS OF VARIOUS SIZES were lined up along the docks at Marine Recovery, Inc., like weary circus elephants too tired to perform one last act. Rust showed through the old gray paint; decks canted to one side or the other as though the ships no longer cared to hold themselves upright. The only working vessel appeared to be a giant tugboat. The air smelled of diesel fuel and rancid oil.

Standing on the deck, Abby wrinkled her nose as Rick piloted *My Settlement* to an empty spot alongside the dock. She tossed a line to a man in overalls who was waiting there. He tied them off to a cleat while she tossed bumpers over the side to protect their relatively pristine blue-and-white boat from scraping against the oily, creosote-covered pilings.

Rick turned off the engines, then joined her on the deck. They climbed up an old wooden ladder to the dock and the workman offered Abby a hand up.

"Thank you," she said.

He touched the bill of his Seahawks cap. "What can we do for you folks?"

"We'd like to talk with Sigfried Hoppe," Abby told him. "Is he around?"

He thumbed over his shoulder toward a one-story, wooden building with a corrugated tin roof that didn't look much better off than the derelict ships. "Sig's in the office."

Nodding her thanks, she and Rick walked toward the building.

"From the looks of things, I'd say maritime salvage isn't a real lucrative business," Rick said.

"Maybe that's why Mr. Hoppe would be tempted to drum up business for himself."

Rick rapped his knuckles on the door, then pushed it open. The interior was as much storage space as office. Rows of shelves held marine parts, hundred-gallon cans of lubricating oil sat on the floor and thick coils of towing rope were stowed in a back corner. On the dock side of the office, beneath the one window, a man sat working at his desk.

"Hello," Abby said. "We're looking for Sigfried Hoppe."

"*Ja*, you found him." He looked up from his work, then stood. He had a big barrel chest, thick arms and a drooping salt-and-pepper mustache. Overall, his physical appearance and slight German accent made Abby think of a brewer from the old country rather than a marine salvager. "You need something?"

"Yes, we need your advice." Abby introduced Rick and herself, omitting her professional title, but telling him they were from Sparrow Island. "We thought, given the business you're in, you'd know quite a bit about what causes maritime accidents and why a lighthouse would stop operating properly."

Stroking his long mustache, he looked puzzled for a moment. "Ah, *ja*, the lighthouse at Wayfarer Point. I heard there was a problem."

"Have you heard any hint of what might be causing the problem?"

His sudden boom of laughter was like a canon shot. "They say, down to da Emerald Tavern in town, that it's some ol' coot haunting the place."

Abby cringed. She'd had no idea Margaret Blackstock's theory would travel this far in so little time.

"Can you think of any reason a person would interfere with the lighthouse on purpose?"

He sobered instantly. "That would be a crazy thing to do."

Rick spoke up. "Not so crazy if the person could benefit financially by a ship going aground or sinking."

"Listen, mister. You think I would do a thing like that? Sink a ship on purpose? Is that why you come here?" He shook his head. "You ever see a body of somebody that was drowned, huh? Somebody trapped onboard a ship as it went down? Their fingers full of splinters because they were trying to claw their way out as the water was pouring over them? *Nein*. Once you see that, you don't want any ship to sink no matter how much money you can make. That would be worse than Judas taking his thirty pieces of silver."

"I'm sorry, Mr. Hoppe," Abby said hastily. "We aren't here to accuse you of—"

"*Ja*, I know why you come here. You think I make money because of somebody else's troubles because I charge a fair price for what I salvage. But I don't make them the trouble. They do that themselves by being stupid. Or maybe just having bad luck. The sea can be a cruel place. I would not tempt the fates of my own boats by sending another man's ship to the bottom."

Contrite, Abby apologized again and so did Rick. They headed back to the dock and *My Settlement*. Sigfried Hoppe had convinced her that he had nothing to do with the lighthouse failures. He felt too strongly about the sea and its victims to be lying about his innocence.

She sighed as they pulled away from the dock.

"Guess I wasted your time, Rick. I'm sorry."

"Don't be. If nothing else, we eliminated a suspect and had a nice boat ride in the process."

"*Hmm*." Under an overcast sky, the ocean remained calm, the swells barely making the boat rock. At midafternoon, daylight was already beginning to fade. "Can you take us home via Wayfarer Point so we can get a look at the lighthouse?"

"Can do." He shot her a grin. "You don't give up easy, do you?"

"Not usually. But I'm sure running out of ideas." Maybe all

those ships' captains, including Neil McDonald, had imagined the lighthouse going dark, just as Senior Chief Bosnik had implied. Or maybe she'd simply have to buy into Margaret Blackstock's ghost theory and let it go at that, unless Henry Cobb or U.S. Customs officials came up with concrete evidence of smugglers at work in the islands.

There was little boat traffic during the winter months in the Strait of Juan de Fuca. In the distance, a ferry boat with its running lights on steamed for the city of Victoria on Vancouver Island in Canada. Behind them, a tanker ship headed northward to the refineries on the Washington coast.

Rick turned on *My Settlement's* running lights.

"Gets dark early this time of year," he commented.

All the more reason the Wayfarer Point Lighthouse was important to the commerce that plied these waters.

They motored along in comfortable silence for a time, then Rick said, "I picked up a couple of sandwiches from Springhouse Café before we left Green Harbor and stuck some canned drinks in the fridge. Figured we might get hungry."

"Come to think of it, I am hungry. I didn't take time for lunch."

"Great. If you'll take the wheel, I'll play ship's steward and serve up the sandwiches. Hope you like turkey."

Her empty stomach growled its approval. "Sounds perfect. Thanks."

He went below deck to the galley and quickly returned with two box lunches in plastic containers. With Abby still at the wheel and keeping their course north-by-northeast toward home, they began eating.

"Look," she said after a while, pointing beyond the bow of the boat. "There's the lighthouse." The flash of white light swept toward them at five-second intervals, a beacon warning of the rocks that lay ahead.

"I'd say we're about five miles off the point," Rick said. "Time to turn to the port, thirty-five degrees."

"Aye, captain." Smiling, she rotated the wheel. The boat responded, slipping in between the swells of the sea change before settling into a more comfortable movement again.

"Abby!"

She turned at his sharp call.

"The lighthouse," he said. "It just went dark."

Unbelieving, she immediately throttled back. "What on earth!"

In the deepening dusk, the silhouette of the lighthouse building was barely visible rising from the point. But no light flashed its warning.

Some way, somehow, someone had turned off the light at Wayfarer Point Lighthouse.

CHAPTER ✿ EIGHT

Dumbfounded, Abby stared toward the lighthouse. "We're not imagining this, are we?"

Rick shook his head. "Not unless we've both got a bad case of hysteria based on the power of suggestion. From what I saw, the light went off, just like that." He snapped his thumb and finger together.

"How?" she asked, knowing the question was rhetorical. Neither of them knew the answer. *But someone did.* Or ought to.

She glanced to the stern of the boat. There, through the cabin windows, she saw the running lights of the oil tanker that had been following them. It was still moving up the strait.

"Rick, do you think that tanker realizes the lighthouse is dark?"

He followed the direction of her gaze. "I don't know. They were a couple of miles behind us and won't turn east where we did. They'll keep heading due north."

A surge of adrenaline kicked through Abby's blood stream. "See if you can raise them on a marine frequency. Warn them about the light."

"Will do."

Meanwhile, Abby let the boat idle while she grabbed for her cell phone. Flipping it open, she checked the signal strength, then punched in the number of the Bellingham Coast Guard Station that she had programmed earlier.

After a young seaman answered, she said, "I'd like to speak to Senior Chief Bosnik. It's urgent."

"I'm sorry, ma'am. The chief's gone for the day."

"Then you'll have to reach him at home or wherever he is. The light at Wayfarer Point has gone out. Again."

"Please hold the line."

Abby waited. She glanced back at the tanker. Rick had reached them on the radio and they seemed to be slowing. If they were imagining the lighthouse being out, so was the captain of the tanker, which wasn't exactly reassuring.

"Bosnik," the chief barked over phone. "What's going on?"

"Chief, this is Abby Stanton. I'm about a mile off Wayfarer Point. As we approached the point, the light went out. We're observing the dark lighthouse now."

"You're on a boat?"

"Cabin cruiser. There's also an oil tanker steaming up the strait. We've warned them about the light and they're slowing."

"Hang on."

Abruptly, he put her on hold. She waited again, watching both the lighthouse and the tanker. A tingle of apprehension trickled up her spine like ghostly fingertips, raising goose bumps. Rick was talking with the tanker. They had a GPS system. The weather was calm. No one was likely to run aground tonight.

"Stanton!" Bosnik barked. "My monitoring equipment says there's nothing wrong."

"Then your monitoring equipment is wrong, sir. You can contact the *Eureka Marie* tanker to confirm our observations. She's almost even with the point now."

Abby could almost hear the chief's mental wheels revolving in search of an answer. At least now she thought they were asking the same question.

"I'll have my crew at the lighthouse first thing tomorrow morning," he announced. "We'll get to the bottom of this if we have to dig up the whole island, I can promise you that."

Expressing her thanks, Abby disconnected. She planned to be at Wayfarer Point when Bosnik's crew showed up. She wanted to be there when the Coast Guard solved the mystery.

Assuming they could.

WHEN ABBY GOT HOME, she found Mary working in her craft room, sorting through old snapshots for the scrapbook she was making for her grandchildren. Finnegan was curled up under the worktable.

"Oh good, you're home." Smiling her welcome, Mary wheeled around. "I didn't know what time you'd get here so I put your dinner in the refrigerator."

"I'll get it in a minute." Looking over her sister's shoulder, Abby admired the decorative way she'd organized the pages in the scrapbook. Each page had a colorful border, the snapshots arranged in creative ways with clever subtitles.

"How'd it go in Port Angeles?" Mary asked.

"Interesting, to say the least. Particularly the trip home." She related her meeting with Sigfried Hoppe, the lighthouse going dark and her conversation with Chief Bosnik.

"Well, thank goodness. It sounds like you finally have the Coast Guard's attention."

Abby agreed. "I'm optimistic the lighthouse will be fixed now."

"Good. That means we only have one mystery left to solve—who sent us the flowers."

Chuckling, Abby picked up a snapshot of Jacob and Mary holding baby Nancy in her arms. Mary's grandchildren, Emily, seven, and Nicholas, three, would love seeing their mother when she was only a baby. Since Abby had been living in New York during most of the years her sister had been raising her children, she'd had mostly a long-distance relationship with her niece and nephew. She regretted that now. She also knew Mary wished she could see her grandchildren more frequently.

"I've pretty much run out of ideas about the flowers," Abby said, putting the photo back on the worktable. "So much so that earlier today I was thinking our mystery benefactor might have been Rick DeBow. But I can't believe he'd send flowers and then not say anything about it."

"Probably not. Though he's a very nice man." Picking up a glossy Florists' Association magazine, Mary flicked through the pages. "Of course, there is another man who could have sent you those flowers."

"Who?" From Abby's perspective, she was fresh out of ideas.

"You know who."

"Mary," she warned sternly. "Tell me who you're thinking about."

Lifting her head, Mary looked up at Abby. "Perry Nelson."

Abby's jaw went slack and she shook her head. "He wouldn't send me flowers."

"There was a time when he certainly could have and would have."

"Well, yes, but . . ." she sputtered. Perry couldn't be the one. An old flame, true, but . . .

"Have you tried to communicate with each other?"

"Not at all. There's no point."

Setting her magazine aside, Mary returned her attention to the scrapbook she was putting together. "Maybe you should drop him a note."

Abby stared at the top of her sister's head. Perry wouldn't have sent her Valentine's flowers and not followed up on the gesture. He was too—what was the expression she was looking for? Too sophisticated to let something like that drop without another word.

Wasn't he?

"Frankly," she said, drawing a deep breath, "I don't think either of us ought to let one mystery flower arrangement keep us awake at night. We'll eventually find out who sent it. Either way, it's in the Lord's hands."

Forget that discovering the source of the flowers had been on her mind for days now. She would simply put that particular mystery out of her mind and worry about other things where she had some modicum of control, like the eagle census.

THE NEXT MORNING when Abby woke, she bundled up against the chill air, poured herself a cup of coffee and went out on the deck to read her morning devotionals. Even on a damp, cool day, she felt nearer to God when she could hear the sounds of nature and inhale the fragrance of the earth and sea around her as she meditated.

The day's devotional message came from Jesus' message in the sermon on the mount. Appropriately, the topic dealt with worry. The lesson concluded, "Therefore do not worry about tomorrow, for tomorrow will worry about itself. Each day has enough trouble of its own" (Matthew 6:34).

As she contemplated the message, she listened to the song of the ocean humming against the rocks below Mary's house. A crow in a nearby fir tree cawed a discordant note, then set off to find its flock. Seeking a bit of attention, Blossom hopped up onto the deck. Purring, she brushed against Abby's legs.

She reached down to run her fingers through the cat's lush fur coat. "No worries for you, huh, Blossom? Just as long as your dish is full and you have a warm place to nap, you're content."

It was harder for humans to halt the stream of worries that tended to plague them. Because of the mystery flowers, both she and Mary had spent far too much time fretting about something of little significance.

Bowing her head, she sought the Lord's comfort, asking Him to lift the day's worries from both her and Mary's shoulders and give them the faith to know He was watching over them.

As she went inside to eat breakfast, her steps felt lighter. She knew, deep in her heart, problems would be solved and worries lifted if she simply gave them over to the Lord.

ANCHORED JUST OFF WAYFARER POINT, a Coast Guard boat bobbed in the swells. Onshore, a half-dozen men in blue overalls, their pants legs tucked into their boots, and wearing ball caps with Coast Guard logos, swarmed around the lighthouse.

They wielded shovels and picks, attacking the ground on the north side of the building with a vengeance. Dirt flew. A few curses too. Senior Chief Bosnik stood off to the side scowling at his men.

The clouds overhead promised another gray day.

"Good morning, chief." From his dour expression, Abby concluded Chief Bosnik wasn't all that pleased to see her. Or he was even less pleased his men hadn't yet found the fault in the lighthouse electrical system.

"We've checked the cell phone telemetry from the Bellingham Station to the substation powerhouse." A muscle jumped in his square jaw. "It's good."

"Which means you can eliminate that as the source of the problem?"

He cut her a look that he might have given a new recruit who was out of uniform.

"From the substation to the light, there's no break— I repeat—*no* break in the power."

"So what are you digging up?"

Abby was absolutely sure senior chiefs were not supposed to growl at local residents. But she forgave him. He was frustrated. It showed in the way he stood, fists on his lean hips, the downturn of his mouth. The Coast Guard had promoted him any number of times and trusted him that the lighthouses under his supervision would operate in the way they were intended. Bosnik was a man who didn't like to fail, either himself or his superiors.

Several cars from town arrived, parking at intervals along the road where Abby had left her vehicle. Word spread quickly in a small town.

William Jensen, the editor of *The Birdcall* wasn't the first to arrive. But he was the most blustery. A thin man, he was all arms and legs as he strode across the uneven ground, a camera dangling from a strap around his neck.

"I'm the press and need to talk to whoever is in charge." He directed his demand to Chief Bosnik.

"No comment," came the chief's terse reply.

"The public has a right to know what's going on here," William persisted. Notebook in hand, he was ready to record the story.

Bosnik glared at him. "I said no comment. You'll have to step back, sir." When William failed to move away, the chief repeated his order, with emphasis. "Now!"

Equally determined, William responded. "This is public land." He slipped the notebook into his jacket pocket and lifted the camera to his eye. "Whatever is going on, it's news and I intend to report it." The camera flash went off in the chief's face.

The seamen stopped their digging, their eyes on their superior.

More cars arrived on the road above the lighthouse.

The chief, his face red with anger, took a threatening step toward the newspaper editor.

"William!" Abby called. She hurried over to him. "Why don't we stand over by the trees out of the Coast Guard's way? I'm sure Senior Chief Bosnik will give you a statement as soon as he has anything to say." Hooking her hand through William's arm, she tried to urge him to move away—for his own safety. Years younger than William, the chief outweighed him by a good many pounds and looked to be in top condition.

If things became physical, it wouldn't be a fight William could win.

Scowling, William resisted her efforts. "Abby, this is a big story. I've got to stay on top of it."

"I know. But if we let these men do their work, I'm sure you'll get the story that much quicker."

"*Humph.* Don't you know, a story would break big here on the island on Wednesday with the paper already out and delivered. This sort of thing never happens on *Tuesday*, does it? Oh no, couldn't happen *before* my deadline. The readers will have to wait a whole week to read about this. By then it'll be old news."

"I'm sorry, William," she said sympathetically, all the while easing him away from the lighthouse and Chief Bosnik. "But it's good that you'll have plenty of time to get all the facts before you have to go to press."

He *humphed* again, but they'd reached the windblown stand of fir trees where the rest of the onlookers had gathered. Ignoring them, William began snapping pictures of the scene and the men who had resumed their digging.

Aaron Holloway, the twenty-five-year-old grandson of the owner of Holloway's Hardware, was in the crowd. "Hey, Abby. What are they up to?"

"They're trying to find out why the lighthouse keeps going dark," she replied.

A man in a turtleneck sweater, who she didn't recognize, laughed. "You mean they're looking for Pettigrew's ghost?"

Others in the crowd joined in the laughter.

Abby grimaced. "I think it's unlikely the problem's due to the late Terrence Pettigrew."

"That's not what they're saying in town," someone called.

In a party mood, the onlookers were laughing and talking

among themselves. Not much that was newsworthy happened on Sparrow Island, and the spectators wanted to make the most of it.

But as the time dragged on, and the sun finally penetrated the cloud cover, Abby began to think her day would be better spent at the conservatory preparing for the upcoming weekend's bald eagle count. It was entirely possible the Coast Guard would dig up the length of the cable from the lighthouse to the power substation without discovering the problem.

Just as she was beginning to wonder if she'd be able to get her car out of the jumble of parked vehicles, one of the young Coast Guardsmen called out.

"Chief!" Shovel in hand, he backed away from the spot where he'd been digging. The young man's eyes were wide with surprise. Or horror. "I found something."

As though of one mind, the spectators surged forward, William Jensen in the lead. Abby was right beside him.

The other seamen gathered around the man who had announced the discovery. Chief Bosnik shoved through their ranks.

He gave a low whistle as he stared down into the three-foot-deep trench his men had dug to get to the buried power cable.

Slipping past the chief, William snapped three pictures in quick succession.

The chief yanked the newspaper editor back from the trench, opening a gap between the men that gave Abby a clear view of the seaman's discovery. She shuddered at the sight.

There, at the bottom of the trench and partially covered by a disintegrated tarp, was a skeleton dressed in an old navy peacoat and a dark knit cap with a few tufts of hair sticking out.

CHAPTER ❦ NINE

Senior chief bosnik appeared as stunned by the discovery as Abby was.

"There shouldn't be a body here," he muttered. "It's government property. Nobody authorized this. I'd know if they had. It'd be in the records." He knelt to examine the skeletal remains more closely.

"Chief, I don't think you ought to disturb the body," Abby said. "Not until we get someone in authority to take a look."

His head snapped up and he scowled at her. "I'm in charge of this lighthouse."

William moved to the opposite end of the trench to snap pictures from a different angle.

"But you're not trained in forensics, are you? This could be a crime scene. We don't want to lose any evidence if it is." Although, given the condition of the body, it would have to be a very old crime.

Looking confused by the unfamiliar situation, Bosnik shot

another look at the bottom of the trench. "This guy could be Navy. You know, from the jacket and cap."

Abby pulled the cell phone from her pocket. "I'll call the sheriff's substation. They'll get someone out here, then we'll know how to proceed."

"If he's Navy, then the investigation falls under the Navy Crime Scene Investigator's office. That's procedure."

She punched in the phone number. "I'm sure our Sergeant Cobb will know the correct procedure to follow." And she hoped Henry was on Sparrow Island this morning, not back at Lopez Island, which was also part of his jurisdiction and where he lived.

The deputy who answered the phone switched her call directly to Henry Cobb; Abby briefed him on the situation.

"I'll bring my crime scene specialist along," Henry told her calmly. "We'll be there in less than thirty minutes. Meanwhile, ask the Coast Guard to clear the area and move any spectators away from the scene. I don't want it contaminated by people stomping around."

"Will do." Hanging up, Abby reported Henry's request to the chief. Not that the scene hadn't already been thoroughly contaminated by thousands of people visiting the lighthouse since the body had been buried.

The chief seemed energized by what amounted to an order. "Men, I want you to establish a perimeter around the scene. Back to those trees and to the water line. Nobody gets closer than that, including that nosey reporter, until the cops get here."

"I'm not just a reporter," William protested as one of the seamen took him by the arm, propelling him away from the gravesite over his vociferous objections. "I'm the editor. I own the paper."

"You'll have to talk to him sooner or later," Abby said mildly to the chief.

"Nobody talks to the press until I get the go-ahead from my CO." With that, he pulled a cell phone from his pocket, snapped it open and walked a few steps away from the grave, presumably to call his commanding officer.

With a critical eye, Abby studied what she could see of the human remains in the trench. Who would bury someone next to the lighthouse? And why? If the deceased was a sailor, why hadn't the Navy reclaimed his body years ago? If someone wanted to hide the body from discovery, they could have taken it out to sea, tied weights around it and dropped him—or her— overboard. If nothing else, they certainly could have buried the body deeper than they had.

A young seaman politely asked Abby to join the rest of the spectators.

She hesitated long enough to offer a silent prayer for the soul of the deceased, then moved away from the scene to wait for Henry's arrival.

Aaron Holloway asked her what was going on.

She shrugged. "I'm not sure. They found a skeleton."

The onlookers *oohed* and *ahed.*

William hurried over to her. "Abby, I love you for poking around with the Coast Guard and making them check out the lighthouse. What a great story this is going to be." He snapped a picture of her.

She blinked, spots in front of her eyes nearly blinding her. "Someone is dead, William. I don't consider that a feel-good story."

"Murder. Mayhem. It's all grist for mill. Newspapers thrive on reporting the dark side of life."

Fortunately, Sparrow Island didn't experience much crime and no murders that she could recall. That her inquiries with the Coast Guard had resulted in turning up a skeleton was hardly a reason for anyone to love her. In fact, she wished William would show a little more sensitivity to the deceased.

Noticing that Chief Bosnik had finished his phone conversation, she eased away from William to talk to the man in control of the scene.

"What did your commanding officer say?" she asked.

"We'll let the local authorities make the initial determination. If they think the dead guy is Navy, the CO will request an official investigation."

"That sounds reasonable. I'm sure Sergeant Cobb will handle his end of the investigation very professionally."

Just then she heard the siren of an approaching police vehicle. A silvery-tan police cruiser with the familiar green stripe on the side came into view on the road, weaving its way around the jumble of parked cars. It stopped and Henry Cobb got out of the passenger seat. His driver, Deputy Mike Bennett, exited the car and retrieved what looked like an oversized fishing tackle box that contained what he needed for his crime scene examination.

Nodding toward Abby, Henry touched the brim of his hat in a quick salute, then introduced himself to the senior chief. They shook hands.

"What have we got here?" Henry asked.

"Sure not anything I was expecting." Chief Bosnik gestured toward the trench and Henry followed him.

The three men—Henry, the chief and Deputy Bennett—peered down into the hole much as Abby had earlier.

Taking off his hat, Henry scratched at the fringe of gray hair on his head. "If that guy died as a result of some crime, it's sure a cold case by now. He's been down there a long time."

"It's a crime to bury someone on government property without authorization," the chief said, apparently a stickler for the rules and feeling proprietary about the small patch of land that was his responsibility.

Henry glanced around. "Guess this area's belonged to the government a long time, huh?"

"Since 1902. That's when the first lighthouse went up."

"A little before my time." Turning to his deputy, Henry said, "See what you can find out. I'll call for some transport."

Letting his man get to work, Henry strolled toward Abby. "Looks like you may have another mystery on your hands."

"I'm sure you and your men will be able to solve this one."

He shrugged. "Maybe, maybe not. After Bennett's done, we're going to have to exhume the remains. I figure Dr. Randolph can do a preliminary autopsy for us. Give us an idea of how the guy died and when."

Dr. Dana Randolph was the director of the Sparrow Island Medical Center and an excellent physician, handling the health care needs of most of the islanders and tourists who developed a problem while visiting the area. Occasionally she filled the role of coroner too.

"The victim could be a woman," Abby reminded Henry.

"I sure couldn't tell one way or the other from looking at the skull. But the jacket and cap look like they'd belong to a man, seems to me."

Finally escaping from the seaman who had him in check, William dashed over to Henry. "What can you tell us, Sergeant? The public wants to know what's going on."

"Can't tell you a thing right now, William."

"Look, Henry. We're friends. This is *The Birdcall* you're talking to."

Henry simply smiled and patted William on the back. "I'll let you know what I find out when I can. Until then, it's no comment."

ABBY OBSERVED THE ACTIVITY around the gravesite for a while longer, then decided she really did have to get to work. She wanted to be sure she had enough volunteers from the conservatory signed up for the eagle census to supplement those coming from the San Juan Islands Birding Society. She'd catch up on the progress of identifying the deceased later.

As she was walking into The Nature Museum, a column of sunlight caught the bigleaf maple tree in the center of the circular drive, highlighting the tips of the branches where the faintest hint of spring buds had finally begun to show. High in the tree, a bald eagle perched on a branch eyeing his surroundings.

"Be sure to come back for the census," she called to him. "Wouldn't want to miss counting you."

Pushing through big double doors, she spotted Wilma Washburn shelving new nature books in the small gift shop near the entrance.

"Hey, Wilma. They have you running the gift shop now along with everything else you do?"

Wilma's dark eyes sparkled as she acknowledged Abby's comment. "Honestly, these books just came in. I didn't see any reason to wait for someone else to shelve them when I wasn't busy at the moment."

"Careful, or Hugo will find some extra work for you."

"It's all right. I like being busy." She arranged the last of the colorful books of nature photographs on the shelf and stood back to admire her work. "I heard the Coast Guard found a dead body out at Wayfarer Point."

"A skeleton, actually."

Rubbing her arms as though she suddenly had a chill, Wilma shook her head. "Any idea who it is?"

"Not yet. Dr. Dana will do a preliminary autopsy. I imagine we'll know more after that. But it looks like whoever the deceased is, he's been dead a long time."

Thoughtfully, Wilma walked back toward the reception desk, which was her usual post. "I remember an old Salish man who used to wander around town making a nuisance of himself. Drunk most of the time. He seemed to get into a fight about once a week and end up in the pokey. Then one day he simply vanished."

"An Indian?"

"Not one of our more outstanding role models, I'm afraid." Wilma was very proud of her Indian heritage. A skilled basket maker, she practiced the ancient craft and participated in tribal affairs.

Following Wilma to the reception desk, Abby checked the clipboard for signups for the eagle census and was gratified by the number of volunteers who were listed. "How long ago was it that he vanished?"

"Let me think. When my nephew, Artie, was just a toddler, old Hank Cultee used to carry him around on his shoulders, when he was sober that is. He wasn't a bad man, just an alcoholic. I think by the time Artie was in school, Hank had gone missing."

Abby understood that alcohol could be a cruel master, one

not every victim was able to escape. And since Wilma's nephew, who worked as a deputy for Henry Cobb, was in his late twenties, Abby guessed this Hank Cultee had disappeared about that many years ago. Long enough that his remains would have decomposed, leaving nothing but bones if he was the skeleton they'd found.

"No one ever heard from Hank after that?"

"Not that I know of." Wilma leaned her elbows on the reception counter. "You think that's who's buried out at the point? He got into one too many fights, got himself killed and somebody wanted to hide the evidence?"

"I don't know."

"Funny, I hadn't thought about that man in years. Now I can see him in my mind's eye as clear as day. His hair was jet black with hardly any gray in it. He always wore a tatty pea jacket and knit cap, and he used suspenders to hold up his pants."

"Wilma! That could be the man! I could even see some hair sticking out from under a knit cap. It was black."

"Really?" She looked amazed and somewhat startled she might have identified the dead man. "Do you suppose it was him?"

"I don't know, but if it is I bet Dr. Dana will discover Hank Cultee didn't die a natural death."

"Well, as Margaret Blackstock might say, wouldn't that beat all." She mimicked Margaret's Brooklyn accent.

Chuckling, Abby took the clipboard with her and headed for her office. While it seemed unlikely Hank Cultee was Margaret's ghost of Wayfarer Point Lighthouse and responsible for the problems out there, it would be a relief to know the identity of the deceased.

She noticed Hugo's door was open and she stopped in to see him. He smiled in greeting.

"Looks like we have a nice group of volunteers to help out with the eagle census," she said, holding up the clipboard. "I'm going to check in with Leanne Van Hoesin to make sure the San Juan birders group is all set to go."

"Excellent. The weather report's good for the weekend, which will make it a pleasant outing for everyone." Leaning back in his chair, he tented his fingers together. "I understand there's been some excitement out at the point this morning, but I haven't heard the details."

Taking the chair in front of Hugo's desk, she briefed him on the morning's grizzly discovery.

"Very interesting. You say the senior chief from the Coast Guard thought the man might be Navy?"

"Yes, but Wilma thinks the deceased might be a Native American who vanished thirty years ago without a trace."

Standing, Hugo paced around the room and finally settled on the edge of his desk in front of Abby. "You're aware, I'm sure, that during World War II there was some military activity here in the Northwest. There were great fears that Japan would attack us, and even some sightings of Japanese submarines off the coast."

"But if it was a sailor who died, wouldn't the military have reclaimed his body for a proper burial after the war?"

"One would think so. But perhaps it was a Japanese sailor who died one way or another, and his crew mates couldn't take him back home."

"Goodness. I hadn't considered that possibility."

"I'm not saying that's what happened, of course. And I'm

sure Dr. Dana will be able to tell from the deceased's bone structure what ethnicity he is, or was."

"Or if it's a woman," she added.

His eyes widened in surprise. "What makes you think that?"

"I don't, really. I'm just not prepared to jump to any conclusions until we hear from Dr. Dana. But it did look like the deceased had long, dark hair, which could belong to either a man or a woman." She shuddered at the thought that someone had been buried there, unknown in an unmarked grave for all those years.

"Perhaps you should put your amateur sleuthing skills to work. You might be able to narrow the possibilities—missing people, lost sailors and so on—which would help Dr. Dana in her efforts to identify the deceased."

Shaking her head, Abby rejected the idea. She had enough on her plate with the upcoming eagle census. Besides, the more important question was to determine why the lighthouse kept going dark. A skeleton that had been in the ground for thirty or more years wasn't the cause, she was sure.

"I think I'll leave identifying the body to the experts," she said.

AFTER RUNNING TO IN STITCHES to pick up some yarn for her projects and handling other errands in town, Mary returned home in late afternoon. She parked her van in the garage, then she and Finnegan rode the lift down.

Removing the dog's harness, she said, "You're off the clock, boy."

Finnegan gave himself a big shake and took off across the

yard at warp speed. Mary had complete confidence he wouldn't go far because he was an amazingly well-trained dog. For a second she envied the freedom he had to run and play in a way she no longer could.

Bobby McDonald came running across the yard. "Hey, Mary!"

Mentally pulling herself back from that negative thought, she said, "Hey, yourself, young man. How was your day at school?"

Finnegan came racing back, and the boy and dog wrestled together for a minute. Finally, Bobby picked up a fallen branch, tossing it for Finnegan to fetch.

"School was okay, I guess. But I'm having more fun with Uncle Robert. I'm learning all kinds of stuff about frequencies and the rules hams have to follow. Pretty soon I'll be ready to take the test to get my own license."

She could see the pride in the boy's eyes. "Good for you."

"He lets me talk on the radio sometimes. He has to be there, though. I'm not allowed to talk until I get my own license."

"I understand. Who have you talked to?"

Frowning, he thought a minute. "There was this guy in Seattle. WA7BAM. That's his call sign. Got his license when he was only fourteen, and that was years and years ago. In 1992, before I was even born."

Mary swallowed a laugh. "You're going to get your license soon and you're only ten."

He grinned. "Yeah. Uncle Robert says I'm smart enough to learn the stuff I need to know."

Mary had no doubt Uncle Robert was right. "What about that funny transmission we heard the night we came over to meet your great uncle. You know, the funny one about no big fish? Have you heard anything like that since?"

Picking up the stick Finnegan had retrieved, Bobby tossed it again. The dog chased after it at full speed.

"I dunno. Uncle Robert gets kinda mad about stuff. You know, being blind and all. And then when somebody on the radio does something stupid, he gets all upset. He did that the other night. We heard him yelling in his room."

"It's not easy losing your eyesight, Bobby." Or the use of your legs, she acknowledged to herself. "You have to be patient with your great uncle."

"That's what Mom says too." Wistfully, he looked back toward his house. "I wish there was some way I could fix Uncle Robert."

Reaching out, Mary hooked her arm around Bobby's waist and drew the boy toward her for a hug. "We all wish that, honey. But I suspect the best thing we can do for Robert is give him all the love and acceptance we can. Getting used to being blind is something he'll have to do for himself. With a little help from God, of course."

The boy lifted his narrow shoulders in a shrug. "I've been praying for him. A lot."

Tears burned at the back of Mary's eyes. After her accident a good many people had prayed for her. She was confident those prayers had made the difference in her recovery and her acceptance of the limitations she'd had to face.

"I know God hears your prayers, honey. And your Uncle Robert feels the power of those prayers, too, even though he can't always tell you exactly how he feels."

"I guess." Bobby escaped from her embrace, eager to chase after Finnegan, who was happily in pursuit of a moth he'd never be able to catch and probably wouldn't know what to do with if he actually caught it.

Mary watched the playful antics of the boy and the dog for a while, thinking about the resilience of youth. While all that energy might not be entirely wasted on the young, she wished she could harness just a fraction of that energy again.

Bowing her head, she reminded herself to be grateful for the blessings she had and not focus on that which had been taken from her.

IT WAS NEARLY DARK when Abby returned home. She found Mary in the kitchen preparing dinner.

"I wish I'd had a roommate like you my entire working career." Abby bent down to give her sister a hug. "Some nights I'd get home from work too tired to open a can of soup. Now I come home to all these wonderful smells that make my mouth water."

Mary stopped grating cheese to return the hug with her free arm. "It's a new pasta recipe I'm trying. It uses whole-wheat pasta, low-fat cheese, chicken and lots of tomato sauce and spices."

"It sounds ever so healthy and a lot more appetizing than a can of soup." Abby pinched a bit of cheese from the dish. "Let me go clean up and I'll set the table for us."

"Henry's coming to dinner too."

"Ah. Thus the new recipe," Abby teased.

Her cheeks flushing, Mary waved off the comment.

Abby hurried upstairs to wash up and change clothes. She enjoyed Henry's company almost as much as Mary did, but sometimes she felt like a fifth wheel. Mary and Henry didn't seem to get much time alone together. Not that either of them had complained. Still, she couldn't help but think matters between them might progress somewhat faster if Mary's little sister weren't hanging around all the time.

Back downstairs again, she set the table and poured the water. The timer announced dinner was ready just as Henry arrived.

"Perfect timing," Mary said, greeting him at the door. "Our dinner's ready and all that's left to do is put it on the table."

"I'll do that," Abby called from the kitchen. "You two can sit down and I'll serve you."

It wasn't long before Abby joined them at the table. Henry said grace, then Abby served up spoonfuls of steaming casserole onto the plates.

Henry sniffed appreciatively. "You two ladies spoil me."

"Dinner was all Mary's doing, I assure you."

The smile he sent in Mary's direction was more than affectionate.

"How was your day, Henry?" Mary asked.

Surprised by the question, he glanced at Abby. "You didn't tell her?"

"I haven't had a chance. I just got home a few minutes before you got here."

"What?" Mary asked. "Is something wrong?"

"Not with either of us," Henry assured her. Then he went on to describe what had happened that morning and the skeletal remains the Coast Guard had found.

"Oh my, that's terrible," Mary said.

"Did Dr. Dana have a chance to examine the body?" Abby asked.

"Nope. This was her day off and she'd gone into Bellingham to do some shopping. We had to store the remains in a refrigerated unit. I imagine she'll take a look tomorrow."

"Well, who on earth do you suppose the poor soul could be?" Mary asked.

"Both Wilma and Hugo have come up with some possibilities," Abby said, telling them about the old Indian, an unknown sailor or someone left behind from the Japanese Navy in World War II.

They ate in contemplative silence for a few minutes, Henry helping himself to a roll and buttering it.

Thoughtfully, Mary looked up. "I remember some years ago there was a woman who lived out at Oyster Bay. Her husband reported her missing, but no one had any idea where she might have gone. There was talk that the man abused her. No proof, however. Do you think . . . ?"

"Anything is possible at this point," Henry conceded.

Both Mary and Henry turned to Abby.

"A perfect job for Abby," Mary teased.

"Now, stop that!" Laughing, Abby pushed her empty plate away. "Henry can figure this one out, can't you?"

"I imagine I can. But I could likely use some sleuthing help. *If* you have the time. It'd be good to have some background information on the possibilities before Dr. Dana gives us her verdict."

Abby wasn't thrilled with the prospect of researching missing persons. But the niggling curiosity about who had been buried at Wayfarer Point was hard to resist.

They finished dinner and Abby cleared the dishes, putting them in the dishwasher. Mary and Henry went into the living room to watch one of Henry's mystery shows on TV. Abby often joined them, but this time she thought she'd give them some privacy.

Feigning fatigue, she went upstairs. She was in the middle of a mystery novel that was quite good. She thought she'd settle down to read a few chapters before bedtime.

But the lure of her laptop computer sitting on her desk was too much to resist. It wouldn't take all that long to do a little searching on the Internet to see if she could come up with some information about missing persons in the San Juans. Or sailors lost at sea—U.S. or Japanese.

Putting her book aside, she walked over to her desk. A few minutes of browsing might not turn up anything at all.

Or maybe it would.

CHAPTER ✣ TEN

SHE'D OVERSLEPT. ABBY threw off the covers, sat up and scrubbed her face with her hands. She'd surfed the Internet until the wee hours of the morning, fascinated by the wealth of information she'd found.

Showering quickly, she pulled on slacks and a turtleneck sweater, then went downstairs for breakfast. Although the sun was out, it had a watery look to it and the day didn't promise much warmth.

Finnegan, tail wagging, trotted out of the kitchen to greet her.

"Hey, buddy," Abby said, giving him a scratch around his ears. "Good morning to you too."

"Goodness, I was about to check to see if your car was gone," Mary said. She wheeled out of the kitchen. "Did you oversleep?"

"I certainly did." Going into the kitchen, she spied some apple-cinnamon muffins on the counter and decided to have one for breakfast.

"That's not like you, Abby. Are you feeling ill?"

"Not at all." She placed a muffin on a plate and put it in the microwave for thirty seconds. While that was happening, she poured herself some juice. "You won't believe all the information I found on the Internet last night."

"About what?"

"About Japanese submarines that were sinking merchant ships here in the Northwest during World War II."

The microwave dinged and Abby retrieved her muffin, carrying it and her juice to the table.

Mary chuckled. "You mean our resident sleuth stayed up all night after all?"

"Oh hush," Abby responded with a grin as she got herself a cup of coffee from the pot Mary had prepared. "It appears to be true that I'm constitutionally unable to resist trying to solve a puzzle. But that doesn't mean I won't rely on Henry to solve this particular mystery."

Mary rolled her chair closer to the table. "So tell me what you found out."

"Well, during World War II a Japanese submarine sank at least one merchant ship in the Strait of Juan de Fuca. It was the *SS Coast Trader* and it was torpedoed in June of 1942."

"So you think the body they found could be one of our merchant sailors?"

"No, that's not what I'm saying. At least not yet. But it's true that all but one of the crew members of that ship survived."

Mary's eyes widened with excitement. "And the missing crew member?"

Forking a bite of muffin into her mouth, Abby shook her head. "From what I read, the outcome wasn't clear for the missing seaman. They may have recovered his body or not. It was hard to tell from the descriptions in the article I read."

"Then the body could have been the American merchant seaman."

"Yes, but there were several Japanese submarines that prowled the Northwest. Some of them had airplanes that they catapulted off the sub, sort of an underwater, mini-aircraft carrier. One even tried starting fires in our Oregon forests."

"Oh dear."

"See, the point is, there was a lot of military and merchant activity going on around the San Juan Islands during that war. Wearing a navy pea jacket would be typical for anyone in the military at that time. So that body—skeleton, really—could be from either side of the war."

"So what you found isn't all that helpful in determining who the body is, or was."

Abby scowled. "Well, in that sense, no. And unfortunately, old issues of *The Birdcall* aren't computerized so I couldn't check out the woman you mentioned who had gone missing some years ago. I'll have to stop by the newspaper office to follow-up on that possibility."

Chuckling, Mary took a bite of her buttered toast. "If that was before William bought the paper—and I think it was—then the chances of the story of a missing woman being in *The Birdcall* are probably slim to none."

"Oh, because of poor ol' Elmira Underwood, the editor before William?"

"Blind as a bat, poor dear. She had so many typos in the paper, it was a game to find them all. And her idea of a big story was when some youngster's pig for a 4H project escaped its pen before the butcher could catch him."

Abby laughed at the memory too. "Well, the pig did get into Archie Goodfellow's produce section at The Green Grocer. He probably wasn't too happy about that."

"You're right. That was a good story after all." The humor of the past gave them both a smile.

"Anyway," Abby said, "I thought I'd drop by the newspaper office this morning before I go into work and see what I can find out."

"I'm sure Henry will be pleased with any information you can dig up."

Abby eyed her sister, trying to determine if Mary was teasing her about her penchant for solving mysteries, whether they were Abby's business or not. But Mary seemed far more interested in clearing the kitchen table than giving Abby a hard time.

And the fact was, Abby had instigated the investigation surrounding the problems at the lighthouse. It was only natural that she'd take an interest in whatever the Coast Guard turned up, including unexplained human remains.

Clinging to that rationale as reason to pursue this new mystery, Abby finished her breakfast and headed into town.

A stiff breeze was blowing down off of Arrowhead Hill, making the flags at the public park snap to attention. Seagulls aimed into the wind, flapping their wings wildly, but were swept back toward the marina. Somehow, Abby thought the birds were enjoying the game of being propelled back to where they had started. Although she admonished herself not to give human characteristics to creatures in the animal world, it was still fun to imagine what they might be thinking.

She pulled open the door of *The Birdcall,* surprised to find Margaret Blackstock standing at the counter talking with William.

"Hey, Abby," William said, "I'll be right with you."

Margaret turned around, her eyes opening wide. "There's the lady of the hour, all right."

"No rush," Abby said to William. "Lady of what hour?" she asked Margaret.

"You know, digging up old Terrence Pettigrew, the ghost of Wayfarer Point Lighthouse, the poltergeist who's been making all that mischief out there."

"Really, Margaret—"

"Now, you can't deny they dug up a body, can you?"

"No, of course not. But that doesn't mean—"

Margaret snorted in disbelief. "And just who else do you think would be buried next to the lighthouse after all these years?"

"Actually, there are several possibilities, none of which involve ghosts or things that go bump in the night."

"I, for one, don't believe any of those other stories. Pettigrew's the culprit or rather his ghost. You can bet your Mets tickets on that, honey."

"This press release looks fine, Margaret," William said. "I'll be sure to get it in next week's paper." He held up a couple of sheets of paper, apparently the information Margaret had brought him in her role as school secretary.

"Thank you, William. The school's cultural arts program is quite important. For some of our children, that's the one place they can shine. Getting their name in the paper gives them a real boost."

Turning to Abby again, Margaret lowered her brows in a scolding way. "You mark my words, Abigail. There's a ghost at work out there at the lighthouse, and we have to let the poor thing find some peace."

"Really, Margaret—"

"If I'm wrong and that wasn't Terrence Pettigrew they dug up out there, then you tell me where *was* that man buried, huh? A smart woman like you should be able to find the body, don't you think?"

With that, her head and bouffant hairdo held high, Margaret whirled and stalked out of the newspaper office. As soon as Margaret was out the door, William nearly leapt over the counter, he was so eager to hear news of the skeleton that had been found at the lighthouse.

"What have you discovered?" he insisted.

"At this point, you know as much as I do," Abby said, still trying to process Margaret's challenge. Terrence Pettigrew must be buried somewhere. But Abby didn't know where. Nor should it be important. The man had been dead for years.

"Don't be coy with me," William said. "I know you and Mary are tight with Henry. He's got to know something by now."

Reaching across the counter, Abby touched William's hand to calm him. His face was so flushed, she was suddenly worried he'd have a heart attack.

"Slow down, William. We won't know anything until Dr. Dana gives us the autopsy report. But meanwhile, I could use your help."

His bushy eyebrows shot up. "How?"

"Mary remembers a woman from Oyster Bay who went missing some years ago. I'd like to check back through your—"

"You think the skeleton belongs to a woman?"

Abby rolled her eyes. "I have no reason to believe that one way or the other. I'm simply following a few leads I've picked up."

"Leads from whom? Who's your source?"

Lowering her head, Abby counted to six. She couldn't possibly make it to ten, given William's agitated reaction. "William," she said very slowly and succinctly, "I'd like to look at back copies of *The Birdcall.* Starting about thirty years ago. Could I do that, please?"

"You know that's all on microfiche, and except for a few years, there's no index," William warned.

Abby nodded, not exactly thrilled at the prospect of having to search potentially dozens of rolls of microfiche film. "I know."

Rather reluctantly, William led her to a small backroom where he turned on the overhead lights. Racks of horizontal poles draped with dusty newspapers lined the walls and there were three large file cabinets. Stacks of aged cardboard boxes were piled haphazardly on the floor near an ancient microfiche machine.

"I want you to keep me in the loop," William said. "If you find anything, you'll let me know, right?"

"I'll certainly try to," Abby hedged. If she found anything of interest, her first responsibility was to tell Henry. The press would have to wait.

Wishing she had asked Mary to be a little more specific about when the Oyster Bay woman had gone missing, Abby rummaged through boxes of film canisters looking for those from about thirty years ago. She plucked one from a box, put the film in the machine and began to scroll. The first headline she came to read: WOMAN'S DRESS STOLEN FROM CLOTHESLINE.

Abby smiled at that, wondering if the culprit had ever been caught.

Looking over her shoulder, William quickly lost interest in her search and went back to his office.

Left on her own, Abby skimmed through articles as they came up on the screen, looking for some telltale clue that would help her identify the deceased who had been found at the lighthouse. The flow of headlines told the story of a quiet community where the big news most often was a school graduation party, community play or a tourist's boat that ran aground on the beach. Crime didn't seem to be a part of Sparrow Island's history, at least not as recorded by the previous editor, Elmira Underwood.

Working her way through several years worth of microfiche, Abby was beginning to wonder if she was on a futile search. Then she found what she'd been looking for: HUSBAND REPORTS WIFE MISSING.

Abby quickly scanned the article. Nathaniel Latori reported his wife, Angel, had been missing for three days. Neighbors indicated often hearing the couple having loud arguments. There was no record of Angel's having left Sparrow Island by ferry and the family boat was still tied to the dock. Police reported no sign of foul play, but they were still investigating.

A photo accompanying the article showed a happy couple on their wedding day, the smiling bride a petite, dark-haired girl of no more than twenty.

"Interesting," Abby murmured.

Like magic, William appeared at her side. "What'd you find?"

"Nothing definitive. But I did find the story about the missing—"

"You think this is the woman they found?" William positioned himself so he could read the article.

"I have no idea." Still, it was one more possible lead to identifying the deceased. Although it would seem odd for such a pretty woman to be wearing a navy pea jacket.

"Abby, this information might help Dr. Dana. We've got to go see her and tell her about—"

"I'm sure the doctor can do her work without our help."

"Well, if you won't go, I will." Stepping into his office, he grabbed his suit jacket and pulled it on. "There's a big story here and I intend to get to the bottom of it."

Abby didn't want William to harass Dr. Randolph and disrupt her work. But she knew when William sniffed a story, he was unstoppable. Like the news bloodhound he wanted to be, he'd run the story to the ground.

With a shake of her head, Abby knew she'd have to go with William to see the doctor. It was the only way she'd have a chance to satisfy her own curiosity and at the same time protect Dr. Dana from being badgered by the local press.

ANXIOUS TO EXERCISE her own investigative skills, Mary decided to research the enclosure card that had come with the mysterious floral arrangement.

She went into Island Blooms where she found Candace in the front area giving the flowers in the refrigerator fresh water and tossing the blossoms that had faded.

"Hey, Mary. I didn't expect to see you this morning."

"Oh, I just wanted to check on something." Releasing Finnegan from his harness, she signaled for him to relax in his usual place near the front counter.

"Hope it's not me you're checking on," Candace said, dropping a handful of old carnations into a trash barrel.

"Goodness, no." Mary laughed. "I have complete faith in your ability to run the shop without my looking over your shoulder. You've proved yourself more times than I can count."

Candace smiled at the praise. "Then can I help you find something?"

"Maybe." Looking at the enclosure card that she'd brought from home, the one that had come with the mystery flowers, Mary read off the name of the stationery manufacturer. "Do you remember a salesman from Reflections Stationery dropping buy to sell us card stock?"

Pausing with her clippers raised, Candace frowned. "I don't remember a salesman, but I think we got a catalog from them a few months ago."

"Do we still have it?"

"I'm not sure. If we do, it'd be in the bottom drawer on the left-hand side of the desk."

Mary rolled over to the desk and opened the drawer in question. The contents were neatly arranged, a variety of catalogues from distributors offering everything from vases to gift cards, all of them filed alphabetically. She marveled at Candace's efficiency and organization. What a jewel she was.

She pulled the Reflections Stationery catalog from its spot and began flipping through the pages.

"Have we ever ordered any enclosure cards from these people?"

"Not that I can remember." Setting her clippers aside, Candace joined her. "What are you trying to find out?"

"I'm still puzzled by the flowers Abby and I received for Valentine's Day." In truth, Mary didn't want to admit the mystery was gnawing at her and waking her in the night.

"Oh. Well, maybe a few sample cards came with the catalog. I could have put them in the rack instead of throwing them away."

Mary's spirits lifted at the possibility. "Do you think that's what happened?"

Twisting her lips into a crooked grimace, Candace checked the rack of cards on the counter. "I can't actually remember doing it or even getting sample cards. But sometimes I get really busy. . . ." She worked her way across the display, then down each row.

"It's all right, Candace. I know how it is when the shop gets hectic." Like it did just before Valentine's Day. Neither she nor Candace had had a chance to take a break, much less to do their jobs methodically.

Candace let her hands drop to her side. "If we did have cards from Reflections, we sure don't have any now."

Nodding, Mary made a page-by-page search of the catalogue looking for a picture of the card she'd received. She found it in a mix of cards that florists order as a group.

She tapped the page with her fingertip. "This card is in their current stock."

"Which means what?"

Mary shook her head. "It means I'm going to call my friend Renea at Friday's Flowers in Friday Harbor. Once in a while the 1-800-delivery service gets confused and selects her shop for a Sparrow Island order instead of finding us."

"Oh, that's a good idea."

Locating the number, Mary placed the call. Since there were few florists in the San Juan Islands, they'd developed a friendship and cooperative spirit. After working with her father for years, Renea had taken over Friday's Flowers a few years ago when he retired.

Renea answered the phone, and they spent a few moments commiserating about the pressure of Valentine's Day.

"I was wondering," Mary said, getting to the reason for her call, "do you use Reflections Printing for your enclosure cards?"

"Reflections? Um, yeah, we do. Are you thinking of going with them?"

"Well, not really. The thing is, we have a tiny mystery on our hands." Excited that she might be onto something, Mary explained about the unexpected floral centerpiece. "Could you have filled a Valentine's order for delivery here on Sparrow Island?"

"Oh gosh, no, Mary. If I get a call like that, I give 'em your number right away."

Mary's momentary optimism deflated.

"Of course," Renea continued, "we had a ton of arrangements that were picked up right here at the shop. I assumed they were all for folks here in Friday Harbor. But I suppose someone could have personally delivered one in your area."

Frowning, Mary recognized her meager investigative efforts had hit a dead end. "Oh, well, it was just a thought. Good to talk to you, though."

"Next time you come to the big city, let's do lunch."

Mary chuckled at the reference to Friday Harbor as the 'big city.' "I'll do that, Renea. I promise."

As she hung up the phone, Mary stared off into space. Unlike the crossword puzzles she liked to solve, the mysterious floral arrangement had her stumped. She'd have to leave the detective work to her sister.

After doing a bit of paperwork, she decided to call it a day and go home.

Driving down Oceania Boulevard toward her house, she noticed Irene Farrand, an elderly neighbor lady who lived down the block, outside using her walker. Since she rarely saw

Irene outside and had been unable to get her involved in any of the craft groups she belonged to, Mary pulled over to say hello.

She rolled down the van window. "Hi, Irene. It's good to see you out and about. How are you feeling?"

"Not all that great," Irene admitted. At close to ninety, she was showing obvious signs of osteoporosis and had many physical limitations. But she still lived alone and apparently preferred it that way. "My great-granddaughter is coming to visit me over Presidents' weekend. I thought I ought to get a little sun on my face while I can so she won't think I'm already a ghost."

Mary laughed. "Good for you, Irene. I'm sure your great-granddaughter will be pleased that you're up and walking about."

"She's a real sweetie, that Kathleen. A real sweetie, always sending me cards and such."

Mary remembered seeing the girl visiting Irene several times over the years. A college student now, she recalled.

"Well, have a good time with Kathleen. Have her drop by to say hello if she has a chance."

"I will." Risking a fall, Irene waved a hand, then gripped the walker before she lost her balance.

Driving off, Mary counted her blessings that in many ways she was more mobile than Irene and far less isolated from social contacts. Her wheelchair and van allowed her to go where and when she wanted—without the risk of falling and breaking a hip.

That was definitely a plus.

CHAPTER ❦ ELEVEN

ABBY FOLLOWED WILLIAM'S small, four-wheel drive SUV to the Medical Center, a one-story building on Harbor Seal Road. As she pulled into a parking spot, she noted that both a Coast Guard vehicle and Henry's patrol car were parked near the entrance. Maybe Dr. Dana had some answers for them.

Exiting his SUV, William marched double-time toward the entrance. Abby had to hurry to catch up with him.

"Easy, William. Our skeleton isn't going anywhere."

He didn't look back at her as the automatic doors swished open for him. "But my story might go up in smoke if she tells all to the cops and leaves me out in the cold."

Shaking her head in amusement at the man's determination, Abby managed to get inside before the doors slid shut again. William headed down the hallway to Dr. Dana's office with Abby on his heels.

Standing behind the reception desk, Mary Ellen Walters, who handled most of the administrative duties for the Medical Center, tried to waylay them. "Dr. Randolph is with the sheriff. You can't—"

William stormed right past her. "The public has a right to know what's going on."

Raising her hand in an apologetic wave, Abby followed in William's wake. Her curiosity was fully as keen as his. Granted, she might not have blustered her way into the doctor's private office as blatantly as he did, but she surely wanted to learn the results of Dr. Dana's autopsy.

Wearing a white lab coat and sitting behind her desk, the doctor had a manila file folder open in front of her.

Senior Chief Bosnik, immediately on guard, snapped to attention as they burst into the room. Sergeant Cobb rose to his feet more slowly.

"I didn't know we'd invited the press," Henry said, eyeing William with little surprise.

"You can let me in on the news or I can file papers under the Freedom of Information Act. Your choice, Henry. I'll get the story either way."

Scratching at the fringe of graying hair, Henry checked with the doctor and senior chief, who both nodded. "We were talking about calling you, William. I guess you sort of beat us to the punch."

Like someone had popped his balloon, the bluster went out of the newspaper editor. "Well, then . . ." He pulled his notepad and pen from his pocket. "Let's hear what the doctor found."

Dr. Dana's office was small, its one window looking out at the fir trees behind the Medical Center. Henry gestured for Abby to take his chair, then stood behind her. William took up a position by the wall where a bookcase was crammed with medical books.

The doctor cleared her throat and shuffled through the papers in her file. Her hands were quite small, almost delicate, although Abby knew they were both strong and sure when treating her patients.

"These are only preliminary results, you understand," the doctor said. "A forensic anthropologist might well add additional information or have a different take on the matter, but as far as I can tell, the deceased died forty or more years ago from natural causes."

"Can you be certain of that?" William asked.

"No. Not entirely. But there's no trauma to the body that I can find. No head injury. No evidence of broken bones, except two very old breaks—one of his wrist, which hadn't healed very well, and another on his jaw. I imagine he suffered from arthritis, both in his wrist and his knees."

"It's a man then?" Abby asked. One who apparently had been in at least one fight that had broken his jaw—possibly a barroom brawl. Which meant the deceased could be the Indian Wilma Washburn had mentioned, although the timing didn't quite jibe.

"Oh, yes. I'm quite sure of that. The pelvic bones are those of a male, likely in his sixth or seventh decade, based on decay and the wear-and-tear on his joints."

That eliminated the missing woman as the deceased, Abby thought with some relief. But it still left several possibilities.

"How long has he been buried?" William asked.

"That's extremely difficult for me to say. A forensic scientist would be able to make a much better approximation, given the state of the remaining clothing, as well as the state of decomposition. I'm estimating forty years or so, although I emphasize that's only an educated guess. It could be plus-or-minus as many as ten years."

"So who is the guy?" William asked.

"I'm more concerned about whether or not the man was Navy," the chief said. "If he was, I need to let my CO know. They'll take over the investigation."

Dana shook her head. "From the condition of the deceased's clothing, I can't be sure if he was wearing a naval uniform or just a jacket and overalls. I simply don't have the forensic training to make that kind of a judgment, nor the necessary knowledge about uniforms. I'm sorry."

"It's okay, doctor," Henry said. "At least I know it's not a criminal matter."

"You can't guarantee that," William insisted. "The guy could have died of poisoning. Or maybe he was suffocated."

Henry chuckled. "A part of you is a ghoul, isn't it, William?"

The newspaper editor sputtered, offended by the accusation. "Just trying to get a story," he said defensively. "If you don't want to pursue every lead—"

Abby interrupted. "Could the deceased be Japanese? From World War II?"

Dr. Dana's otherwise smooth brow furrowed. "Oh no. The facial bone characteristics are definitely Anglo. A straight nose, angular jaw. Not Asian at all."

"How about Native American?" Abby asked.

Dr. Dana shook her head. "The facial bone structure doesn't fit, although if the person were of a mixed racial background, the answer might not be so clear-cut."

"Whoever he is, the guy shouldn't have been buried on government property," the chief reiterated. "That's a crime."

Henry shrugged. "A misdemeanor, maybe. One that's forty years old. Hardly worth prosecuting."

The room was quiet while they all contemplated the autopsy results and puzzled over who the deceased might be.

Henry decided to summarize. "What we do have, then, is a male Caucasian, sixty or more years old, who died of natural causes."

"I'd say, based on my examination, that's an accurate statement," Dr. Dana agreed.

"Then why was such a man buried next to the lighthouse in a shallow grave?" Abby asked. "Why not at Green Acres Cemetery here on the island?"

No one seemed to have an answer to that.

As they all stood to leave, William seemed particularly disappointed not to have some gruesome tale to relate. Whatever headline he wrote for the next issue of *The Birdcall*, it wasn't likely to stir up a whole lot of excitement among the residents of Sparrow Island or earn him a Pulitzer Prize.

The senior chief held open the office door for Abby and they walked together toward the exit.

"Did you discover anything while recovering the body that might be causing the lighthouse to operate incorrectly?" she asked him.

"Not a thing. We didn't find a single break in the cable. *Nada*. My men dug up the entire length, clear back to the substation, and you can bet they weren't all that happy about it. There's nothing wrong with the connection."

"So we still don't have an explanation for the light going out or why there have been several near misses in the strait."

Despite his large physique, he seemed to shrink into himself. "No, ma'am."

Abby was as thoroughly puzzled as the Coast Guard. Given that she didn't believe in ghosts, as Margaret Blackstock suggested, she didn't know how else to proceed. The thought that a ship might go aground or that two ships might collide because the lighthouse was malfunctioning gave her the shivers. The environmental damage could be catastrophic, which didn't include the possible loss of life in a collision.

Returning to her car, she sat quietly for a moment. The interior was warm despite the cool air outside. Clouds had begun to roll in from the north and the sky was lowering. Another storm coming.

Oddly, her thoughts kept returning to Margaret's insistence that the culprit—the poltergeist—was Terrence Pettigrew, set on revenge because he'd been fired as the lighthouse keeper. That had happened so many years ago that the theory made no sense, forget the ghostly element.

Still, she couldn't help but wonder where Terrence had been buried. Surely his son, Bryant, had seen him peacefully into his grave at Green Acres Cemetery just off Cross Island Road.

Shaking her head, she knew she ought to get back to The Nature Museum to be sure she had everything in order for the eagle census on Saturday.

But as she pulled out of the parking lot, she found herself turning toward the cemetery. It would only take a few minutes to verify Terrence Pettigrew had indeed been buried at Green Acres—not left in a shallow grave beside the lighthouse he had long tended.

THE ENTRANCE TO GREEN ACRES boasted a six-foot tall wrought iron gate anchored by two ornate pedestals formed out of red brick. The chapel to the right of the entrance was also built of brick and had a sloping cedar-shingled roof that echoed the angle of the fir tree branches that framed the building.

Parking, Abby walked toward the adjacent office building and went inside.

The carpet muffled her steps; subdued oil paintings on the walls added a touch of class as did the warm wooden paneling and fragrant floral bouquets from Island Blooms that Mary supplied twice a week.

As though he had sensed her arrival, Leonard Meekem, Jr., the current director of the cemetery and a man she'd gone to high school with, stepped out of his office. It took just a moment for him to recognize her. And like his father before him, the flexible features of his face seemed capable of expressing whatever emotion grieving families would best appreciate—one of deep mourning or even a joyful recognition that a loved one had gone to be with the Lord.

He looked concerned as he said, "Hello, Abby. How can I help you?"

She suspected he was waiting to determine if someone she loved had passed away, or if hers was a social or business call.

"I hope I'm not interrupting anything, Lenny," she said, calling him by the nickname everyone in town used.

"Not at all." Extending both his hands, he clasped hers in a warm, reassuring grip. "It's always good to see you."

"If it's not too much trouble, I'd like to check on someone who I think was buried here at Green Acres some years ago."

"Of course. Someone you cared about?"

"No, not really. I don't actually recall knowing him."

He lifted his brows, which were showing the same flecks of gray as his dark hair. "Who might that be?"

"Terrence Pettigrew."

"Ah." His light brown eyes focused into the distance as though sorting through a directory of gravesites in his cemetery. "As I recall . . . I believe he was buried in one of our earlier sections, Serenity Place."

"Would it be possible to see the gravesite?" she asked. She wanted to confirm that Terrence had actually been buried here.

He nodded slightly. "Of course. It would be my honor to escort you."

As they went outside, Lenny made small talk, inquiring about Mary and her children, as well as Abby's parents. He seemed perfectly at ease and knowledgeable about the latest events in town.

"I understand you'll be leading an eagle census this weekend." He cupped her elbow to assist her into an electric golf cart for the ride to Pettigrew's gravesite.

Surprise had her hesitating before stepping into the car. "Yes, that's right."

"There's an old-growth fir tree at the top of our property. My father insisted no one fell it, no matter how jagged the upper branches looked. I believe we have a nesting pair there this year."

"Really?" She grinned, grateful for his father's foresight. "I'll be sure that a team of our volunteers include the cemetery in the route they check."

Asphalt paths wound gently through the rolling acreage, a variety of trees dotting the well-cared lawns: Douglas fir, lodgepole pine, bigleaf maple and Pacific madrone. The sections closest to the chapel were marked with upright headstones engraved with dates reaching back to the early 1900s. In newer sections, plaques honoring the deceased were flat against the ground for easier maintenance. Bouquets of flowers marked scattered plots that had been recently visited, and there were several red Valentine's balloons floating above the graves of loved ones.

The ripe scent of recently mowed grass permeated the air.

Somewhere out of sight, the growl of the lawnmower indicated the gardener was still at work.

It didn't take long before Lenny pulled the golf cart to the side and nodded toward a group of gravesites resting beneath a Pacific madrone.

"If memory serves, Mr. Pettigrew's final resting place is just over there."

Leaving the electric cart on the path, they walked a few paces across the damp grass. The markers were a mix here, some standing upright while others were flat to the ground. With unerring certainty, Lenny stopped in front of the gravesite with a flat granite marker engraved, TERRENCE PETTIGREW, 1896–1968. A small image of a lighthouse was etched below the date.

"I believe this is the gravesite that interested you."

Nodding, Abby contemplated Terrence Pettigrew's final earthly resting place. Like many of the nearby graves, the ground had begun to sink over the casket, leaving the lawn uneven in spots. There were no flowers in the holder, no sign anyone had visited the site in years.

She suddenly wished she had thought to bring flowers to brighten this somber section of the cemetery.

"It appears that Mr. Pettigrew is indeed buried here," she said.

"Was there some question?"

"No, not really. But an old skeleton was found out by the lighthouse—"

"Yes, I heard about that. Such a shame, not to be properly returned to the earth from which he came."

"There are those who thought it might be the remains of Mr. Pettigrew."

"I can assure you, no one has disturbed this gravesite in my memory. Mr. Pettigrew is where he was laid to rest in 1968."

The marked gravesite supported Lenny's assertion and tended to dispel Margaret's theory, which still left the identity of the deceased very much up in the air.

AFTER A DAY OF RAIN, Saturday dawned to a clear blue sky and chilly temperatures. Rather than reading from her book of daily devotions, Abby picked up her Bible and opened it to Isaiah 40:30–31, one of her favorite passages and particularly appropriate for the day's eagle census.

Alone in her room upstairs, she read the verses aloud. "Even youths grow tired and weary, and young men stumble and fall; but those who hope in the Lord will renew their strength. They will soar on wings like eagles; they will run and not grow weary, they will walk and not be faint."

She was certainly no youth and she knew well about being weary, but Abby's faith in the Lord had given her strength for many years. Her heart soared when she gave herself over to His will.

Closing her eyes, she prayed that those who joined her this morning would find the strength, energy and determination to complete the eagle census, that none would be injured as they tramped across often uneven ground, and that all would feel uplifted by the spirit of God, as symbolized by one of His most magnificent creatures—the bald eagle.

With an ironic smile, she acknowledged she was ever so pleased Benjamin Franklin had lost his bid to make turkeys the national bird. Not that turkeys weren't wonderful birds, of course, but as a symbol, they did their best work at Thanksgiving.

After breakfast with Mary, Abby gathered her clipboards with maps of the island, the routes well marked for the volunteers, and all of her bird-watching gear. Knowing she'd have to transport some of the volunteers to the starting point of their routes, she'd left her compact car at The Nature Museum the previous evening and borrowed the center's big ten-passenger white van. Relishing the brisk morning air, she drove toward the ferry landing where all the volunteers—those from the San Juan Birding Society and her own Nature Museum volunteers—would meet.

Several of the local volunteers stood in a cluster in the parking lot. Ida Tolliver, an attractive blonde who worked at Springhouse Café and filled in part-time as receptionist at The Nature Museum, spotted Abby first and waved.

Parking the van, Abby joined the group.

"Good morning all. Thank you so much for coming."

"We've already identified one nesting pair." Ida pointed toward the tree-covered peninsula beyond the marina and an old-growth tree whose jagged top rose above the rest.

"Yeah, does that mean we can go home now?" Billy Joe Beck, a sixteen-year-old new volunteer asked. "It's freezing out here."

Everyone laughed, including Abby.

"Not quite yet, Billy Joe. How 'bout I find you some ear muffs instead?" Abby offered.

"Billy Joe is so full of hot air." Rebecca Cody, another teenage volunteer who'd made a specialty of studying trees, teased her friend and elbowed him. "He can keep us all warm."

That comment caused more good-natured laughter.

The temperature was hovering in the mid-forties, and the volunteers were all dressed in warm jackets, knit hats and gloves, most of them with binoculars dangling around their necks. And, like Abby, they wore jeans and sturdy hiking boots. When they laughed, the damp air combined with the low temperature to make their breath fog. Later in the day it would warm into the fifties.

The ferry from Friday Harbor rounded the point and announced its imminent arrival with its ear-splitting horn. The workmen on the dock moved into position to secure the heavy lines the seamen onboard would toss to them. Drivers of the dozen or so cars waiting to depart returned to their vehicles.

Shading her eyes with her hand, Abby scanned the upper decks for the San Juan birders. Leanne Van Hoesin's height made her stand out from the group. Abby waved, but she didn't think Leanne saw her.

While the ferry eased up to the dock, Abby organized her clipboards by map coordinates for easier distribution. It didn't take long before cars began rolling off the ferry. Several turned into the parking lot rather than taking the road up to town. Almost twenty members of the San Juan contingent joined the local group.

Abby gave Leanne a big hug. "Looks like your people turned out in force."

"Oh, they love this sort of activity. Gives us an excuse to bird-watch that even our spouses can't argue about."

Understanding exactly what Leanne meant, Abby laughed. Dedicated birders could spend every spare hour pursuing their hobby, sometimes to the detriment of their families. Having a specific reason to be out bird-watching got them a free pass from their other responsibilities.

As Abby gathered the group around her, she noted that Justin Foote had enlisted three of his youthful friends for the morning's effort—two girls and a boy, all of them handsome young people with bright eyes and intelligent expressions. Gray-haired Wulf Walkenhorst was among the group as was Pamela Folz, her guide dog Harriet and her friend, Maureen O'Leary.

Abby welcomed them to Sparrow Island. "I'm so pleased you could all come today. I think there are plenty of us to thoroughly cover the entire island before lunch and we'll be able to work in groups of three or four, so we won't miss any sightings. I would like us to all get acquainted though, so I'm going to mix you up a bit. If it's all right with you, I'll pair up Sparrow Island volunteers with a couple of you from Friday Harbor." She'd also try to put the less experienced birders like Ida with someone like Leanne, who'd been at the hobby for years.

"That's a good idea," Leanne confirmed. "That way my people won't get themselves lost."

"Now, Leanne," Wulf said, "you know we all have an unerring sense of direction and would never get lost."

"Except that one time when we had to send Pamela and her dog out to track you down on Lopez when you didn't come back in time for the ferry."

"I certainly wasn't lost." Looking amused, the older gentlemen shrugged. "Can I help it if the day was warm and I decided to take a nap under a tree?"

Again the group chuckled, probably because many of them had enjoyed a similar experience on a nice summer day.

Breaking them into small groups, Abby handed out the clipboards and briefed them about marking the maps. "Circle the spot where you see the bird, give it a number and indicate on the other sheet of paper what the bird was doing. If it's sitting on a post or in a tree or on the ground, or if it's sitting on its nest—probably brooding a couple of eggs this time of year. If you spot an eagle flying, note the time and direction of flight. That way we won't be double counting any birds."

"What about other raptors?" someone asked.

"Yes, let's count those too," Abby said. "But be sure to note the type. We may have some golden eagles and, of course, hawks of various sorts."

"Have any of the baby eagles hatched yet?" Ida asked.

"Not yet. That's why we're sure to catch the mom and dad around their nest. Eagles are very devoted parents."

When everyone seemed to understand what they were to do, the groups climbed into their respective vehicles and set off to their route's starting point.

Abby led the group with Pamela and her guide dog, her friend Maureen, and Justin's teenage friend, Kirk Zumbrowski, a youngster with big brown eyes and a ponytail. Their route would lead them along the base of Mount Ortiz.

CHAPTER ✤ TWELVE

Abby drove them through Green Harbor, the streets quiet at this hour, then turned onto the road that led to Wayfarer Point Lighthouse. The two women had elected to sit in the backseat along with the guide dog, which left Kirk up front next to Abby.

"Do you and your friends ever come over to Green Harbor to hang out?" she asked the young man.

"*Hmmm*, yeah, sometimes." He squirmed in his seat, glancing out the passenger side window to check the stores along the street. "You know, things get pretty boring at Friday Harbor sometimes."

"I remember feeling that way when I was a teenager too. 'Ah, if only I lived in the big city with all those movie theaters and malls,' I used to think."

"Yeah, like that." He shot her a lopsided grin.

"And then I'd remember how much I loved the outdoors here with all the boating and nature right at my fingertips, then I'd decide mall crawling wasn't my thing after all."

"Yeah, well, I'm really into nature, too, you know. Protecting the environment and stuff like that. Justin's really big on that too."

"Good for you both."

As Abby drove along, sunlight cut through the branches of the fir trees, dappling the roadway in a jigsaw puzzle of light and shadow. In a spot where the forest opened up to a grassy area, two black-tailed deer lifted their heads from grazing to watch the van pass by. A moment later, one of the island's non-native rabbits dashed across the road, his original ancestors brought here by well-meaning people who thought they'd make good hunting. Since there were few predators, the population of rabbits had flourished, to the detriment of some of the local flora. Fortunately, raptors had found them to be a tasty meal if their favored fish treats weren't readily available.

From the backseat, Abby heard Maureen describing the scenery to Pamela.

"Are you still in school?" Abby asked Kirk.

"Yeah. I'm a junior. A year-and-a-half and I'm outta here."

"What will you do then?"

"University of Washington, I guess. Computer science probably."

"You must be pretty smart."

He shrugged off her assessment. "Justin's the real computer whiz. You know, games and stuff. He had to drop out of school 'cuz his dad died and his mom doesn't make a lot of money. So he's helping out by writing code and doing some freelance computer security work for big companies. Man, he knows all there is to know about hacking into businesses and protecting systems from viruses."

"Wow! He's a handy guy to know. I'll keep him in mind if my computer gets infected." She did have virus protection on her laptop at home, and The Nature Museum did too. But there were times when a virus could sneak through even the best firewalls. Not that she had a clear understanding of the process or why anyone would create a virus meant to destroy the work of others.

But she appreciated Kirk's hero worship of Justin, a young man who knew the ins-and-outs of the computer business.

Abby turned off the main road and headed inland. A few minutes later, they arrived at Summit Stables. She parked and her passengers got out.

"Oh dear," Pamela said. "We're in search of eagles, but I think we've found horses instead."

Abby laughed. "Your olfactories are in good working order, Pamela. This is Summit Stables. A friend I went to high school with owns the place. She won't mind if we park here and walk up the trail toward Mount Ortiz."

"In my case, walking is a better choice than riding a horse, I should think. Harriet wouldn't care to be mounted on another animal's back."

From the well-trained way the guide dog behaved, Abby suspected Harriet would go wherever and however her mistress wanted her to. Among other things, the dog barely spared a glance at the horses in the corral. She was entirely focused on Pamela's well-being, much as Finnegan looked after Mary's needs.

Abby handed Kirk the clipboard. "How 'bout you be in charge of noting whatever sightings we get?"

He grinned, pleased with a job to do. "Yeah, sure. I can do that."

"The path's a little rough," Abby said to Pamela, "but I think you'll be all right."

"Harriet won't let me get into too much trouble. Neither will Maureen, for that matter."

A blush colored Maureen's cheeks as she shook her head in denial.

Suddenly, Pamela raised her hand, asking for silence. "Red crossbills," she whispered, pointing toward the top of a stand of lodgepole pines. "Hear that *kip-kip-kip*?"

"I do," Maureen said.

Abby smiled, watching the flock of small birds dart through the treetops. "That's amazing. How do you do that?" Although she had recognized the birds' distinctive call as well, the sound hadn't particularly registered with her.

Waiting a moment before she responded, apparently enjoying the undulating sound of the birds, Pamela finally said, "The good Lord gave me five senses. He only took one away, so I assume He intends me to use the rest of them as best I can."

"Wow. That's way cool, ma'am," Kirk said, his gaze following the flight of the crossbills.

With an appreciative smile, Pamela said, "Lead the way, Ms. Stanton. We're here to spot eagles, not crossbills."

"My pleasure."

Abby started off and Pamela gestured for Harriet to follow. The trail led around the end of the corral, where horses eyed them with only mild interest, and was wide enough for Abby to walk next to Pamela. Walking with confidence, the woman had a firm grip on Harriet's harness.

"How long have you had Harriet?" Abby asked.

"Almost two years. I would have gotten a dog sooner, but for quite some time I had enough residual vision that I could get around on my own. You have to be entirely blind before you apply for a guide dog. Then Harriet and I trained together."

"You seem to have adjusted very well to your handicap."

"I was fortunate. As soon as I was diagnosed with macular degeneration, I started looking for resources and learning adaptive behaviors."

Amazingly, Harriet led Pamela around the drooping branch of a fir tree that hung over the trail. The obstacle was well above the dog's normal line of vision, but apparently Harriet still knew it would be a hazard for her mistress.

"I'd say it was more a question of you being determined to keep your independence," Abby said, "rather than being fortunate."

"Ever since I was a little girl, people have described me as being stubborn," Pamela said with amusement. "I suspect that turned out to be my saving grace. My stubbornness became an asset."

Abby imagined that was an accurate statement.

The forest here was mixed, dominated by Douglas fir with lodgepole pines in smaller stands, particularly where the ground had been disturbed. On this south-facing slope, there was little undergrowth.

Keeping a close eye both on the trail and the sky, Abby spotted a Cooper's hawk, distinguishable by its size and rounded tail, perched on top of a power pole.

"Look," she said quietly, pointing and raising her binoculars to her eyes.

"It's a hawk, right?" Kirk asked.

"But what kind?"

Both Kirk and Maureen studied the bird through their field glasses.

Finally Maureen ventured an answer. "I think it's a Cooper's hawk. It seems too big to be a sharp-shinned hawk but not as big as a goshawk."

"Well done, Maureen," Abby said.

"I told you she was a quick learner," Pamela said in praise of her bird-watching apprentice.

"How do you want me to mark him on the map?" Kirk asked.

Abby showed him what she wanted and they walked on up the trail. Although the air remained cool, they were warm enough when they kept moving. Kirk took off his cap, stuffed it in his pocket, and unzipped his jacket.

"How did you go about finding help in adapting to your blindness?" Abby asked Pamela as they continued up the hill.

"You mean besides praying day and night?" she said with a laugh.

"Well, yes. Rehabilitation programs, that sort of thing," Abby added.

"I started with my doctor and just kept asking questions. I even enrolled in a six-week program at Stanford University for mobility training." She cocked her head toward Abby. "You seem unusually interested in the subject. Is there someone you know who is going blind?"

"He's already completely blind." Abby told her about Robert Weatherford and his difficulties adjusting to the devastating results of an explosion.

"The cause of his blindness is tragic, and a terrible loss," said Pamela, "but as long as he continues to think of himself as a victim, he'll have trouble moving forward with his life."

"I'd love for him to have a chance to meet and talk with you. Your courage inspires me. It might help him too."

"Then let's arrange it," Pamela said cheerfully. "You pick a date, and Harriet and I will take the gentleman on a bird walk."

Just then the path turned and the landscape opened up before them with a breathtaking forest scene.

"Look there!" Kirk raised his glasses to his eyes and gazed out across the tops of the trees. "That's gotta be . . . Wow, look at that! *Two* bald eagles sitting on a gigantic nest. Is that cool or what?"

With matching enthusiasm, Maureen joined the young man. "I bet they're brooding a couple of eggs in the nest. I wish we could see them."

"Come back in a few weeks and you'll see them hatched," Abby suggested.

She wasn't immune to the striking sight of two such magnificent birds any more than the newer bird-watchers were. Her heart soared with a combination of pride and love for these creatures God had created to populate His forests and bring joy to those who were fortunate enough to view them.

Although this was a known nesting site, it didn't dim anyone's excitement, particularly when the male took wing and soared overhead in his search for a meal for his mate.

As they walked on, Maureen spotted an immature eagle circling the same nest.

"Probably last year's hatch from the same pair," Pamela explained. "They're staying close to home longer these days because the population has grown so large. That one will help feed the new chick."

"Improving its chances of survival," Abby added.

Dutifully, Kirk noted the sighting, and they continued walking along the base of Mount Ortiz. One of the other groups would hike to the top of the mountain to look for nesting activity at higher elevations, but Abby had considered this lower route more appropriate for Pamela, in particular. However, she may have underestimated the woman.

Soon they completed their designated route and it was time to return to the van. Although they hadn't spotted many eagles, Abby considered the morning a success, both in terms of the census and her concern for Sandy's great uncle. She had Pamela's phone number and intended to connect her with Robert Weatherford.

By the time they arrived at The Nature Museum, several of the other groups had returned as well and were lounging around in the meeting room where box lunches of sandwiches and fruit had been laid out, and canned drinks stored in an ice chest. The animated conversation among the volunteers and exchange of sighting information indicated the day had been a grand success. The two groups of bird watchers had gotten along well, as Abby had anticipated.

"Hey, there's Justin," Kirk said as he waved to his friend. "Hey, old man." He turned back to Abby. "Want me to give him our map? He said he was gonna computerize the whole thing."

"Let me talk to him first." Abby took the clipboard from Kirk, amused that he'd refer to his friend as an 'old man.' "You did a good job today. Thanks."

He shrugged. "No sweat. It was kinda cool, you know? Seeing the eagles and stuff."

Cool indeed, Abby mused as she crossed the room.

"How'd your route go?" she asked Justin, who she'd assigned to a group that hiked a section of the north shoreline.

"Two nests, two eagles and a screamin' red-tailed hawk that was showing off for his girlfriend. He put on an awesome display." He took a big bite of his sandwich and chewed it down in one gulp.

"Sounds like your group had a good morning."

"Yeah. It was great."

"If you're still willing to computerize our results, could you stick around until all the groups return? I want to take a look at what we've got and make copies of all the reports."

"Sure. No *problema*."

Thanking Justin, Abby then circulated among the volunteers, expressing her appreciation to each one.

She found Ida sitting with her group of birders. "How'd it go for you folks?"

Everyone echoed *great*.

"We found two active nest sites," Ida told Abby.

"That's wonderful. Was one of them at Green Acres Cemetery?"

The young woman's eyes widened. "You knew about that one?"

"Lenny Meekem told me about it two days ago, but I didn't take time to check it out. Glad you spotted it."

The small group of newly formed friends nudged each other, assuring themselves that they were super-alert birders.

Hugo arrived, greeting each volunteer and handing them a tan Nature Museum ball cap and a ballpoint pen with The Sparrow Island Nature Conservatory stamped on it—a small token of thanks.

As he worked his way around the room, Hugo stopped to talk with Abby. "It appears your morning went well."

"Very successful, I'd say."

Looking around the room, he nodded thoughtfully. "Did you hear what happened out past the lighthouse last night?"

A sense of dread twisted in Abby's midsection. "A collision?"

He nodded again. "Nearly. It was raining, the visibility was poor and apparently the lighthouse had gone dark again. An oil tanker was heading south and came within inches of a power boat that he hadn't seen."

Abby groaned. "Was anyone hurt?"

"No, evidently the tanker just missed the side of the power boat. But it could have been deadly. The Coast Guard's investigating."

For all the good that would do! Abby thought. Why couldn't the Coast Guard come up with some answers? The next time there might actually be a collision and the ships and people involved might not be so lucky.

Just as bad, the natural environment along the islands' coastal regions could take a devastating hit.

"Well, I guess we should be grateful there were no injuries," she said to Hugo. "Next time it could turn out differently."

AN HOUR LATER, Abby was still shaken by the news of the near miss. Numbly, she made copies of the reported eagle sightings, but her mind worked at solving the question of who and why someone would create such a dangerous situation.

"You almost got the stuff together?"

Justin's question made Abby jump. He stood at the office doorway. His baggy pants and overly large T-shirt made him look much younger than his twenty years.

"Oh yes. I'm sorry. I'm almost done." Most of the volunteers had already departed for home, either on Sparrow Island or via the ferry back to Friday Harbor. She hadn't meant to keep Justin so long.

A copy of the last report slipped out of the machine and

Abby stacked them together, keeping the originals for herself. As she'd glanced at each report, she'd seen what a good job the volunteers had done. There'd been an amazing number of nesting pairs sighted; she'd count them up later.

"Here you go, Justin." She handed him the pile of reports.

"Are you all right?" he asked, frowning as he took them from her. "You look, like, a little worried."

"I'm fine. Just troubled about—" She shook her head. "An oil tanker nearly ran over a smaller boat last night in the straits between Sparrow Island and San Juan Island. It's just lucky a collision was avoided."

Justin's nostrils flared and his faced paled for an instant before his dark eyes sparked with an emotion that was hard to define. "Was anyone hurt?"

"No, thank the good Lord."

He silently exhaled. "Then maybe those tankers will think twice before transporting oil on that route between the refineries and Seattle."

The way he seemed so upset about the tankers and where they traveled, Abby looked at him strangely. "What other route would you have them take?"

"How 'bout we use a heck of lot less oil and save them from transporting anything? At least the tankers could stay way out in the ocean where they couldn't muck up the shoreline."

While Abby didn't want any shoreline spoiled, Justin's ideas seemed pretty pie-in-the-sky to her. She was all for saving the environment and stewarding natural resources, but the world's economies were now dependent on oil. Stepping back from that would have them all living as they had a hundred years ago. It wasn't a picture she could support anymore than she could understand those who seemed to believe in unbridled consumption. Somewhere there had to be a compromise that would benefit people and protect the environment.

With a shake of her head, she decided now was not the time to debate Justin about the future of planet earth.

"Let's take a look at what we've got," she said. "Then I'll let you decide how best to display all this information so the public can understand our eagles and view the nesting sites."

"From a distance," Justin added as he began to sort through the reports.

She eyed him carefully. Like a good many young people, Justin saw things in black-and-white with no room for compromise. It took a degree of maturity to realize you might not always be right.

"How long do you think it'll take you to put the data together?" she asked.

He flipped through the pages. "Not long. I'm sort of between projects. I think I can get it done by next Saturday. Would that be okay?"

"That'd be great. Give me a call when you're ready to get together and I'll come over—"

"It's okay. I'll come to the museum. You'll be able to see how it'll look as a display."

"That's wonderful, Justin. I really appreciate your help." She touched him lightly on the arm as she thanked him. "You know, The Nature Museum does have a budget to pay for technical assistance. Not huge, you understand, but we'd like to cover some of the time you put into the project." Now that she knew his family's financial situation, she wanted to help Justin as best she could.

"Not necessary. Sometimes you gotta do stuff because it's the right thing to do."

"You're a very generous young man, Justin. But at least let us reimburse you for any out-of-pocket expenses you have, like supplies and ferry tickets. Not one of us wants you to go in the hole on this."

He shrugged. "That sounds fair enough. I'll keep track of what I spend."

They chatted a few more minutes about how to lay out the display, then Justin left.

Abby took the original reports into her office and sorted through them, getting a clearer picture of the raptor population on Sparrow Island. After checking her phone messages, she headed for home. Or rather to the sheriff's substation in Green Harbor.

She felt sure a criminal action had caused the near-collision of the two boats in the strait. If that crime had been initiated on land, surely it fell under Henry Cobb's jurisdiction.

CHAPTER ❧ THIRTEEN

ABBY FOUND DEPUTY MIKE Bennett working behind the counter at the sheriff's substation. A tall, slender thirty-year-old, he wore his crew cut and uniform with equal military precision.

"Hi, Mike. How are you?"

He welcomed her with a broad smile. "Doing good, Ms. Stanton. How 'bout you?"

"I could be better. Is Henry in?"

"No, ma'am. It's his day off. Is there something I can do to help you?"

Disappointed Henry wasn't there, she frowned. Of course, he deserved a day off, but— "Do you know if he's investigating the incident between the oil tanker and a small boat last night?"

"I heard about that. Could have been worse, I guess. But the Coast Guard has jurisdiction in the case of maritime accidents."

"What if it wasn't an accident? What if a crime on land caused the two vessels to get that close to each other?"

"Well, then, I guess we'd be looking into that." Thoughtfully, he ran his palm over his smoothly shaved cheeks and angular jaw. "Is that what you think happened?"

"I certainly don't think it's an accident that the lighthouse goes dark when there's a ship in the strait, particularly an oil tanker, and then turns itself back on. Someone, or something, is causing the problem."

"Gee, Ms. Stanton, I guess I can ask the Sarge when he comes back to work on Monday if we're going to do any investigating. He hasn't said anything to me so far about the situation."

Maybe she could call Henry at home. Or perhaps he was seeing Mary this weekend and Abby would have a chance to talk to him.

"I did hear Sarge say that guy they dug up out at the lighthouse, the remains anyway, are going to be shipped to the mainland for cremation," the deputy said.

"Cremation?" she echoed.

"Yeah. They gotta do something with the remains. Since nobody knows who he was, cremation and internment at some public cemetery over there is the best they can do."

"That's sad, isn't it? There won't even be a name to record, a totally anonymous person."

"There's no way to I.D. the guy. Doctor Randolph tried, I guess, but there wasn't much to go on."

"No, there wasn't." Feeling dejected, Abby thanked Mike for his help and left for home.

If Henry didn't want to or thought he couldn't pursue the lighthouse problem, she could talk to someone else who might be knowledgeable about how such things operated. Since she had an ulterior motive for seeing Robert Weatherford, the lighthouse would provide a good excuse to go calling on the neighbors.

The McDonald's small SUV wasn't in the driveway when Abby arrived home. But she parked her car and crossed the lawn to their back door anyway. To her relief, Bobby answered her knock.

"Hi, Abby. Do you know if two-hundred volts is applied to a hundred-ohm resistor, what the current through the resistor will be?"

Abby blinked. "No, I don't think I do."

"It's two amps. I just figured that out. It's an Ohm's law thing." He held the door open for her to step into the kitchen. "Did you know if you had a ham radio license, you'd be called a YL? That means 'young lady' in ham lingo. I'll be an 'old man.'"

Amused, Abby chuckled at Bobby's enthusiasm. "I take it you're studying for your licensing test."

"Uncle Robert's helping me."

"Oh dear. Maybe I shouldn't interrupt. Is your mother here?"

"Naw, she went to the grocery store and Dad's at work. But it's okay. I let Uncle Robert have a nap earlier, but he probably needs another break. Mom says I can be pretty...um... taxing."

That did indeed seem like a real possibility, particularly for a man who wasn't used to having children around. There were times when Bobby's constant questions and extraordinary curiosity made Abby wonder how Sandy had the energy to survive.

Bobby led her into the living room where Robert was sitting on the couch. Papers, pencils and an amateur radio study guide were strewn on the coffee table.

"Hello, Robert. It's Abby from next door."

"Please tell me you've come to rescue me from this young genius. I'm having trouble keeping up with him."

Bobby plopped himself down on the floor in front of the coffee table and picked up his pencil. "No, he isn't. Uncle Robert knows all there is to know about this stuff."

Abby chose the overstuffed chair beside the couch and sat down. "If you don't mind the interruption, I have a bit of a technical problem I could use your help with."

Robert's graying brows rose above the frame of his dark glasses. "I thought your specialty was birds."

"It is, but we have a situation here that's troubling. You recall how the lighthouse went dark when you were out fishing with Neil."

"I was there too," Bobby said. "It was really weird."

She smiled toward Bobby. "It happened again last night." She told him about the incident in the straits. "Since the Coast Guard can't seem to come up with a reason for the problem, I thought maybe you, as an engineer, might be able to suggest what's causing it."

"I'm a structural engineer, not electrical."

"But you've had a broad range of experience. Have you ever heard of anything like that happening elsewhere?"

He considered her question for a moment. "I gather it's an intermittent problem."

Abby nodded, then realized she had to answer out loud since Robert couldn't see her. "Yes, that's how the electronics specialist from the Coast Guard explained it to me."

"Do you know what the source of power is? Where the electricity comes from that runs the light?"

She thought back to her conversation with Petty Officer Houston. "The young man I spoke with said there's a dedicated line from the substation here on Sparrow Island out to the lighthouse. They monitor it by cell phone and he says there's never been so much as a glitch in the current."

Running his hand around the back of his neck, his hair in need of a trim, Robert seemed to ponder the problem. "Is the light computer-operated?"

"I think the light is activated when it gets dark."

"*Hmmm*, like street lights," Robert said.

"How do they do that?" Bobby asked.

"A celluloid measures the light level. When it gets dark, a switch is closed and the light goes on."

"Would there be a way for someone to interfere with that?" Abby persisted.

"Only if they were in the lighthouse at the time."

"I don't think that's possible. The building has been boarded up for years, and it doesn't appear anyone has broken in or had access." She shook her head. "Why did you ask about computers?"

"Hackers," he answered quickly. "They're the ones who are causing the most havoc these days. On the Internet and every-where else they can think of."

Someone who knows a lot about computers and computer security, she mused. Someone like Justin? According to his friend Kirk, Justin did freelance computer security work. "But how could they turn the power on and off without the moni-toring equipment showing anything going wrong?"

"Simple. They'd hack into the Coast Guard computer and bypass the monitoring program."

"Hack into the Coast Guard computers?" she asked, aghast. "Wouldn't that affect national security?"

"It could," Robert conceded.

Bobby popped up to his knees. "Maybe it's terrorists that are messing with our lighthouse. Maybe we should call the President or somebody."

Holding up his hand, Robert silently gestured for the boy to calm down. "Let's not jump to conclusions, junior, until we know the facts. Right now, this is all speculation."

"But what if—"

"If you're going to be a scientist, you can't go racing off like you've got a wild hair—" Stopping abruptly, Robert thought better of his comment. "You need to consider all the facts at hand. The truth is, we don't have adequate data at this point."

"Except something's going on and the Coast Guard can't figure out what," Abby said.

"Well, we do know that intercepting signals from cell phones is easy," Robert pointed out. "The government does it all the time. If the transmission isn't encrypted or if the hacker can break the codes, then he'd be able to reprogram the computer that operates the dedicated power line to the lighthouse."

Abby sat back in the chair and looked up at the ceiling, thinking. "I know of a young man who is very good at computer codes and does some security work for large companies."

"Then he's a guy who could help you figure out what's going on better than I can."

She flashed on the memory of Justin becoming so upset when discussing the oil tankers and his concern for the environment. "Unless he's the one doing it."

Robert turned his head toward her. "This man you're thinking of, could he be the one?"

"I hope not." Standing, she paced around the living room. Her heartbeat accelerated as she tried to deny the possibility that Justin was involved. "He's helping me out with The Nature

Museum's bald eagle census, doing some computer work for me. He's very into environmental protection. I can't believe—"

"The people who blew up the dam in Mali, and blinded me in the process, did it in the name of saving the environment." His words rang with bitterness. "As far as I'm concerned, the world would be better off without do-gooder environmentalists who don't understand the consequences of their actions."

Although Abby was a dedicated environmentalist, she didn't take his comment personally. He'd been hurt. Badly. And the perpetrators had, at the very least, been misguided if not radical extremists with a destructive agenda.

But could Justin, and perhaps his friends, be just like that? How would she know? Without any evidence, she couldn't accuse them of what amounted to a criminal act.

She walked across the room to look out the front window. A crow was perched on the branch of a pine tree out front; she could barely hear his warning caw through the double paned glass.

"How would whoever's doing this know when there were oil tankers or other ships in the strait?" she asked.

"They'd have a lookout. Someone to spy on what's going on," Robert said.

"And let their coconspirators know what's happening by cell phone?"

"Maybe. But I'm told that cell phones here on the island aren't terribly reliable. There are a lot of dead spots. Plus, they can be traced."

"What about those funny radio transmissions we've heard?" Bobby asked. "You know, that dumb stuff about big fish, little fish?"

Abby whirled and looked at Bobby. "Did you hear that last night?"

"Well, yeah," he stammered. "I mean . . . Uncle Robert?"

"We did." Robert nodded his head. "I wonder if that was around the time that the two ships passed each other?"

"Did the radio operators identify their call signs this time?"

"Nuh-uh," Bobby said. "Uncle Robert says that's not good procedure."

But maybe it was if you wanted to keep your identity secret. Although no one had said Justin had a ham radio license, she was still suspicious—despite the fact she hated the thought he might be guilty of putting seagoing vessels at risk.

She did a mental double take. Justin's friend Kirk had called him "old man." Did that mean Justin was a ham? Or was Kirk simply teasing Justin because he was a few years older than his friend?

"Robert, how would you go about catching whoever is messing with the lighthouse, if that's what's going on?"

He gave her question some thought before responding. "I'd set a trap."

"How?"

"On the next foggy or rainy night, I'd secretly post people out at the lighthouse to see if the light went off. Meanwhile, I'd have someone listening to the radio, see if there was another transmission like the big fish, little fish about the time the light goes off. Then you'd know if the two are connected."

"But we wouldn't know who's doing the transmitting."

"No, but I think you have a suspect in mind."

She did and hated the possibility. Justin was such an intelligent young man. How could he be risking his whole future—

and the environment he claimed to value—by pulling such a crazy stunt? *If* he was the culprit, she had no choice but to try to stop him.

From the kitchen, Abby heard Sandy returning home.

"Hey, anybody here?" Sandy called.

"We're in here," Abby responded.

"Mom! We're gonna set a trap for some terrorists!"

Abby rolled her eyes and Sandy appeared in the doorway, her expression wary.

"You're going to do what?" Her glance shot from her son to Uncle Robert and then to Abby.

Abby grinned. "It's not quite like that. Honest."

Sandy didn't look all that reassured.

Both Robert and Abby tried to explain the situation, but it was clear Sandy wasn't entirely onboard with their plan. Abby decided it was time to leave, that making plans for catching the culprit would have to wait until another time, then she realized she hadn't approached the second reason she'd wanted to talk with Robert.

"Robert, I've met a woman I think you'd enjoy getting to know," she said. "Is there a time next week when I could get you two together?"

His lips quirked into a half smile and his brows lifted again. "Sandy, you didn't tell me your neighbor's such a talented person. Not only does she chase after would-be terrorists, she's a matchmaker too."

"No, no," Abby hastily countered, laughing, before explaining why she wanted Robert to meet Pamela Folz.

Robert's lighthearted smile turned into a scowl. "I'm not about to spend the rest of my life being led around by some smelly dog."

Immediately stepping up to her uncle's side, Sandy laid a firm hand on his shoulder. "Uncle Robert will be delighted to meet your friend and will be *polite* and listen to everything she has to say. Won't you, Uncle Robert?"

His acquiescence was less than enthusiastic, but Abby took it as the best he could manage under duress. She promised to get back to him about the date, gave Sandy a reassuring wink before saying good-bye, and headed back across the yard to Mary's house.

She had a great deal to think and pray about. She truly didn't want Justin to be guilty of putting ships at risk in the strait. Nor did she want Robert to blow off the wisdom and experience Pamela had to offer.

Tonight she'd take her worries to the Lord and hope He would lead her along the right path to resolving her dual problems.

SUNDAY WAS ANOTHER CLEAR DAY. The parishioners filled Little Flock Church as though the gift of sunshine had given them hope that true spring would soon arrive.

At the close of the worship, Rev. Hale asked the congregation to join him in singing the hymn "The Glory of Spring How Sweet" by Thomas Gill. His baritone voice led them in praise of renewal, and Abby felt uplifted by the song's message as she exited the church with Mary and their parents.

Outside, however, the chill air reminded her that spring would arrive in God's own time.

"How are you, girls?" Ellen Stanton asked as they gathered on the walkway. She tugged her full-length coat more snugly around her, her light-blue eyes filled with a teasing light. "Any more flowers delivered lately from mysterious suitors?"

George Stanton knelt to give Finnegan a good pet and chin scratch.

"Oh, Mother," Abby laughed. "That's one mystery I've given up on." Although the flowers still piqued her curiosity, she had other, more serious matters on her mind.

"You're worried about the lighthouse and the safety of the ships in the strait, aren't you?" her father said as he stood, perceptive as always.

"I am. I'm also troubled that the human remains the Coast Guard found are going to be cremated and disposed of before the person is identified." She almost wished Margaret Blackstock were right, that it was the ghost of Terrence Pettigrew who was haunting the lighthouse, not Justin and his friends doing the damage. At least that might explain the body being buried there.

"Did either of you know Terrence Pettigrew?" Abby asked impulsively.

Ellen shook her head, but Abby's father nodded.

"I knew him vaguely," George said. "When I took my charter boat clients out around Wayfarer Point, I'd often see him near the lighthouse. He was very conscientious. As far as I know, he never once let the light go out while he was in charge."

"Things have certainly changed in that regard lately," Mary commented.

"I remember that Pettigrew was very upset when the Coast Guard took over," George continued. "He stormed around town for days, shouting and arguing with anyone who would listen. I think he'd intended to spend the rest of his life there and never leave."

"His son buried him at Green Acres," Abby told them.

Ellen nodded as though she sympathized with Terrence

Pettigrew. "The poor man. He probably would have preferred to be laid to rest right at the foot of his beloved lighthouse, right beside the skeleton that was found. It sounds like the Coast Guard didn't handle the situation very well back then, just turning Mr. Pettigrew and his son out onto the street to fend for themselves."

That was when they'd taken up commercial fishing, Abby recalled. But their hearts hadn't been in it. The two men, father and son, continued to long for the life they'd been forced to leave.

If she hadn't seen Terrence's grave with her own eyes, she could easily believe Bryant had followed his father's heart's desire, burying him beside the lighthouse.

But what if that were true?

No, she'd seen the grave.

But not what was under the ground or inside the coffin.

She shook the thought aside. Convoluted reasoning would get her nowhere. And she wasn't about to ask Lenny Meekem to dig up the grave and check.

"What are you thinking?" Mary asked.

"Nothing. A pure flight of fancy."

Or maybe not. . . .

Planning to follow George and Ellen home to Stanton Farm for supper, Abby took hold of Mary's wheelchair and began pushing her toward the parking lot, Finnegan leading the way.

Sandy McDonald, wearing a wool skirt and cardigan sweater, came running toward them. "Before you leave," she said breathlessly, "I have a huge favor to ask of one or the other of you."

Mary stopped her chair. "Anything, Sandy. What do you need?"

"I should have asked yesterday when Abby was over, but I forgot Neil was working tomorrow."

"You need someone to watch Bobby after school?" Abby asked. She or Mary often looked out for Bobby on days that Sandy had to stay late at school because of her teaching job. It was no burden. In fact, Bobby had become a frequent volunteer at The Nature Museum. Abby was sure she could find some way to keep him busy, if need be.

"Actually, a little more than that," Sandy said. "They're giving a ham radio licensing exam tomorrow afternoon at the Community Center. Uncle Robert says Bobby's ready to take the test."

"Goodness!" Mary said. "Bobby hasn't been studying for the exam for very long and he's only ten years old. Does your uncle really think he can pass so soon?"

"Uncle Robert says so. I think Bobby has learned the electronics part so fast because his teacher last year had him working on an extra-credit unit about electricity. So he had a head start."

"He's also one very smart youngster," Abby added.

"True, but he's been studying hard too." Sandy's cheeks flushed with pride. "Anyway, I have in-service teacher training tomorrow that's going to last until about six. And Neil's working."

"You want one of us to take Bobby to the exam?" Mary asked.

"If it wouldn't be too much trouble. Otherwise, he'll have to wait at least a month. And I'm not sure Uncle Robert will be here that long."

"I could take him," Mary volunteered. "Monday's are never busy at the shop. Candace can manage on her own."

"Are you sure it's okay, Mary?" Since Abby had planned to spend Monday examining the data from the eagle census, it would work better for her sister to take the boy to his test. *If it wasn't an imposition.*

"No problem at all. Shall I pick him up at school when he gets out?"

"That would be perfect. I really don't know what I'd do without you two." Sandy gave Mary a hug and squeezed Abby's hand. "Is it all right if Robert comes along too? I think he'd like to be there to support Bobby's efforts. Teaching him ham radio, well, it's the only thing that seems to have engaged his interest since the accident."

"Then he should definitely be there for Bobby," Abby agreed.

So did Mary. "I'll treat him to a ride in my van and promise not to terrorize him."

Abby laughed. "You're a fine driver or I wouldn't ride with you all the time."

Looking relieved that she'd worked out arrangements for Bobby to take the test, Sandy said, "I'll ask Uncle Robert to be ready to go at 2:45. Just pull into the driveway and honk. He'll come out on his own. Then you can pick up Bobby at school."

"We'll be fine," Mary assured her. "And I'm sure Bobby will pass the test with flying colors."

"Neil and I have heard so much about Ohm's law and the rest of it, I think we could pass it ourselves." Laughing, Sandy thanked them both again and hurried off to rejoin her family.

Abby and Mary continued on to the parking lot, both anxious to enjoy their own family gathering.

With her remote, Mary lowered the van's lift and then rode it up. Finnegan jumped in beside her.

"I'd like to impose on your time next week too," Abby said as she climbed into the passenger seat.

After securing Finnegan, Mary locked her chair in place behind the wheel. "Impose away."

"I managed to get Robert Weatherford to agree, albeit reluctantly, to meet with the blind lady from the San Juan Birding Society, Pamela Folz. I think she'd be a real inspiration to him."

"Yes, he does need to see that being blind isn't a death sentence."

"I thought I'd call her tonight or tomorrow, and find out when would be good for her this coming week. I also promised her dog Harriet a play date with Finnegan."

The dog's ears perked up at the mention of his name and Mary laughed. "So you'd like me to get them together?"

"If you don't mind. You and Robert could pick Pamela up at the ferry, then they'd have a chance to visit."

"I think that's an excellent idea. Robert needs all the encouragement he can get."

Abby gave her sister a big smile. Sandy's scheduling conflict had been easy to resolve, and bringing Pamela and Robert together looked like it would work out. She could only hope and pray that her other concern about Justin and the lighthouse would be as easily cleared up with no lasting damage done.

So far the chance of that was not looking good.

CHAPTER ❦ FOURTEEN

After a beautifully prepared meal of pot roast, potatoes, cabbage-and-apple salad and fresh rolls, as well as a nice visit with their parents, Abby and Mary returned home just after dark.

Mary wheeled herself into the living room. Blossom jumped down from her favorite chair and strutted over to greet her, tail raised high.

"Hi, sweetie." Patting her thigh, Mary encouraged the cat to leap into her lap. "Did you miss us?"

Blossom contemplated the invitation a moment before accepting. With a graceful leap, she landed lightly in Mary's lap, then began kneading Mary's leg.

Abby hung up her coat in the front closet. "You'd think after all these years, I'd learn not to eat so much at Mom's house. I'm stuffed."

"Me too. She surely likes to spoil us."

"Guess that comes with being a mom." Sitting down on the couch, Abby stretched out her legs and patted her tummy. "I'm going to have to go back to doing situps every morning or start working out with Sandy. If I don't, pretty soon I won't be able to get into any of my clothes."

"I know the feeling. Confined to this wheelchair, I don't get nearly enough exercise."

"Except your arms are stronger than mine these days."

"That may be true, but it doesn't do much for my waistline." The doorbell rang.

Groaning, Abby said, "I'll get it." They didn't usually have callers on Sunday evening, and she hoped it didn't mean trouble.

She opened the door to find a young woman wearing jeans and a University of Washington sweatshirt standing on the front porch.

"Hi," the girl said. "I hope I'm not interrupting anything. I'm Kathleen Farrand, Irene's great-granddaughter. She lives down the street."

"Yes, of course." Abby opened the door wider. "Please come in."

"I won't stay long—"

"I hope there's nothing wrong with Irene."

"No, she's fine. I just had a question." Smiling shyly, the young brunette with big, brown eyes followed Abby into the living room, where Abby introduced her to Mary.

"I spoke to Irene just the other day," Mary said. "She was very excited that you were coming to visit."

"I feel sorry for Nana-Gram—that's what I call her. She lives alone and all. So when I can, I like to come visit for a couple of days."

"She certainly appreciates it," Mary said.

"Is there something we can do for you or Irene?" Abby asked. An older woman living alone often needed some extra help, and Abby was more than ready to do what she could.

"Well, this is a little odd, I admit." Her cheeks flushed an attractive shade of pink. "You see, I wanted to send Nana-Gram flowers for Valentine's Day, and I've got this friend who lives on San Juan Island. She said she was going to be here at Green Harbor that day and would pick up an arrangement for me and deliver them to Nana-Gram."

"Oh dear." Smothering a laugh, Abby sat down heavily.

Kathleen's brows pulled together in confusion as she continued. "Anyway, Nana-Gram never got them. So I called my friend. She said she'd left them on the porch, but when I asked her what the house looked like, I knew she'd dropped them off at the wrong place."

"And I'll bet the house where your friend left the flowers looked exactly like our house," Mary concluded, her own effort not to laugh crinkling the corners of her eyes.

"Well, pretty much. I know you two are good neighbors to my great-grandmother, so I don't want to accuse you of anything."

"But we *are* guilty," Abby confessed, chuckling, more at herself for the machinations she'd gone through trying to figure out who had sent *her* flowers than the fact that Irene had missed receiving her rightful arrangement.

Kathleen's big eyes widened. "You got the flowers?"

"I'm afraid so," Mary confessed.

"Wasn't there a card?" Kathleen asked.

"Oh yes," Mary said. "But there was no name on the envelope and the card said 'Love always.' But we couldn't read the signature, so we didn't know who'd sent them."

"I thought maybe they'd been misdelivered," Abby admitted. "I even called the neighbor next door, thinking her husband might have sent them." Remorseful, she shook her head.

"I'm so sorry. I should have made more of an effort to find out where the flowers belonged."

"No, not at all. It was my friend's fault. I gave her the address, but she wrote it down wrong."

"But poor Irene." Mary rolled toward Kathleen, her movement causing Blossom to jump to the floor and trot off. "She should have had that lovely bouquet to enjoy on Valentine's. I must say, it was a perfect complement to our table that night. They're still quite lovely, if you'd like to see them. The arrangement's still on the table."

"No, it's okay. Honest. I just couldn't figure out what went wrong. Nana-Gram is cool with it."

"I'll tell you what, young lady." Mary took Kathleen's hand. "In case you didn't know, I happen to know the florist here in Green Harbor rather well. I'll have her send out a beautiful bouquet to Irene tomorrow to make up for the one that didn't arrive."

"Oh, you don't have to do that. I mean, I don't want you to go to any expense on account of my friend who messed up."

"Not to worry. I've got the local florist in my back pocket. She owes me, so it won't cost me a dime, I promise. You can reassure your friend about that."

Abby worked hard to suppress a giggle. Her sister's kindness tickled her. She'd never think of burdening a young woman with an ounce of guilt—either Kathleen or the friend who had delivered the arrangement to the wrong house.

"Well, gosh, that's really nice of you." The girl glanced from Mary to Abby and back again. "Mostly I'm just glad I found out what happened. And you've been so nice."

"I think we both appreciate a great-granddaughter who

takes the time to visit someone who loves her," Abby said. "That's a very special thing to do."

Kathleen blushed again. "I'd better get back, but I can't thank you enough."

Coming to her feet, Abby escorted the young woman to the door and saw her out, sending her regards to Irene.

Returning to the living room, she collapsed onto the couch again. "I feel *so* foolish!" She leaned her head back and closed her eyes. Her cheeks were hot with embarrassment.

"Why do you feel foolish?" Mary asked. "We had no idea who sent those flowers. We would have had to go up and down the whole block before we discovered they were intended for Irene. And even if we'd asked at the time, Irene might not have known she was supposed to receive flowers."

"But for almost a whole week, I've been fantasizing about who might have sent them. I suspected every man who looked at me for more than two seconds, and a couple who didn't even glance in my direction." Bending over, half laughing, she buried her head in her hands. "Good grief! I've reverted to being an adolescent."

"Well, if it's any consolation, I did a little sleuthing trying to find out who had sent them too."

Abby lifted her head. "You did?"

"Not that I thought they'd been meant for me, you understand."

"Mary Ellen Stanton!" Abby cried out, using her sister's maiden name. "You didn't!"

Laughing, Mary could hardly catch her breath. "We are quite a pair, aren't we? Don't women ever get too old to worry about men?"

Going to her sister, Abby knelt next to the wheelchair and hugged Mary. "Apparently not. But I'm so glad we have each other."

Mary stroked Abby's tidy hairdo. "Do you regret you never married and had a family of your own?"

"Oh, I don't know. There were moments when I came close to marrying, but the timing never seemed right. I was too involved in my work or he was. Now it seems clear that I'm exactly where the Lord wants me to be."

They hugged again. The way they held each other was a validation of the joy of sisterhood, the spirit that two women would always share because they were part of each other.

THE NEXT MORNING, Mary let Candace know about the very special order to be delivered to Irene Farrand.

Later in the day, precisely at 2:45 in the afternoon, she pulled into the McDonald driveway and tooted her horn for Robert.

Using a long, white cane that he tapped in front of him, he gingerly came down the porch steps. Dressed informally, he wore khaki wash pants, a wool shirt and a windbreaker. Dark glasses covered his eyes.

Mary rolled down the passenger side window. "You're right on time."

"Let me know if I'm going to fall off the edge of the earth, will you?" he called, walking cautiously toward the van.

"You're doing fine. About six more steps and you'll reach the van."

"Probably smack right into the side of it." Waving the cane from side-to-side, he took one hesitant step after another.

"Almost here. Couple of steps left."

From his place behind Mary, Finnegan stood up to watch Robert's progress as though he wanted to help. His tail wagged in encouragement.

Robert reached out toward the van with his hand. When his cane knocked on the van, he grabbed at the air and caught the side mirror, then searched for the door handle. Feeling his way, he climbed into the seat and collapsed his cane.

"I feel like I just crossed the Gobi desert."

"A few small steps for you," she said, paraphrasing Neil Armstrong's words on the moon, "and a giant step toward independence."

He *humphed* at her, unimpressed by her comment or his accomplishment.

"You want to close the door and buckle up? Wouldn't want you falling out when I take all those sharp corners at ninety miles an hour," she teased.

Complying with her request took a moment as he fumbled to find the door handle and the seatbelt latch.

Mary waited patiently. She knew the more Robert learned to do on his own, the happier and more independent he would become.

When he was settled, she backed the van out of the driveway. "I bet you're as excited as Bobby about him taking the licensing exam."

"I'm such a nervous wreck, I probably couldn't pass the test right now myself. But Bobby's one cool customer and smart as a whip. I think he'll be all right. He had me quizzing him last night until Sandy insisted he had to go to bed."

"I imagine he studied so hard because he doesn't want to disappoint you."

"He won't. Whatever happens."

"We'll say a little prayer that he does his best."

Robert turned his head away from her. "If God doesn't care about crazies blowing up dams and innocent people getting killed or starving to death, then I doubt He cares about one little boy taking a ham radio exam."

"I believe God cares about each of us."

"Did He care about you when your car went off the road and you were paralyzed?" he challenged.

Although she knew Robert couldn't see it, her smile was ironic. "I said I believe He cares about us all. I didn't say I understood why bad things happen. But I have faith that He has His reasons."

He grunted an unintelligible sound.

Obviously, Robert's faith had been shaken by the tragedy that had struck him. Mary could only hope and pray he'd find his way back to the Lord. For some, it wasn't an easy path to travel, nor a short one.

Green Harbor Public School was a two-story structure on Municipal Street. There were two play yards, one for the primary-grade students and another for the older youngsters that included a basketball court and a soccer field. At the moment, the students were all inside. Mary pulled up to the curb to park behind another waiting car and shut off the engine.

"We're here a couple of minutes early," she said. "Would you like to go inside to get a look at the school?"

He turned his head sharply toward her. "Considering that I wouldn't be able to *see* the school, that would be a waste of time, wouldn't it? And I have no interest in having little kids either gawk at me because I'm blind or run me down because I can't get out of their way."

Grimacing, Mary shook her head. "You know, English is a funny language, and words can be either a blessing or a curse depending upon how they're used. People are always asking me if I'd like to walk over to the Springhouse Café for lunch. Or walk down to the beach with them. Obviously, they don't mean that literally. Granted, right after my accident, it bothered me when someone said that. But I realized they weren't being thoughtless. I was the one being overly sensitive. In fact, I learned to take that sort of remark as a compliment. It showed they were so interested in me, in having my company, that they'd actually forgotten that I could no longer walk."

"That's a very pretty speech," he said. "But it's different for me."

"It's different only because you haven't had time to come to terms with the new you. Give yourself a chance."

He didn't have a retort for that.

The dismissal bell rang, effectively halting their conversation, which was probably for the best. Mary remembered how tired she'd become of people telling her everything would be fine after her accident. It hadn't been. But she'd adjusted and learned to appreciate the differences in her new life.

A moment after the bell sounded, children began bursting out of the school like dandelion seeds scattered by a breeze. Free at last, they hitched their backpacks over their shoulders or dragged them on wheels along the ground. Laughing and shouting back and forth, the students' youthful energy had been unleashed after a long day.

Bobby emerged from the throng and raced toward the van.

"Hey, Uncle Robert. Hi, Mary," he said, climbing into the van and greeting Finnegan with a warm hug and pets before ridding himself of his backpack.

"You all set for the exam?" Robert asked.

"I think so."

Mary started the van. Slowly, she maneuvered away from the curb, taking particular care for children who might dash out in front of her, as well as the other parents there to pick up their offspring.

How well she remembered picking up Nancy and Zack here at the same school. They'd come flying out of their classrooms, full of talk about the day's trials and successes. Nancy, of course, had been the more verbal one. But there'd been days when Zack couldn't hold back either. She'd had to listen with both ears, one for each child. Only a mother could manage the cacophony of two children speaking at once and still be able to respond to each.

She sighed, recalling those years with fondness. She wished her children and grandchildren didn't live so far away. Nancy with her two children—Emily and Nicholas—in Florida, and Zack often on the road pursuing his musical career as a keyboard artist.

But they were both successful and happy in their own ways. She couldn't ask more than that.

The Community Center was located on Cross Island Road, not too far from the school. A large, one-story stucco building, the facility served Sparrow Island as a social center for events such as the Harvest Festival Celebration on Halloween and the annual Autumn Dance. In addition to one large room, smaller meeting rooms could be created with moveable partitions.

With Finnegan's help, Mary wheeled herself toward the entrance while Bobby served as Robert's guide. The older man rested his hand on the boy's shoulder. A posted sign indicated the Ham Licensing Exam would be held in a room off to the side of the larger auditorium-sized space.

"Hello," Mary called as she rolled into the room. "I think we've come to the right place."

A gray-haired gentlemen in his sixties with a goatee gave her a smile. "You have if you're looking to take the test for a ham license."

"I'm taking the test," Bobby announced, introducing himself. "And this is my neighbor, Mary Reynolds, and my great-uncle Robert. He's already a ham."

"Nice to meet you, old man," the gentleman said, extending his hand to Robert before realizing, when he didn't reciprocate, that Robert was blind. "The handle here is Ted, W7DH— otherwise known as W7 Dashing Hero, according to my wife who loves to read romance novels." He laughed at his own joke.

"W7PQ." Robert provided his call sign and nothing more.

"W7 Pretty Quick, huh?" Ted quipped. "I'd like you to meet the other guys." He pointed toward a man about his same age, who was well over six feet tall and rail thin. "That tall drink of water is Manny, W7 Awful Ancient. And our youngest volunteer examiner is Justin, W7 Wicked Playboy. He got that handle 'cuz he's pretty good with the ladies." Again Ted laughed, amused by his own cleverness.

The younger man with straight blond hair to his shoulders waved and shook his head, denying he was either wicked or a playboy.

About that time, two high-school boys arrived to take the test as well as a husband and wife. The couple wanted to be able to talk to their son who was in the jungles of Peru translating the Bible into an obscure native language. Ham radio was the only means of communication for the mission outpost—and then only when they had enough gasoline for their small generator.

Ted gave the examinees forms to complete, which would later be sent to the Federal Communications Commission, assuming they passed the test.

After waiting a few more minutes for any additional test takers, Ted announced it was time to begin. He asked Mary and Robert to step out of the room so there'd be no question of Bobby getting extra help.

"You'll have to lead me," Robert whispered. "I don't have any idea where I am."

"No problem. Take hold of my wheelchair. I won't let you bump into anything."

Pointing the way for Finnegan, Mary rolled slowly toward the building's entrance so she could see outside. Clouds had begun to form around the top of Mount Ortiz and the sky looked like it might be planning to rain.

"How long do you think the test will last?" Mary asked.

"If Bobby knows the answers like I think he does, it won't take long. Maybe a half hour. But then the examiners have to check the answers."

"Looks like I should have brought along a book to read or some knitting." A member of a knitting club, Mary had been working on a child's pullover sweater for her Warm Up America project. She'd just started on the sleeves last week and could have used the waiting time productively.

"A book sure wouldn't do me much good," Robert said.

"It would if you knew Braille or had a book on tape to listen to. And there are certainly other crafts you could learn to do, like ceramics and basket making. Or you could take up a musical instrument like guitar or—"

"You sure are full of ideas about how to run *my* life, aren't you," he shot back.

"Sorry." Mary grimaced. Obviously, she was sticking her nose in where it wasn't wanted. "If you'd like to sit down while we wait, there's a folding chair about three paces to your left up against the wall."

Using his cane, he made his way to the chair and sat down heavily.

Mary's natural instinct was to feel sorry for the man. But that wouldn't help him regain his independence. Still, it was really none of her business. She silently bowed her head.

Please Lord, she prayed, *help Robert find a way out of his dark valley and find the light of Your goodness and love once again. Amen.*

Finnegan yawned and stretched out on the floor as they waited for Bobby to finish his exam. Mary watched the changing shape of the clouds forming around the mountain and the way the edges crept lower on the hillside. Although Robert seemed stoic, his back ramrod straight, she noticed his foot tapping out an impatient beat. He wasn't as calm as he wanted to appear.

Finally, Bobby came racing out of the exam room. "Uncle Robert! I passed!" He flew into his uncle's waiting arms. "I only missed two, Uncle Robert. The examiner said that was good."

"It's wonderful, junior. It's terrific!" His voice trembling with pride, Robert clung to Bobby. When he finally let the boy go, he lifted his glasses to wipe his eyes. "You did good, junior. I'm proud of you."

Emotion filled Mary's throat, too, both for Bobby and his great-uncle.

"Hey there, young man. Do I get a hug too?" Mary asked.

Bobby whipped around and all but climbed into her lap. "Thanks for bringing me here. Mom and Dad will be excited that I passed the test."

"I'm sure they'll both be as proud of you as your uncle."

"Yeah." He grinned.

"When will you know what your call sign is?" Mary asked.

"The FCC will post his call sign at their Web site in a couple of days," Robert explained.

"I'm gonna bookmark that Web site as soon as I get home so I can check it every day," Bobby said.

Mary laughed at the boy's eagerness.

The three of them headed back to the van, with Bobby smiling from ear to ear.

When Mary returned home and sorted through the day's mail, she found a lovely thank-you note from Irene Farrand. Since it carried no stamp, Mary guessed Irene's great-granddaughter Kathleen had dropped it in their mailbox before returning to the mainland and her school.

Irene raved about the flower arrangement Candace had sent to replace the misdelivered Valentine's Day gift and said it was like extending the occasion for an extra week, particularly since Kathleen could enjoy it with her.

Tucking the note back in the envelope, Mary smiled to herself. She and Abby could put the mystery of the unexpected flowers behind them now and bring it out when they wanted to have another good laugh at themselves.

CHAPTER ✿ FIFTEEN

B OBBY WAS TERRIBLY excited and so was his Uncle Robert," Mary said to Abby as they ate dinner in the kitchen later that evening. "In fact, Robert seemed very emotional about the whole affair, and very proud."

"I'm proud of Bobby too. He's one smart youngster." Abby served herself some salad and passed the bowl to Mary. There were spring-like place mats on the table this evening, bright yellow with an appliquéd bouquet of colorful flowers in the center, a gift from Ana Dominguez, who owned In Stitches where Mary bought much of her knitting yarn.

"Who administers the ham test?" Abby asked. "Is it the school district?"

"No, the examiners were licensed hams. Two gentlemen, who looked a little older than we are, and a young, slender fellow with straight blond hair. Justin was his name. All three were very polite and encouraging to Bobby."

Abby's forkful of salad stopped in midair. "Was the young man Justin Foote?" Her primary suspect in the lighthouse caper?

"I don't think any of them mentioned their last names, just their first names and call signs. Justin's was something about W7 Playboy, though he didn't look much like a playboy to me. A slender, academic sort, if you ask me."

"Long, blond hair and blue eyes?"

"Why, yes, I think so. Do you know him?"

I know someone who calls him 'old man.'

Mentally, another puzzle piece fell into place, and Abby nodded. "He's one of the volunteers who helped with the eagle census. He's even doing the computer plotting of the nesting sites we located to use for our display board. According to one of his friends, he's quite an expert on computer security." Which probably meant he knew both how to protect a computer, as well as hack into one.

"Then he must be a nice young man and smart too. But that's not why you're frowning. What's wrong?"

Abby resumed eating, and between bites told Mary about her suspicions based on Justin's prowess with computers. "Now that you've confirmed he's also a ham radio operator, I'm pretty sure that must be how Justin and his friends are communicating. When there's a large ship in the strait, whoever's watching the area refers to it as a big fish. Then Justin does his computer magic, hacks into the Coast Guard cell phone line that monitors the power, leaving no trace that he's been there, and turns off the lighthouse."

"I remember Bobby saying he and his uncle had heard a curious radio transmission about big fish. But Justin seemed like such a nice young man. If he's the one, doesn't he understand what he's doing is dangerous?"

"As well as illegal. The good news is that no one's been hurt yet."

"Only by sheer coincidence," Mary pointed out.

"Oh, I forgot to tell you. Henry stopped by the conservatory today. The Coast Guard's finished investigating that accident. It turns out the owner of the fishing boat had been drinking and didn't have his running lights on, which was why the tanker didn't spot him in the storm. They gave the man a citation. Fortunately, that means the lighthouse's going dark didn't cause the near miss." Abby imagined Senior Chief Bosnik was relieved about that. Better to assess blame on the boat owner rather than Coast Guard equipment, or someone who had hacked into a government computer system without their knowledge.

"Sounds to me like Justin's lucky he wasn't responsible."

"Still, what he's doing is wrong and he needs to be stopped."

Selecting a roll, Mary broke it in half and spread butter on it. "Are you going to report him to the authorities?"

Abby considered the question as she finished the last bite of her breaded chicken patty. "So far, no great harm has been done. If I report him and he gets arrested and into the judicial system, his future—certainly his career in computers—will be over. He won't be able to get a job anywhere, not even working freelance. His mother's already in financial trouble because his father died unexpectedly, according to his friend."

Normally, Abby believed in following the letter of the law. But there were times when an exception could be made.

She wasn't sure whether this was one of those times or not, and wouldn't know until she and Robert snared Justin and his friends in the trap they were concocting. Something they would have to do soon.

And they needed a dark-and-stormy night in order to set the trap.

Standing, Abby carried her plate to the sink and rinsed it. "I talked with Pamela Folz today. She said the day after tomorrow, assuming it's not raining, would be a good day for her to come to Sparrow Island. Is that good for you?"

"My calendar's clear."

"Good." They discussed the details and Abby said she'd let Robert know about the plan.

Robert would be going home soon, so Abby wanted him to feel more optimistic about his future before he left. Pamela seemed the right person to give him a big boost.

THAT NIGHT ABBY PRAYED for guidance about Justin, but woke as uncertain about what she should do as she'd been when she went to bed.

Waiting for the Lord to provide answers required patience, she reminded herself.

The morning was overcast, but the weather report didn't call for rain. This was one time when Abby would welcome a storm so she and Robert could set their trap.

Because she knew Henry and Dr. Dana were planning to ship the remains of the skeleton found at the lighthouse to the mainland soon, she felt compelled to have one more chat with Bryant Pettigrew. Although she'd seen his father's gravesite, she couldn't get past the feeling that Bryant was hiding something.

That something could be that he'd secretly exhumed his father's body and moved it to Wayfarer Point. Under normal circumstances, that would be a crazy notion, one she'd laugh at if Margaret Blackstock brought it up. Now, she wasn't ready to dismiss the idea without talking to Bryant one more time.

Wearing slacks and a jacket, her hands stuffed in the pockets for warmth, she walked through the marina. The low tide revealed crustaceans clinging to the pilings. A rock dove—a bird most people called a pigeon—strutted along the water's edge, head bobbing up and down as it foraged for breakfast. Except for the occasional creak of a boat rubbing against the dock, the marina was eerily quiet.

Bryant was nowhere in sight when she reached the *Princess Lola.*

"Mr. Pettigrew! Are you here?"

When she received no answer, she looked around the marina for some sign of Bryant or someone who might know where he was. It was past the time Bryant usually went for breakfast at the Springhouse Café. He should be back by now.

"Bryant!" she called again. "It's Abby Stanton. I'd like to talk to you." ·

There was no answer, but the boat rocked unnaturally as though someone was moving around inside.

"It's about your father," she called. "I won't take up much of your time."

She waited a moment, then the cabin hatch opened a few inches.

"My pa's dead. What else do you need to know?"

"May I come onboard? There's something I have to tell you."

He opened the hatch wider. "You can tell me from where you're at."

She didn't necessarily want all and sundry to know what she suspected about Terrence Pettigrew's remains, but she had little choice other than to stay put. No one else seemed to be around anyway.

"I thought you'd want to know that the remains of the person we found at the lighthouse are going to be shipped to the mainland for cremation."

He stepped out onto the deck. His gray hair was mussed, his peacoat hanging open over a wool shirt and oil-stained work pants. "Why in tarnation are they going to do that? Couldn't they just leave him alone where he was?"

Despite the lack of an invitation, Abby used the wooden steps next to the boat to climb onboard the *Princess Lola*.

"Why did you dig up your father from Green Acres and move him out to the lighthouse?" she asked gently, believing the best way to find the truth was to confront him. Her heart ached for the pain she knew Bryant was experiencing.

His eyes filled with tears and his whiskered chin quivered. "Because that's what he wanted." He sat heavily on a wooden crate that had been turned upside down. "That was his own, the lighthouse was. The only place he wanted to be. He talked about the lighthouse all the time, even after when we were out fishing. He'd wanted to stay there until he died and then be buried right next to it. I promised him I'd see to it and I did."

She crouched down in front of him. "I'm so sorry, Bryant."

"They shouldn't have fired him. That was *his* place and Grandpa's before him. My pa and me were both born there. Nobody cared about all those years—" He pulled a white handkerchief from his pocket and blew his nose. "It wasn't fair."

"I know. What they did wasn't right. But I don't think you want his remains sent to the mainland now."

He shook his head. "What else am I gonna do? I don't have any money to bury him again. And I can't tell anybody what I did. They'll put me in jail or something. Over at the café, I heard people saying what I did was against the law."

Surely the café customers had been talking in generalities, not because Bryant had confessed to them what he'd done.

"I don't think you have to worry about going to jail," Abby said. "Henry Cobb told me burying your father out there was nothing more than a misdemeanor and no one would want to prosecute you after all these years." Even the Coast Guard couldn't be so cold and unsympathetic as to send an old man to jail for following his father's wishes.

"You sure he said that?"

"Yes, I'm quite sure. And I think if I talk with Lenny Meekem at Green Acres, he'll find a way to put your father back into the casket you bought for him originally. I don't think the owner of a cemetery would want it to get out that they've been missing a body for almost forty years and didn't know it was gone."

Bryant's lips twitched with a half smile. "I snuck in there in the middle of the night. It scared me to death, digging up the grave and thinking somebody might spot me. Or one of them other dead folks might pop up right out of the ground and pull me down with 'em. *Whew!*" He shook his head and closed his eyes at the memory. "Wouldn't want to go through that again, I'll tell you that for sure."

Shivering at the thought, Abby could understand his reluctance to dig up any more bodies, even if she didn't believe in ghosts and goblins.

Pushing herself to her feet, she said, "I'll talk with both Henry and Lenny Meekem, and see what we can work out. I don't want you to worry, Bryant. Your father's remains will be well cared for."

"Somebody should've at least thanked my pa for all he did. Tended that light for nearly fifty years and nobody respected all his hard work. They just made him turn over the key and shut him out. Shamed him, they did, acting that way." He hung his head. "Now it turns out with them digging up my pa, I've broken my promise after all. Didn't mean to."

Lightly, she placed her hand on Bryant's shoulder. "I'm sure your father understands you did the best you could."

What a shame, Abby thought as she walked back to her car. A man needed respect for his life's work. Operating the lighthouse protected the safety of sea-going vessels long before niceties like Global Positioning Systems were invented. To ignore the contributions of a man who'd devoted his life to protecting others didn't seem at all fair.

A little recognition of Terrence Pettigrew's efforts would go a long way toward easing Bryant's guilt about fulfilling his father's last wishes.

Idly, she wondered how Senior Chief Bosnik would feel about that.

At The Nature Museum, she waved to Wilma as she walked past the reception area on the way to her office. After hanging up her jacket on the back of the door, she sat down to make some phone calls.

She reached Henry at the sheriff's substation.

"What would you say if I told you I know who the skeleton at Wayfarer Point is and how he got there?"

There was a long moment of silence on the other end of the line. In the background, she heard a deputy talking on another phone.

"I'm listening," Henry finally said.

"I wouldn't want this treated like a criminal case."

"Did you uncover some kids' prank?"

"Not exactly."

"Abby, you're going to have to tell me what's going on before I decide if a law was broken."

Leaning back in her chair, she adjusted her glasses, and looked up at the poster on the wall above her desk—a mature bald eagle in flight. "The deceased is Terrence Pettigrew. His last wish was to be buried next to the lighthouse."

"And his son carried out his wish," Henry concluded on his own.

"After he first had him buried at Green Acres, then he dug him up and moved him. Under the circumstances, you or I might have done the same thing. Terrence wasn't treated very well by the Coast Guard when the lighthouse was automated."

"I can't recall hearing that you've exhumed any bodies lately and I sure haven't. Without court approval, you can't go around digging up relatives and planting them wherever it strikes your fancy, particularly on government property."

"There were extenuating circumstances in this case."

"I know." He exhaled a long sigh. "What do you want me to do, Abby?"

"Nothing, really. I just wanted to keep you in the loop. With any luck, Lenny Meekem will agree to quietly rebury Terrence where he belongs and no one will be the wiser." She explained her reasoning that a mortician like Lenny Meekem wouldn't want it known around town that a body had been missing from his cemetery for a good many years without him knowing it.

"You have a devious mind, when you set yourself to something, Abby. I'm glad you're not a criminal or I'd have a hard time catching up with you."

Abby laughed.

Her phone call to Lenny Meekem went well. After a little sputtering and complaining, he saw the wisdom of being circumspect about the loss of one of the bodies in his care. He agreed to contact Dr. Dana to release the remains to him for reburial and invite Bryant to be present for the private occasion. No charge.

That left only one more phone call on her list for the day.

"Chief Bosnik," she said when he answered his phone, "I'd like to talk with you about the Coast Guard honoring the last lighthouse keeper on Sparrow Island for his years of faithful service."

"I don't know what you're talking about, ma'am."

She explained the situation to the chief and the history of the lighthouse at Wayfarer Point. "I think it would be nice if there were a plaque on the structure honoring all the keepers."

"A plaque? Ma'am, that kind of a decision would be above my pay grade."

"Who would have the power to authorize that?"

"I don't know. I'd have to start with my CO. But it could take somebody as high as the Secretary of Navy to get something like that approved."

Abby rubbed at her temple where a headache was beginning to bloom. She might have bitten off more than she could chew.

"If you'll give me the name and phone number of your CO," she said, "I'll start with him."

"It's a her, ma'am."

"Even better." But even a sympathetic Coast Guard Commander might be hard to convince that putting up a plaque honoring lighthouse keepers was in the best interests of the service. Abby was going to need a carrot to dangle in front of the Coast Guard.

CHAPTER ❦ SIXTEEN

THE FOLLOWING MORNING, Mary parked her van in the lot near the ferry landing.

"Let's walk down to the dock," she said to Robert, who sat in the passenger seat showing no enthusiasm at all for the day's activities. "We'll meet Pamela there and bring her back to the van."

"You go ahead. I'll wait here."

Robert couldn't see her frown, but surely he could feel her disapproval. He wasn't even trying to deal with his blindness. While she understood how difficult the adjustment must be, there was much he could do to help himself. Starting with prayer.

With a sigh, she unlatched her chair and motioned for Finnegan to join her on the lift. "The ferry should be rounding the point at any moment. You'll hear the horn sound. I'll be back as soon as I can."

"I'm not going anywhere."

Shaking her head, she exited the van. Pamela Folz would need a miracle to get Robert to respond to her in a positive way. The man was so deep into depression, it would take a full-time effort on God's part to pull him out of it.

She wheeled down to the landing, Finnegan trotting along at her side. A brisk breeze was blowing, lifting white caps in the open sea beyond the harbor, and Mary pulled her jacket more tightly around her. Her short hair fluttered in the breeze and she smoothed it back from her face. She hoped the ferry's passage hadn't been too rough for Pamela's taste.

A few minutes after the ferry rounded the point, Neil McDonald, wearing his crew member's uniform of dark blue coveralls and a matching jacket, escorted Pamela and her dog off the ship.

"Hi, Neil." Mary waved to him. "Over here."

He spoke to Pamela, then angled in Mary's direction with his passenger holding his arm, her golden retriever guide dog at her side. "Here's your special delivery, Mary. Direct from Friday Harbor."

Mary thanked Neil, then directed her attention to Pamela. "It's so good to meet you, Pamela. My sister spoke very highly of you after the eagle census."

Pamela extended her hand, which Mary took in both of hers, warming Pamela's.

"Abby did a wonderful job organizing that project," Pamela said. "I enjoyed birding with her."

"And this must be Harriet. You're beautiful, young lady." Mary held her hand out for the retriever to sniff. Finnegan was all but quivering to get acquainted too, so she introduced both Pamela and Harriet to her dog.

Neil looked around the dock area. "Where's Uncle Robert?"

"He's waiting for us in the van." She gestured toward the parking lot.

"I imagine he's uncomfortable walking around strange areas," Pamela said. "It's very disconcerting when you first go blind to be in unfamiliar surroundings."

"It's been a problem for Sandy to even get him out of the house," Neil said.

"After the morning I have planned for him," Pamela told them, "he may decide he can manage better than he thought he could."

Mary raised her brows, wondering what Pamela had in mind. "What are we going to do? Abby didn't mention your plans."

Chuckling, Pamela's smile was filled with confidence. "Robert and I are going bird watching, of course."

Stunned, Neil nearly choked. "You've gotta be kidding, right?"

"Not at all." Pamela didn't appear in the least offended by his question. "It's a lovely day for birding."

Neil shot Mary a questioning look. "Well, I'll leave you two on your own then. Good luck to both of you. I know Sandy really appreciates you trying to help her uncle. He's always been special to her."

They thanked Neil for his assistance, then headed toward the van. Pamela placed her free hand on the wheelchair and helped push.

"I hope the ferry trip wasn't too rough for you," Mary said. "It looks pretty choppy out there today."

"Oh, it was smooth as glass in that big old ferry. My husband used to have a charter service and we went out in all kinds of weather. I still love to go boating. Almost as much as I love birding."

When they reached the van, Mary made the introductions.

Robert was barely civil while Pamela and her dog settled into the backseat, and Mary locked her wheelchair in place. She silently prayed it would *not* be a long, stressful morning.

"Is there somewhere in particular you'd like to go?" she asked Pamela.

"To the stables, if that's all right with you."

"What? Are we going riding?" Robert asked.

"We could later, I suppose," Pamela said cheerfully. "But I have something else in mind first."

Bird-watching, Mary thought with an ironic twist of her lips. She had no idea how Pamela would manage that with Robert being so resistant to improving his mobility.

There was very little conversation en route to Summit Stables. When Mary pulled to a stop near the corral, Pamela started to get out.

"Come along, Robert," she said. "We're going for a walk."

Mary had a moment of panic. "Pamela, the ground here is too uneven for my chair. I don't think I can—"

"Oh, I thought I had explained. Just Robert and I are going birding. You'll have to wait for us here. I hope you don't mind."

Open-mouthed, Mary stared at the woman. She wasn't talking about the lame leading the blind. She had in mind the blind leading the blind.

"Are you sure?" Mary asked.

"Quite sure. Harriet and I know this path well. It's where Abby brought us last weekend."

Robert strenuously objected to the plan. "I have no intention of walking around out in the woods with someone who can't see."

"I assure you, Robert, Harriet has perfect vision. Out of the car and we'll have our first lesson right here."

"You're nuts, lady." Reluctantly, he climbed out of the van. "If Sandy hadn't insisted, I wouldn't be here at all."

Pamela ignored his complaint. "What do you smell, Robert?"

"A barnyard. It stinks."

"Well, yes, but I don't think the horses object. Now then, do you feel the wind on your face?"

"Yes." His forehead puckered above his dark glasses.

"Which way is the wind blowing from?"

"From my right."

"Perfect. We have two of our senses that are working at full tilt. Now, how far away from the stables do you think you'll still be able to smell them?"

"How the heck would I know?"

"Why don't we find out? We know if we can smell the horses, we can always find our way back here, can't we? Meanwhile, we'll put our hearing to good use as well. I already hear a noisy pair of sparrows scraping and *pishing* in a nearby clump of grass. Do you hear them?"

"I suppose."

"Good. Then, we're off." After waving good-bye in Mary's general direction, Pamela had Robert take her right arm while she held Harriet's harness with her left hand. Robert extended his long cane in front of him.

Together, the two of them started off toward the path that was clearly visible to Mary . . . and, apparently, to Harriet. Robert's steps were hesitant, Pamela's confident.

Mary reached behind her in the van to pet Finnegan. "What an amazing woman she is, boy. I do believe Robert's eyes are going to be opened to a whole new way of life today."

After a few minutes, Mary undid Finnegan's harness and let him off the clock so he could get out of the van to stretch a bit.

She really was going to have to bring her knitting with her whenever she went out. She hated being idle.

Still this was a pleasant place to park. With the van's windows open, she could hear the wind shifting through the tops of the nearby fir trees and the restless movements of the horses in the corral. A black bird—Mary could never remember the official names of birds as well as Abby—perched on the fence railing for a time, eyeing her before flying off to investigate something of more interest.

Winter rain had encouraged grass to grow under the canopy of trees, and the shoots were the bright, effervescent green of spring. By mid-summer that same grass would turn brown and go to seed, the shoots perfect to use in a dried flower arrangement.

Silently, she thanked the Lord for these moments of peace where she could reflect on His natural world and its beauty. She realized this was a blessing she should enjoy more often, just as her sister did, and not fret about having idle hands.

Nearly an hour after they'd left, Pamela and Robert came striding back down the path. Robert's shoulders were back, his head held high, and he seemed to be leading them.

"Hey, you two," Mary called out. "Did you have a good time?"

"I heard an eagle screech," Robert responded, his grin speaking volumes about his new attitude. "It sounded just like one I heard in the Sahara years ago."

Thank You, Lord, for giving Robert a miracle.

As the two of them climbed back in the van, Pamela asked, "Do you know a nice place to eat lunch in town? I thought I'd treat you and Robert to a bite to eat. Abby, too, if she can join us."

"Going on a bird walk and eating out all in one day. You're pushing things, Pamela," Robert complained but with a half smile. "I'll warn you, though, that I'm likely to spill half my food down my front."

"Oh, *pshaw*," Pamela said. "Everyone spills things once in a while and you won't get any better at it if you don't practice. Besides, our walk made me hungry."

Pamela was such a dynamo and so confident, Robert didn't object further. In fact, he seemed almost eager to give it a try.

"The Springhouse Café is good for sandwiches and salads," Mary told them. "I'll give Abby a call." Reaching into the big denim bag fastened to her wheelchair, she pulled out her cell phone and punched in Abby's number at The Nature Museum. Abby eagerly agreed to meet them at the restaurant. She'd be there as soon as she finished some paperwork.

The short ride back into town brought them to the Springhouse Café.

"The café has a nice view of Randolph Bay and the marina," Mary commented as she exited the van. The chill wind still blew sharply, sending the gray clouds overhead scudding westward. "They also have a ramp for wheelchair access. If you two will grab hold of my chair, you can help push and Finnegan can lead us."

Successfully navigating the ramp as far as the entrance, Mary pressed the button that opened the doors automatically.

"The front of the café is a small gift shop," she explained, eyeing the array of upscale items such as lotions and soaps. "There're a fair number of breakables, like crystal glassware, and the aisles are a bit narrow. It'd be best if we entered single file."

"I hope they've got breakage insurance," Robert commented.

"Use your cane to measure the width of the aisle," Pamela told him. "I'm sure there's ample room to walk. Harriet and I will bring up the rear. She'll keep me from stumbling into the displays."

Mary reached the hostess's podium. Ida Tolliver arrived to greet them. As usual, she wore navy pants, a neat white blouse and a ruffled apron.

Smiling cheerfully, she took in the group. "Hi, Mary. Three for lunch?"

"We'll be four. Abby will be along shortly."

"How 'bout the big table by the window? There'll be plenty of room for you and your doggies."

"Sounds perfect." Following Ida, Mary led her contingent of hungry souls to a large round table. A few of the customers looked surprised to see a pair of dogs inside the restaurant, but most smiled their approval.

Pamela took the seat with her back to the view and Robert sat beside her, Mary on the opposite side of the table. Probably out of habit, Ida gave them all menus and left one for Abby at the vacant place. A rose print tablecloth was set with heavy flatware and matching rose-covered napkins.

Always well behaved in public, the two dogs took up positions next to their respective mistresses, almost as though they were competing to prove each was the more attentive of the two.

Ida said, "I'll be right back with your waters and I'll be happy to answer any questions you have."

"Thank you, Ida." Mary smiled up at her young friend. "We're in no rush."

"I suppose you're going to read the menu to me," Robert said to Pamela, running his fingertips across the plastic-covered menu after Ida had left.

"I don't need to. I already know a good deal about what they serve here."

Robert's brows lowered. "You've been here before?"

"No, but I can use my sense of smell to tell me what's cooking. Tell me what you smell."

He gave that some thought. "Hamburgers and French fries."

Pamela laughed. "Grease gives itself away every time. But concentrate on what's below that scent, a fragrance that's not so potent."

In awe of Pamela's use of her remaining senses, Mary concentrated too. She smelled fish, no doubt the Fresh Catch of the Day. And something spicy, maybe a salsa for the café's chicken-and-cheese quesadilla.

"I get fish," Robert said. "That's all I can pick out."

"That's good for a beginning. The other scents are more subtle, which is why it's nice to have our sighted friend along to read us the menu."

"I'm happy to oblige," Mary said. She ran through the general categories on the menu. Robert decided a turkey sandwich would be the easiest for him to handle; Pamela opted for an Asian salad with chicken and wonton strips. Mary chose the clam chowder with half a meatloaf sandwich.

They'd just reached their decisions when Abby arrived.

"Sorry I'm late. I got stuck on the phone with the wildlife biology professor at the University of Washington." She made her way to Pamela to give her a hug. "I'm so glad you could come to visit."

"We've had a grand morning," Pamela said. "Thank you for inviting me."

Abby touched Robert on the shoulder, then took the chair next to Mary. "So what did you three do this morning?"

"*Those* two went birding. Alone!" Mary announced with a grin.

Abby gaped at Pamela. "You really did?"

"The truth is, Pamela has opened a whole new world to me." Robert reached out to touch his blind friend and found her hand. "And this fine lady has given me a serous kick in the rear end. Which I well deserved."

Mary felt tears well in her eyes. What giant strides Robert had made in a few short hours.

"She's also told me about a mobility program at Stanford that I plan to enroll in, and I'll hook up with services for the blind in Seattle, where I live. Those militant activists in Mali may have blinded me, but there's nothing wrong with my other senses. Or my brain, for that matter. Pamela has convinced me that giving up on myself only lets them win the battle." He seemed to sit a little straighter in his chair. "It's high time I start fighting back."

That was the longest speech Mary had ever heard Robert make, and it was powerfully emotional. She caught Abby's eye and saw that her sister had been moved by it as well.

"Good for you, Robert," Mary said with heartfelt relief and pleasure because of his new outlook on life. "Go get 'em, tiger!"

Everyone laughed, breaking the somber mood, but there were still tears in Mary's eyes when Ida returned with four glasses of water, ready to take their orders.

AFTER LUNCH, Abby took Pamela back to the ferry and Mary drove Robert home. She pulled into the McDonalds' driveway to let him out.

"I owe you a great deal for putting up with my miserable disposition," he said. "Sandy and her family too. I'm not sure how I'll make it up to all of you who've showed me such kindness."

"I'm sure Sandy would agree you don't owe us a thing except finding your own happiness again. That's what we've all been praying for."

"It looks like your prayers are being answered. Thanks."

Mary watched him get out of the van and make his way to the front door with far more confidence than he'd had earlier that morning. She couldn't help but think they'd all been God's messengers. The McDonald family, herself, Abby and, most of all, Pamela Folz had brought the light of the Lord back into Robert's life.

Later that afternoon, while she was knitting and watching a talk show on TV, someone knocked excitedly on the kitchen door. Checking the time and noting school had been out for a bit, she suspected her visitor was Bobby.

"Well, hello there, young man," she said, opening the door for him.

"Look what I got, Mary. It's a radio, a two-meter rig. Uncle Robert bought it for me on eBay. It came today!"

"Goodness, come on in and let me look at it."

Finnegan trotted over to see what all the excitement was about.

"I can't use it till I get my official call sign." He handed Mary the radio. "But see, it's got knobs so I can change frequencies and talk on the repeater."

"My, my, that's very exciting."

Bobby rattled on, using jargon Mary couldn't quite follow.

But that didn't diminish her ability to share the boy's excitement. Having his very own radio was another milestone in his young life.

THURSDAY, ABBY WAS AT THE MUSEUM when the storm that had been threatening for several days began. The sky darkened and rain spattered against the high windows of her office. Picking up her phone, she called Robert.

"The weather report calls for rain through tonight and into tomorrow morning," she told him.

"Then let's hope there's some major shipping activity in the straits tonight. We'll set our trap and see what we catch."

Excitement rippled through Abby's midsection along with dread about who they might catch in their trap. "Should I start monitoring the lighthouse now?"

"No, I think we can wait until full dark. I doubt the culprits will turn off the light until then. If I can get Sandy's approval, I'd like Bobby to go with you and monitor activity on the ham repeater. Then you can report if and when the light goes dark. I'll record all the transmissions from here so we'll have their voices on tape."

"Will it be dangerous at the lighthouse? I don't want to put Bobby at risk."

Robert hesitated a moment. "I don't believe whoever is watching for ships is at the lighthouse. More likely they've chosen a spot at a higher elevation where they can see ships coming from both directions and not be observed themselves."

"Somewhere on Mount Ortiz?"

"That would be my guess. Possibly a location where cell phones don't work. By using ham radio, they avoid any record of calls on their cell phones. And by not using their call signs, they're hoping to be totally anonymous."

If Abby had her way, they wouldn't be anonymous for much longer.

DARKNESS ARRIVED EARLY that evening.

Abby packed sandwiches and hot chocolate for herself and Bobby, and picked him up at his house. Wearing a yellow slicker much like her own, he ducked into her car and pulled his small hand-held radio out from under the protection of his rain gear.

"I got my license, Abby. It was posted on the Internet when I got home from school. WB7KIM. Kids Inherit Millions. How's that, huh?"

Despite her anxiety over the coming evening and how it might play out, Abby laughed. "Did your dad think that up for you?"

"Nope. It was my idea."

Leave it to Bobby. He was a real Cracker Jack. "Sounds like wishful thinking to me." Even in the darkness inside the car, Abby could see Bobby's grin.

"Yeah, but it's easy to remember."

"Why do you have so many more letters in your call sign than your uncle?"

"That's 'cuz he's an extra class. I'm just a technician now. When I pass the code test, I'll be a general class operator. And some day, when I know a lot more about electronics and stuff, I'll take another test and become an extra class like Uncle Robert. Then they'll give me a new two-letter call sign."

She loved the boy's sense of self-confidence. With Bobby it

was never *if* he would pass a test or accomplish some goal, but *when*. She was equally confident of his future successes, both in ham radio and in life.

The windshield wipers struggled to keep up with the steadily falling rain. The windows fogged and Abby turned on the deicer. Despite the heater being on, she shivered. A bad case of nerves, she told herself. She and Bobby would be safe. If the lighthouse went dark, she'd be able to notify the Coast Guard and they would warn any ships in the area to use extra caution.

The road to the lighthouse was pitch dark. No street lights shone and there were no houses along this stretch of roadway. Only the car headlights cut through the rain, and then only for a few feet.

As she thought of the mission ahead of them, Abby recalled the verses from 2 Samuel 22:28–30 that she'd memorized as a young girl.

"You save the humble, but your eyes are on the haughty to bring them low. You are my lamp, O Lord; the Lord turns my darkness into light. With your help I can advance against a troop; with my God I can scale a wall."

She didn't expect to have to scale a wall or even climb the lighthouse stairway. Nor did she anticipate battling a troop of those who would see ships collide and sink in the sea. But she was counting on the Lord to be her lamp in the darkness and help her catch those haughty enough to put the lives of people and the welfare of God's innocent creatures at risk.

CHAPTER ❧ SEVENTEEN

Abby reached the end of the road near the lighthouse and pulled over. So far, the light was slicing an arc through the rain at its regular five-second interval.

"Do you have your radio on?" she asked Bobby.

"Yep. You want me to see if anyone's listening to the frequency?"

"No. Let's keep it a secret that we're here. If they know we're eavesdropping, they might call off their plans for the night. Assuming they're up to their mischief tonight."

Given that the 'mischief' could be dangerous to others, Abby had mixed feelings. She wished Justin and his friends had been shaken by the recent incident, even though it hadn't been their fault, and had given up on their scheme to halt the tankers from using the strait.

Even more, she hoped the perpetrator was someone she didn't know. A stranger she didn't care about.

She had an uncomfortable feeling that wouldn't be the case.

Adjusting her seat, she stretched out her legs as best she could. The rain beat a steady rhythm on the car, the water running off the windshield in sheets, distorting the view of the lighthouse. No other cars were in sight and no people, either. She and Bobby were very much alone here at Wayfarer Point.

Abby tried to keep her anxiety at bay.

"Are you ready for a sandwich and hot chocolate?" she asked.

"Sure." He placed his radio on the console between them. "This is like being private detectives on a stakeout, isn't it?"

She reached into the backseat to get the thermos. "I guess it is." *And maybe Bobby has been watching too many detective shows on TV*, she thought.

"How long do you think we'll be here?"

"I don't know. It's a school night, so I hate to keep you up too late. But if there aren't any ships coming our way, then maybe nothing will happen tonight." She'd tried calling a couple of tanker firms to ask about their schedules, but no one would provide that information. She wasn't surprised.

"So then we'd have to come back tomorrow night?"

She poured two cups of hot chocolate and put them in the cup holder. "You seem pretty eager to stay up all night."

"It's cool. You know, being out in the dark and all, and trying to catch criminals. Maybe I'll be a cop when I grow up."

She grimaced. "I thought you were going to be an astronaut."

"Well, yeah, or a scientist. Maybe a civil engineer like Uncle Robert."

She handed him a turkey sandwich, without mayonnaise, per Sandy's instructions. "I think you're smart enough to be anything you want to be, a police officer, astronaut or an engineer.

God's given you a lot of abilities. He expects you to make the most of them, whatever you do with your life."

"I think it's going to be hard to decide. I mean, I like to do a lot of different stuff."

"You have lots of time before you have to make a decision about your future. Meanwhile, enjoy exploring as many different paths as interest you. God will lead you to the right one, I'm sure."

Certainly her decision to pursue ornithology from an early age had led her down a fulfilling career and life path. Over the years, she'd often felt God's hand at work in her life, no more so than when she'd returned to Sparrow Island to stay with Mary and discovered new challenges right here at home.

Bobby's radio came to life and Abby started at the sound.

"W7AX, W7PU, are you around, Charlie?"

A moment later, another ham responded. "I'm here. W7AX. What's up, Phil?"

"Just checking in on you. How's your XYL?"

Bobby whispered, "XYL means his wife."

Abby nodded. *An eX-Young Lady.* The two voices were not those they'd been waiting to hear.

"Not too good."

The two men chatted back and forth for a while, then signed off with their call signs.

"I've heard them on the air before," Bobby said. "They 'rag chew,' according to Uncle Robert, almost every night."

"Sounds like they're good friends. Ham radio keeps them in touch."

As the minutes ticked by, Abby stared out the window at the lighthouse. Perversely, she wished the thing would go dark so she and Bobby could close their part of the trap and go home to bed. Bobby was already having trouble keeping his eyes open, the hour now past his usual bedtime.

A rap on the side window of the car had Abby nearly jumping out of her skin.

"Abby, it's me. William."

Good grief! *The Birdcall* editor was standing outside the car, his rain hat pulled down tightly over his head, his poncho dripping with water.

She rolled down the window. "William, you nearly scared me to death! Get in the backseat before you drown."

Bobby jerked awake. "What's going on?"

"Nothing's wrong, honey. It's just Mr. Jensen from *The Birdcall.*"

William squeezed into the backseat and took off his hat, slapping the rain from the brim.

"What on earth are you doing here, William?"

"Same thing you are, I imagine." He slammed the door closed, but not before a gusher of rain water found its way into the car. "Doesn't take a genius to know the hooligans who are playing Hobbes with the lighthouse like to strike during dark and rainy weather."

That was true enough. But Abby hadn't expected a crowd to show up.

"What have you got there, Bobby?" William asked.

"My new ham radio. I got my call sign this afternoon. WB7KIM—Kids Inherit Millions."

"Is that a fact?" William nailed Abby with a curious look. "What's ham radio got to do with the lighthouse?"

"Maybe nothing," she hedged. "We were just watching the light, thinking the same thing you do, that a rainy night would be optimum for our mysterious electrical outage."

William clearly wasn't buying her ploy. "You know something I don't. Give it to me, Abby, or I'll find out myself. One way or another."

"I don't know anything for sure. Not at this point." She also didn't want to jeopardize Justin and his friends if they weren't guilty. If they were, she wanted a chance to talk to them herself before turning them over to the authorities. Although the thought of the police, and possibly federal officials, arresting Justin and his friends caused her stomach to knot. Their bright futures would undoubtedly be severely limited if they were guilty of a federal offense.

"You're holding out on me, Abby, and the press has a right to know," William warned.

"I'm not obligated to tell you anything, William. For the moment, you'll just have to trust me."

At that very instant, a female voice spoke on the radio. "There's two big fish! Two of 'em!"

"Roger, copy two fish," came the response. "Here we go."

Abby's gaze shot to the top of the lighthouse. The light swung in its usual arc, left to right, illuminating the rain that continued to fall.

Suddenly the light went out.

"That's it! Tell your uncle Robert," she ordered Bobby while at the same time pulling her cell phone from the holder on her belt.

"W7PQ, this is WB7KIM." Bobby's voice shook on what was his first ham radio transmission.

Abby punched in the number for the Coast Guard Station at Bellingham.

"WB7KIM, this is W7PQ," Robert responded. "I heard the signal. Go ahead."

"The light went out, Uncle Robert. It's dark out here."

"Good boy. I got it on tape," Robert responded. "W7PQ clear."

"WB7KIM, clear." Bobby swallowed hard. "We caught 'em, didn't we, Abby?"

"What's going on?" William wanted to know. "Somebody cut the power to the lighthouse."

Abby reached the Coast Guard Station, and after a few switches, the Officer of the Day answered. He'd been briefed, and a few moments later he told her their monitoring equipment showed no glitch in the power to Wayfarer Point Lighthouse.

"It's dark. You need to warn the ships in the passage."

"Senior Chief Bosnik is with the cutter cruising that area now. He's already sent out an alarm to all ships in the vicinity."

"He has?" She looked out to sea and spotted blinking warning lights not far off shore. Apparently Chief Bosnik was several steps ahead of her and had taken up a position in a way that his Coast Guard cutter would serve the same purpose as the lighthouse until the power returned.

"Thank you," she said to the duty officer on the phone, but he had already disconnected.

William leaned forward between the two car seats. "Abby, you have to tell me what just happened. What was that about two fish?"

She couldn't. She'd recognized Justin's voice announcing "Here we go." She had to give him one last chance to admit the dangerous game he'd been playing and grasp the potential consequences of his actions. And then she'd have to examine her conscience and pray for guidance as to what she should do.

Unless the two ships in the strait collided. Then there would be no way she could hold back the truth and the evidence, Robert's tape of the ham radio transmission.

Both the Coast Guard and Sergeant Cobb would have to be informed.

Although William was persistent, Abby refused to tell him what she knew. Grumbling, he got out of the car.

"I'm going to talk to Henry Cobb," he warned. "He'll make you spill the beans."

"Goodnight, William."

When she started the car, the newspaper editor slammed the door and jumped out of the way. Backing around, she made a U-turn and headed home.

"Are you gonna tell Sergeant Cobb what we heard on my radio?"

"Not just yet. I want to talk to them first and I want your uncle to be there too."

"You know who it is?" Bobby asked, surprised.

Sighing with regret, Abby said, "I'm afraid I do."

"Who is it?"

"I need to be absolutely sure before I accuse anyone, Bobby. I don't want to start a rumor and then find out I'm wrong about who's been doing this. It wouldn't be fair to anyone."

The boy wasn't happy with her evasive answer. But he'd have to be patient. And Abby was still holding out hope she could convince Justin and his friends to see that what they'd been doing was wrong.

When they arrived at the McDonalds' house, Abby followed Bobby inside.

"We heard 'em, Mom! And then the light went out."

Sandy gave her son a hug. "So I understand."

Robert appeared from the back of the house wearing jeans and a flannel shirt.

Breaking away from his mother, Bobby zeroed in on his great uncle. "Did I do all right?"

"Your transmission was perfect, junior. You're well on your way as a ham operator."

"Robert, I'd like to talk to you," Abby said.

He shrugged. "Go ahead."

"Justin, and hopefully his friends, are due to come to the museum Saturday morning to deliver a project he's been working on for me."

"And that's when you're going to nail him?"

"I have in mind showing him and his friends the evidence we have and getting them to see the light about what they're doing."

"You're going to let them off the hook?" Agitated, Robert plowed his fingers through his hair. "People could have been killed, like they were when that extremist group blew up the dam in Mali."

"That's exactly why I want you to be with me when I confront them with the facts."

"Me?"

"I think that's a good idea, Uncle Robert," Sandy said. "There's no one who knows better than you do about the consequences of such a rash act."

"And what do you want me to do? Strangle them? That would be my first impulse."

"But that's not what you'd actually do." Abby took a deep breath. "If I simply *tell* them what could happen if they keep on trying to stop the oil tankers, they might shrug my words off as being naive, or just plain foolish. If you come with me, you *show* them how things can go seriously wrong." Justin's reaction and that of his friends would clarify her next step. If they expressed remorse, that was one thing. But if they became belligerent . . .

"Okay," Robert said reluctantly. "I'll be your bad example."

"And when they fully understand the enormity of what could have happened right here in the San Juan Islands, I want you to forgive them. And the extremists whose actions blinded you."

His head snapped up. "No way. Those people practically ruined my life. As it is, they killed two other innocent people and nearly did the same to me."

"Uncle Robert." Bobby took his hand. "We learned in Sunday school the other day about forgiveness. How you have to love your enemies and turn the other cheek and stuff like that."

Out of the mouths of babes, Abby thought, her chest tightening with pride for her young friend.

"The teacher said forgiving somebody who hurts you makes you feel better," Bobby continued. "It's like that lady who took you for a walk in the forest made you feel better, even when you didn't want to go. Forgiving those bad people in Mali might make you feel real good. On the inside, I mean."

Standing nearby, Sandy pressed her fingers to her lips and there were tears in her eyes.

Robert pulled the boy closer. "You're asking me to do a hard thing, junior."

"Learning about ham radio was hard for me, but you said I could do it. And I passed the test the first time."

Abby held her breath. She and Bobby were giving Robert a difficult test indeed. She wasn't sure he was ready to forgive yet.

But she did know forgiveness would heal him and bring him an inner peace that nothing else could provide.

THE NEXT MORNING she confirmed with Justin that he was on schedule to bring the computerized map of eagle sightings to The Nature Museum the following day, Saturday. She encouraged him to invite his young bird-watching friends to come with him.

She couldn't believe any of them actually wanted to hurt others. *They were misguided,* she thought.

At least she hoped that was the situation.

Her next call was to her pastor, Rev. James Hale. She needed help deciding what to do about Justin and his friends. Rev. Hale was not only a man of God and easy to talk to, he had a good head on his shoulders. He'd be able to advise her.

Fortunately, he agreed to see her before she went in to work that morning.

At the church, Janet Heinz was already at her desk opening mail and arranging her day's activities. A mixed bouquet of yellow roses, white iris and daisies from Island Blooms sat on the corner of her desk.

She looked up from her work and smiled. "Good morning, Abby. I didn't know you were coming in this morning."

"I called Rev. Hale and asked to see him."

"Oh." Worry lines formed above her brows. "Nothing wrong, I hope."

"I just need him to be my sounding board," Abby assured her friend.

"He's a good one for that. Go on in." She gestured toward the door that led to the reverend's office. "Say, I heard the lighthouse went dark again last night. It sure is strange, what's been happening out there."

"Yes, it is," Abby agreed, mildly surprised that Janet had already heard the news. Between the church secretary and Margaret Blackstock, there was almost no need for Sparrow Island to have a weekly newspaper. They spread the news as quickly and easily as scattering birdseed.

With a quick wave of her hand, Abby headed toward Rev. Hale's office. She knocked on his open door and stepped inside.

"Hope I'm not interrupting your work," she said as he stood behind his desk.

"Not at all. Just putting the final touches on my Sunday sermon." A tall, slender man with sandy-blond hair, he indicated the comfortable chairs beside the window. Before he joined her, he closed the door of his office.

"Now then," he said, sitting opposite her, "what can I do for you?"

Overnight, Abby had done a lot of thinking and praying about her situation. And Justin's. Doing the *right* thing, the caring thing, appeared to conflict with being a law-abiding citizen.

"Would it be all right if we spoke in hypotheticals for a moment?" she asked.

The hint of a smile curved his lips. "Preachers are very good at hypotheticals. It's when we get down to brass tacks that it gets complicated."

Returning his half smile, she sighed. "Yes, that does seem to be my problem. At any rate, I'm wondering, if you knew of some well-meaning, intelligent young people who have become involved in something illegal, what would you do?"

He lifted his brows, indicating she had his attention, but he didn't speak.

"So far these young people haven't hurt anyone or caused any real damage. But they could have."

"Did they intend to?" he asked.

"I don't know. My feeling is that their intent is well-meaning, but they're misguided and don't really understand what the consequences of their actions could be."

"Have you talked to them?"

"Not yet, but I plan to."

The preacher sat leaning forward in a thoughtful pose, his elbows on his thighs, his hands clasped between his knees. "I can see you're very troubled about these young people. Have you prayed about it?"

"Oh, I'd say something like full-time since I realized what was happening and who was doing it," she said with a wry smile.

"And you haven't found a clear path yet?"

"I'm terribly torn. On the one hand, if I report these *hypothetical* young people to the authorities, they'd very likely be arrested, probably on federal charges."

"*Hmmm*, that's very serious."

"I know. That's why I'm so torn. If this situation goes on their record, their entire lives will be affected. They might have to serve jail time. And even if they get probation or community service, it would still limit their future careers. And they seem to be such bright youngsters, I'd hate for that to happen to them."

"Because of their foolish mistakes."

Suddenly unable to speak, she could only nod. Tears of concern for Justin and the others burned at the back of her eyes, yet her throat felt thick with guilt over the thought of withholding information from the authorities, including Henry Cobb.

"I understand your dilemma," Rev. Hale said. "Your heart is telling you that you hold the futures of these young people in your hands, and you don't want to hurt them. At the same time, your natural inclination is to report the crime they may have committed."

"That's about the size of it."

He leaned back in his chair. "I'm afraid I can't tell you what to do."

She glanced away. Outside, a stiff breeze waved the branches of the fir trees and sent gray clouds scudding across the patchy blue sky. The clouds looked almost as confused by what direction they should take as she felt.

"I wish you could tell me which way to go," she said.

"I don't think I have to. I know that you have a good heart, your instincts have always been right on and your faith is strong. There may not be a *right* answer in this case. Only the answer God gives you after you talk with these, um, *hypothetical* young people."

She returned her attention to the pastor. "What if He doesn't provide the answer?"

"He will." Extending his hands, he took hers in his, sharing his strength and confidence. "Let's pray together."

Closing her eyes, Abby listened as Rev. Hale asked for the Lord's blessing on her and prayed for His guidance, that she would know what the Lord wanted for the good of both the young people she cared about and the community as a whole.

When he finished praying, Abby still felt anxious about her meeting with Justin in the morning, but stronger too.

RISING EARLY ON SATURDAY MORNING, she showered and dressed, and went outside for her morning devotionals. She needed to be as close to God as possible today. Outside, among His wonders, was where she belonged.

Beyond the back fence, the yard sloped down to the sea and she could hear the waves washing against the rocks. The rising sun cast ribbons of silver across the undulating ocean. Above her, the sky was a pale blue, promising a cloudless day. A phalanx of double-breasted cormorants streaked by en route to their morning feeding grounds.

Abby bowed her head. Taking a deep breath, she prayed for the Lord's guidance that she find the right words this morning to touch Justin's heart, that Robert would find in his heart the spirit of forgiveness and that the Lord would show her the path she should take regarding all the young people.

Finally, she went inside to join Mary at breakfast.

"You look worried," Mary commented. She had oatmeal cooking on the stove and served up a dish for each of them.

Abby poured herself a cup of coffee. "I am worried. A great deal could go wrong when I meet with Justin this morning."

"Are you sure you don't want Henry there? What those young people were doing must be illegal."

"Probably. Interfering with maritime trade is very likely a federal offense. But Justin and the others are just kids. If I report them, their lives and their futures are effectively changed forever."

"I hate keeping secrets from Henry."

"I know. So do I." Sitting down, Abby sipped her coffee.

Mary poured milk over her oatmeal and sprinkled it with brown sugar. "I know you've been praying about Justin and his friends. I'm confident whatever you decide to do will be the right thing."

"I hope you're right."

Abby finished her breakfast and rinsed her dishes and Mary's, putting them in the dishwasher, then prepared to leave.

"Good luck," Mary called to her as she went out to her car.

To Abby's surprise, Robert was waiting for her in the driveway near the garage.

"Good morning, Robert. I was going to come pick you up."

"After Pamela got on my case about being more independent, I decided I was perfectly capable of walking fifty paces to the neighbor's house on my own without falling down or getting lost."

Abby's spirits lifted considerably. If Robert could take such a giant step forward, perhaps he could also find the courage to forgive those who had injured him.

"Good for you! Another ten steps straight ahead and you'll be at my car."

He straightened, extended his cane and walked forward.

Wanting to cheer, Abby issued a silent *thank You* to God instead and smiled as Robert reached the car on his own.

"Do you have the tape with you?" Abby asked as he buckled up in the car.

He patted his jacket pocket. "Right here."

The day could not have been more spring-like. The temperature had warmed by several degrees from the previous week and the buds on the big maple in front of The Nature Museum had begun to bloom.

Justin and his friends hadn't arrived yet, so Abby introduced Robert to Wilma at the front desk, then gave him a brief tour of the museum. They hadn't gone far when she stopped abruptly.

"Robert, you've given me an inspiration. I don't know why I haven't thought of it before."

"Oh-oh. I hope you're not thinking of sending me up a tree to check on bird nests. I'm not *that* independent yet."

She laughed. "No, nothing like that. I've just realized that we have a few touchable exhibits where visitors can actually feel how sharp bird claws are or how feathers feel, and we have a birdsong display where visitors can listen to the bird calls. But we don't have any Braille signs to explain the exhibits."

"That wouldn't do me any good. I don't read Braille."

"Not yet," she pointed out. "But you may learn Braille later, and a lot of young children start off early to learn to read that way. It should be included in our museum. And there should be signs marking our outdoor nature trail as well and even a guide rope to aid the visually impaired."

"Sounds to me like you've just created a whole lot of work for yourself."

"True enough." Sighing, she rolled her eyes. "And created a need for more funding as well. And it's all your fault," she teased.

His laughter warmed her heart. "Fine thing, blaming me for inspiring you."

She took his arm and led him toward her office and the workroom. "We won't be able to create a facility that's visually handicapped-friendly overnight, but I think I'll put it right up there on my wish list. Who knows when we might have an opportunity to implement the concept, once we've recognized the need?"

She noted Robert's amusement, but her responding smile froze on her face when she saw Justin and his friends pushing through the front doors of the museum.

The next hour would determine the future for four young people. She prayed it would be a happy one for them all.

CHAPTER ✿ EIGHTEEN

Her mouth as dry as uncooked oatmeal, Abby greeted Justin and his friends. Acid attacked the lining of her stomach. She so wanted these next few minutes to go well. *Please, God, help me do Thy will.*

She had to clear her throat before she could speak. "I'm glad you could all come this morning." Turning to Robert, she introduced him as her neighbor's uncle who was visiting for a few weeks.

Carrying what looked like an artist's folio, Justin shook hands with Robert then did the introductions of his friends. "Abby, you know Kirk Zumbrowski from the eagle census. This is Shayla Medivore and Loretta Sanchez. They helped with the census, too, but I'm not sure if you met them."

"I do recall seeing you during lunch." The two girls looked exceptionally young with their long dark hair, big brown eyes and little makeup. No more than fifteen or sixteen, she suspected. Too young to lose their futures because of a foolish mistake in judgment.

Loretta managed a shy smile while Shayla giggled self-consciously. "You were pretty busy that day."

No one commented on Robert's blindness, perhaps because they all knew Pamela Folz and her uncanny abilities.

"Well, let's see what we've got," Abby said.

"I'll need a big table or something to spread the map sections on," Justin said.

"We've got a worktable that should do it." Asking Robert to take her arm, Abby led them all past the reception area and through the door that read Private.

"Here we go," she said when they reached the workroom and the table where she studied bird specimens and prepared displays. Boxes of equipment and materials for rotating exhibits filled cupboards along one wall. A window let in natural light to supplement the florescent fixtures recessed in the ceiling.

A stuffed albatross with a broken wing sat on one end of the long worktable.

"Cool," Kirk said. He gently lifted the wing and examined the break. "What happened to him?"

"Originally, he broke his wing by hitting a power line, we think, and then he died. We'd repaired the wing for our display, but he got knocked over during a cleaning operation. I'll have him back on his perch by next week."

Opening the folio, Justin laid out six map pieces, fifteen-by-fifteen-inch squares that he'd blown up from the maps Abby had provided to the eagle census takers. Roads and walking trails were well marked as were the major landmarks such as Mount Ortiz, Arrowhead Hill and the town of Green Harbor. He'd added nest locations as red circles; green arrows indicated the flight of the single eagles they'd spotted. Along the bottom of the map he'd provided a key to explain the symbols.

Except for Robert, the others gathered around the table to admire Justin's work. Robert stood to one side listening quietly.

"This is perfect, Justin." Her heart in her throat, Abby praised the young man and hoped she wouldn't be the one to end his promising future. "You've done a wonderful job."

"I figure you'll want to mount it behind Plexiglas," he said. "I didn't know if you had someone who can do that or not."

"I can find someone, I'm sure. Thank you so much. All of you for your hard work. You're the kind of young people, concerned with the environment, who can be role models for others."

They all seemed pleased with her tribute.

"*If,*" she added, "you don't carry your beliefs to an extreme that can actually harm others."

Their expressions shifted to puzzlement and they glanced from one to another.

"Robert, why don't you tell Justin and his friends what happened to you in Mali."

He cleared his throat and straightened his shoulders. "I'm a civil engineer by training and I've consulted on major projects in a dozen developing nations around the world." He told them of living in the Amazon jungles and working in the most northern reaches of Siberia.

"In many of these countries there is unrest," he continued. "That goes with the territory. But recently there have been environmental extremists who've been taking matters into their own hands. Sometimes they do more damage to the environment than all the greedy corporations combined that they oppose."

Justin began to fidget with his folio and looked uneasy. So did his friends.

"A few months ago, I was inspecting a dam in Mali. A development crucially needed to provide both power and water to the indigenous population in that arid country. It was a random inspection. No one knew we were coming. But our timing couldn't have been worse. A group of extremists blew it up just as we started to walk out on the catwalk."

Shayla drew in a quick breath; Loretta's cheeks paled.

"That's a shame, Mr. Weatherford," Justin said, his gaze darting from Robert to Abby. "But I'm not sure why you're—"

"Because you're extremely fortunate you haven't hurt anyone yet with your pranks at the lighthouse." Robert withdrew the small tape recorder from his jacket pocket and pressed Play.

"You were the guy on the radio!" Justin gasped in recognition.

All four young people listened in shock as they heard the clearly identifiable voices of Shayla and Justin setting Thursday evening's event in motion.

Shayla looked like she might cry. "We didn't intend to hurt—"

"Be quiet," Justin ordered.

Abby directed her attention to Kirk. "The first time we heard a similar transmission, I believe it was your voice. You were the one doing the spotting from Mount Ortiz that night."

His jaw dropped open. "How did you—"

Robert's hands flexed into fists. "Your actions put people's lives in jeopardy and could have caused uncounted damage to the environment you claim you want to protect."

"Are you going to arrest us?" Loretta blinked back tears. "My mom will be so—"

"I think what happens to you now depends a lot on what Justin does." Cocking her head, Abby looked directly into his striking blue eyes. "I want to know exactly how you hacked into the Coast Guard computers and turned off Wayfarer Point Lighthouse."

For a moment, he looked like he was going to deny everything.

"Tell her, Justin," Kirk said. "If you don't, we're all toast."

"Come on, Justin," Shayla pleaded. "You told us nobody would get hurt. But look what happened to this man, and he hadn't done anything wrong."

Justin appeared to shrink in size, his shoulders hunching forward as he stuffed his hands into his pockets. "I hacked into their cell phone connection, not their main computers. It wasn't all that hard. Their peripheral security stinks."

"Go on," Abby urged.

"Then I put a patch across the cell phone line so the monitoring equipment wouldn't know I'd broken into their system. The next step was a piece of cake." He shrugged. "I hacked into the dedicated power line that comes from the substation. It was easy. In fact, one morning I was playing around and hacked into another power line, kind of accidentally." A half grin lifted the corners of his mouth. "I'll bet the power company had crews out all over the island trying to figure out what went wrong."

Abby thought back to the morning the power had gone out here at The Nature Museum and the Mount Saint Helens exhibit had gone a little nuts. *Not the ghost of Terrence Pettigrew. Instead, Justin had been the culprit.*

"What did you expect to accomplish by turning the lighthouse off?" she asked.

"I thought, I mean, we all thought that if the tanker companies decided the strait was too dangerous, they'd send their ships farther out to sea where, if there was an accident, the oil spill wouldn't make it as far as land to mess up the environment."

"But it would eventually," Robert pointed out. "Or damage the creatures on the ocean bottom. And by forcing the tanker to travel farther, they'd be consuming more refined oil, not less."

It was clear that Justin and his friends hadn't considered those consequences.

"Justin, I believe what you've done is a very serious crime— and all of you have been his accomplices." Abby made her point as sternly as she could. "There are those who think I should notify the federal authorities."

"I've been one of those," Robert admitted.

"Oh, please, Ms. Stanton—"

"We were only thinking about what an oil spill would do to the shore birds and stuff. We didn't actually want to hurt anybody. We're sorry, honest we are."

"If you tell, we'll all get expelled from school."

"My mom will kill me."

While the others pleaded for mercy, Justin continued to study the tips of his well-worn sneakers. Finally, he lifted his head.

"I'm responsible. For everything. You don't have to blow the whistle on these guys. I'll swear I did it all on my own."

"So you're willing to take all the blame and go to jail for what you've done?" Abby asked, eyeing him carefully.

"When you tell my mom,"—his Adam's apple bobbed up and down, and he struggled to speak—"tell her I'm sorry."

Abby exhaled in relief. In a surge of faith, she knew what God asked of her. *Justice tempered by the light of mercy.* Justin was no hardened criminal standing there, near tears. Instead, he was a bright young man who had taken a wrong path. He could still turn himself around.

"Justin," she said softly. "How could you use your computer skills to make up for what you've done or tried to do?"

"Huh?" He looked confused by her question.

"Is there any way you could suggest changes in the Coast Guard system or the power company, for that matter, that would prevent someone else from doing what you did or worse?"

Using both hands, he plowed his blond hair back from his face. "I guess I could give them the codes I used to break into the system. But they'd need to upgrade their overall security too." He rattled off technical phrases about traps and system configuration, viruses and Trojan horses, that Abby couldn't understand.

"How long would it take you to do all that?" she asked when he finished his explanation.

He glanced around at his friends as though wanting to apologize. "I don't know. A week or two if I work at it full time."

"Would you be willing to do all that work if it meant no one would learn what you and your friends attempted to do?"

Kirk took a step toward Justin. "I could probably help some. You know, run test programs to see if they work. That kind of thing."

Resting his hand on his friend's shoulder, Justin nodded. "Yeah, we could do it."

Holding each other's hands, the two girls both looked weak with relief.

"I'm going to hold you to that, Justin," Abby said. "In two weeks, I want a complete report, including all the technical codes, on how you hacked into the Coast Guard cell phone connection and the power company equipment, and a detailed proposal on how that can be prevented in the future. I'll take the information to the Coast Guard."

His eyes widened with fear. "If you do that, they'll know who's been messing around and toss me in jail for the rest of my life."

"Not if you remain anonymous."

"You mean you're not going to tell 'em it was me?"

"I'm giving you a second chance. All of you," Abby pointed out. "In the process, I'm sticking my neck out a mile. I won't be able to help you"—*or myself,* she realized—"if you mess this up."

"Messing up includes pulling another stunt at the lighthouse," Robert pointed out. "Or anywhere else. If you do, I won't wait for Abby to act. I'll report you myself. You can't put any more lives at risk."

"Yeah, I get that. Look, I really appreciate what you're doing—"

"Then two weeks from today I'll expect to see you back here with everything the Coast Guard needs to know in order to protect their system from any further interference."

The four young people seemed more than grateful for the reprieve. They swore they'd never try anything like that again. They simply hadn't realized. . . .

After they left, Abby's knees felt so weak, she sat down heavily in a nearby chair and buried her head in her hands.

Robert leaned back against the worktable. "You've done an amazing thing, Abby. Very courageous."

"I don't know about courageous. I just hope it was the *right* thing to do."

"It was." Idly, he twisted his long cane between his palms. "I could hear their remorse. When they realized what they'd done and how badly it could have gone—it's strange, really—I forgave them."

She looked up. "You did?"

"Yes. Listening to those kids, realizing they weren't bad or evil, that their intentions had been good even if they were way off base, I understood what you and Bobby were trying to tell me."

"About forgiveness?"

"About forgiveness and letting go." Straightening out his cane, he tapped his way around the table to where Abby was sitting. "By forgiving those extremists who blew up the dam, whether they're remorseful or not, frees me to look toward the future. And like Bobby said, that feels good on the inside."

Emotion closed Abby's throat and all she could do was nod that she understood.

TWO WEEKS TO THE DAY, Justin returned to the Nature Museum with a file filled with computer jargon that only another computer whiz would understand. There were dark circles of fatigue under his eyes, but he'd done what she'd asked of him.

As he left, Abby smiled to herself. Now she had the leverage and the perfect carrot to talk with the Coast Guard about putting up a plaque in honor of Terrence Pettigrew's service as lighthouse keeper. Then both he and his son Bryant would be able to rest in peace.

CHAPTER ❧ NINETEEN

ABBY PARKED HER CAR in a line with others near the Wayfarer Point Lighthouse. Awkwardly, Bryant Pettigrew got out of the small hybrid. He wore a dark suit that had long since gone out of style and a narrow tie with red, white and blue stripes. His white shirt was yellowed with age but carefully pressed.

Wearing a navy-blue pants suit and low-heeled shoes, Abby walked around to the passenger side of the car. "Are you all right?"

He shot an anxious glance in the direction of the gathering crowd at the base of the lighthouse. "There're a lot of people here."

"They're all here to show their respect for your father and grandfather and the other keepers of the lighthouse."

He fiddled with his tie, the knot neat against the too loose collar. "He'd be real pleased, don't you think?"

"I'm sure he would be."

Taking Bryant's arm, she walked him over the uneven ground toward the lighthouse. The cloudless sky formed a Wedgewood-blue backdrop for the forty-foot-tall structure and small adjoining house.

Two Coast Guard vehicles were parked nearby and a Coast Guard cutter stood just offshore as honor guard. The flag on its bow fluttered in the breeze.

Captain Bette Studer, Commanding Officer of Group Seattle, stood at attention at the foot of the lighthouse. Senior Chief Bosnik and his men, wearing their dress uniforms, flanked her on the left. The public, including many people Abby recognized from Sparrow Island, had formed a half circle around the military contingent. In particular, she spotted Rev. Hale at the front of the group, his height and distinctive blond hair making him stand out.

She smiled, recalling his faith that she would find God's answer to her dilemma about Justin and his friends. The young people were notably absent from this event, wisely keeping a low profile in Friday Harbor.

William Jansen broke from the crowd and hurried toward Abby. Lifting his camera, he snapped a shot.

Bryant flinched and held out his palm to ward off any more picture taking.

"Big day for you, Bryant," William said. "How does all this make you feel?"

He grunted noncommittally.

"How 'bout you, Abby? You had a hand in all this, didn't you?"

"It was the Coast Guard's decision to recognize the valuable service the lighthouse keepers here at Wayfarer Point provided for many years."

"Aw, come on, Abby. Give me a quote."

"I'm sure Captain Studer will make some comments before the unveiling. She's waiting for us."

Urging Bryant past William, Abby moved to the front of the circled onlookers.

"Mr. Pettigrew," the captain said sharply, "would you please join me?"

Going rigid, Bryant effectively dug in his heels.

"It's all right. She's going to have you unveil the plaque." Abby nudged him forward.

After taking two steps, he straightened his arthritis-plagued body as best he could and saluted.

Smiling, Captain Studer closed the distance between them and extended her hand. "I am honored to meet you, sir," she said graciously.

If Bryant replied, Abby wasn't able to hear his response. She knew he was feeling overwhelmed by the situation and all of the people who had come to witness the unveiling.

The captain drew Bryant beside her and they faced the audience.

"Rev. Hale, will you start us with a prayer please?"

The preacher raised his hand in benediction and closed his eyes. "Dear Lord, we are here to give thanks for those who have committed their lives to serving and protecting others, both on land and on the sea. We ask that You accept their sacrifices and welcome them into Your loving embrace. Redeem us, as well, Lord, and let Thy light shine through our works and our prayers. Amen."

The gathered crowd echoed his *amen* as the minister stepped back to rejoin them.

"Ladies and gentlemen." The captain's voice carried across

the rocky point of land. "Sometimes we forget that technology hasn't always been a part of our lives. That there actually was a time when Global Positioning Systems were not in every ship and half the cars on the road."

The audience chuckled at that.

"During all those centuries before technology arrived, ships that ventured to sea sailed with only rudimentary navigation equipment. On dark-and-stormy nights, they were effectively blind. A rocky point, such as the one where we're standing today, could doom a ship and its crew if they went aground, which they did all too often.

"But brave, determined men and their families chose to live often solitary lives to protect and warn those at sea of the hazards they faced.

"This lighthouse was built in 1902, but even before that, men and women volunteered for the rigorous duty of manning the lighthouse. Sometimes it was only a bonfire kept burning throughout a long night that saved the lives of seamen.

"It is those men and women we are here to honor today." The captain nodded toward a soloist from Little Flock Church. In a clear tenor voice, he began to sing the hymn "Lighten the Darkness."

Lighten the darkness of our life's long night,
Through which we blindly stumble to the day,
Shadows mislead us; Father, send Thy light
To set our footsteps in the homeward way.

In the silence following the hymn, the captain nodded to Bryant. "Would you do the honors, please, Mr. Pettigrew."

Slowly, with a shaking hand, he removed the cloth that had covered the bronze plaque where his father and grandfather's names were now engraved alongside the dates they had served as keepers of the light.

As Bryant studied the plaque, he wiped his eyes with the back of his hand, and Abby felt tears well in her eyes as well.

When Captain Studer dismissed them, the crowd began to disperse, some to their cars and others to congratulate Bryant and admire the plaque.

Margaret Blackstock joined Abby. "You know, I was sure it was Terrence Pettigrew who they dug up next to the lighthouse and that he'd been haunting the place, but there hasn't been any trouble out here in months."

"I can assure you, there was no haunting going on here. And Terrence is buried right where he belongs, at Green Acres." She'd checked with Bryant and Lenny Meekam to be sure that task had been quietly accomplished some time ago.

Margaret still didn't seem entirely convinced. Shaking her head, she headed toward her car.

With an amused smile, Abby watched her go, then walked up to the lighthouse to join the others. She extended her hand to Captain Studer.

"Thank you for arranging the plaque and the presentation today," Abby said. "I know it means a lot to Bryant."

"In my view, it's an overdue honor. I meant it when I said that lighthouse keepers performed a great service for those who went to sea." Despite the uniform cap she wore squarely on her head, the breeze caused the ends of her graying hair to flutter around her face.

"As does the Coast Guard serve us all."

"We think so." The captain glanced around the diminishing crowd. "I'd like to meet the person who provided the computer work to secure our cell phone monitoring equipment if he—or she—is here. My computer people tell me it was excellent work."

"I'm afraid that individual prefers to remain anonymous. Think of it as a service to the country."

"Yes, well . . ." The captain eyed Abby suspiciously. "If you happen to see that individual, please express our appreciation. We are fortunate that the wrong person didn't hack into our system and affect more than just the security of the lighthouse."

"I'll pass on your message if I have the opportunity."

After a moment, Captain Studer smiled. "You know, if that information about the weakness in the security of our cell phone monitoring system had come to us from anyone with less credibility than you have, the outcome might have been quite different."

"I appreciate your faith in me, Captain. And your discretion."

The Captain studied Abby a moment longer, then nodded and wordlessly led her troops to their vehicles.

Exhaling a sigh of relief, Abby smiled, confident both the Wayfarer Point Lighthouse and Justin Foote would enjoy a long and productive future.

A NOTE FROM THE EDITORS

THIS ORIGINAL BOOK WAS created by the Books and Inspirational Media Division of Guideposts, the world's leading inspirational publisher. Founded in 1945 by Dr. Norman Vincent Peale and his wife Ruth Stafford Peale, Guideposts helps people from all walks of life achieve their maximum personal and spiritual potential. Guideposts is committed to communicating positive, faith-filled principles for people everywhere to use in successful daily living.

Our publications include award-winning magazines like *Guideposts, Angels on Earth, Sweet 16* and *Positive Thinking,* best-selling books, and outreach services that demonstrate what can happen when faith and positive thinking are applied to day-to-day life.

For more information, visit us online at www.guideposts.org, call (800) 431-2344 or write Guideposts, 39 Seminary Hill Road, Carmel, New York 10512.